THE DEMONS BENEATH

A DI GRAVES THRILLER

WD JACKSON-SMART

BLOODHOUND
— BOOKS —

www.bloodhoundbooks.com

Print ISBN 978-1-5040-6864-2

To Luke and to my parents, for all their support and help with my writing, and for making The Demons Beneath as fun, thrilling and tense as it could be.

CHAPTER ONE

Janine Morris was wide-eyed and pale, her body shaking. Her mouse-grey shoulder-length hair was a mess, and the dark circles under her eyes pronounced. Her brain throbbed and she felt weak. She was aware of the neighbours hovering nearby, all eyes on her, and the small, but noticeable, camera crew outside her house. Her stomach churned. She wanted to sit down, worried she would pass out at any moment. She regretted not having made herself more presentable, then dismissed the thought. There were far more pressing matters at hand.

'Thanks, Bobby,' the maroon-suited woman holding the microphone suddenly piped up. The early morning sun glinted off the huge lens of the cumbersome video camera next to her. Janine snapped her attention back to the professional vlogger and tried to rally herself for the task at hand as the woman continued.

'I'm here in Arnos Grove, north London, with local resident Janine Morris, who claims that her family is being haunted after a string of mysterious events. Thank you for speaking to us, Mrs

Morris. Tell me, what exactly have you and your family experienced?'

The microphone was thrust into Janine's face. Her mouth was suddenly as dry as the cracked paving and browning sprigs of grass underfoot, and she struggled to get her words out.

'Well, erm, it ... it began last week – last Saturday. My youngest daughter, Emma, came running into our bedroom screaming and crying. She said there had been something in her room with her, something watching her.'

'Oh my,' the interviewer answered dramatically, her lips a ring of glossy lipstick. Janine felt horribly self-conscious, could feel the blood hum around her body. She flexed her fingers, trying to push out the nerves.

'She was terrified. Wouldn't go back in her room. In fact, she hasn't been in there since. My husband Darrell checked it over but there was nothing there. We dismissed it at first, but she just wouldn't go in there after that. Then the rest of us began to feel things in the house too.' Janine could feel beads of sweat dripping down her back and wished the interview was over already, but she knew she must finish. It was too important.

'What sort of things?' was the natural question. A few of the neighbours edged closer to Janine's front garden. From somewhere Janine registered a camera flash, and she squinted as she tried to maintain a semblance of composure.

'Freezing cold chills, even though the windows were closed or it was sunny outside. Strange smells that we couldn't find the source of. And you know when you see something out of the corner of your eye, but when you look there's nothing there? We found strange marks in the back of Emma's closet, like scratches made by an animal, but we couldn't find any trace of an animal that might have done it. We've been trying to ignore it all, but the kids are so worked up and it's really starting to affect us.

We're barely sleeping and now the kids will only sleep in our room. It's a nightmare, truly.'

The interviewer pulled a face of exaggerated mock-fear as she glanced at the camera. Janine could tell that the woman thought she was crazy.

'Wow, that does sound scary, like a horror film or something. But don't you think there's a simple explanation for everything?'

The camera whirred as the lens zoomed in on her. She knew people would doubt her, doubt her stories, maybe think she had lost the plot entirely, but she couldn't let that get in the way.

'No. No, I don't. I can understand why people wouldn't believe us. I really can, it sounds, well, nuts, but I can't shake the thought: what if Emma didn't imagine it? What if something really was in her room? We didn't imagine those smells, the cold chills, the marks.' The muscles in her shoulders were rigid with tension. As the interviewer turned and spoke to the camera once more, the breeze lifting her curled blonde hair, just one thought spun around Janine's mind.

Someone, please help us!

Detective Inspector Daniel Graves stood watching one of the crime scene examiners lean in close to get a better look at the bloodied cadaver. His stomach was a bubble of anxiety at the state of the body and he swallowed, tasting bile in the back of his throat. He ran his hand through his short brown hair.

Since accepting a promotion and transferring to the Homicide and Serious Crime Command of the London Metropolitan Police Service permanently four months ago, he had already worked on three murder investigations. His mind had settled into the new position quickly but his gut was yet to adapt, and the sight of a dead body was still enough to make him gag. The heaving city was a world away from Buxton in Derbyshire, where he had been based before. It already seemed like decades ago. His skill on four homicide cases in Buxton, three domestic and one related to an individual with severe mental health issues, had earned him the transfer, but his new position had forced him to get used to seeing dead bodies far more regularly than he had in his previous role. But he wasn't even close to getting used to it. He wasn't convinced anyone ever really did – except perhaps for morticians. For now, he was content to work on not being sick at every crime scene. He had done exactly that more than once at the start of his career and knew it was not the best impression to give. So far, today he'd kept his breakfast down. That was progress. He was keen to play down just how badly he was affected by proximity to dead bodies. It didn't look good if the detective on scene looked pale as a sheet. He was also in no rush to share with his colleagues the flashbacks he had whenever he saw a body.

'Hi, I don't think I introduced myself. DI Graves. What can you tell me about this guy, then?' he asked the woman kneeling over the body. He kept the back of his hand over his mouth as a precaution, if nothing else. The woman gently prodded a piece of bloody flesh around the edge of a horrific stomach wound, pursed her lips and turned to look up at him, squinting in the sunlight. She did not seem bothered by his evident reluctance to get closer to the body.

'Well, we can rule out a stabbing – a traditional one, anyway. The wound is too ragged, too large. There are some small striations along the costochondral junction here,' she said, pointing to glimpses of white visible through the gore. Daniel risked a fleeting glance at where she was pointing.

'Possibly a crowbar, based on the striations, but I can't say for sure yet, since we haven't found the weapon. It was a violent attack, though. Likely happened in the small hours of this morning, maybe around six hours ago judging by the state of the body and the minimal insect activity. I'd say it was quite spontaneous, certainly not done with any precision, probably fuelled by a burst of extreme anger.'

Daniel looked out across the running track of the Finsbury Park Athletics Centre. The sun forced him to shade his eyes with one hand as he surveyed the scene. A high green fence surrounded the place. He could see no obvious gaps, but the fence would be fairly easy to climb over. Surely neither the victim nor the attacker would have had keys to the gate. A movement to the right caught his attention, and he turned to see his partner walk past the stand next to the entrance and head towards him. DI Charlie Palmer's perfectly styled hair shimmered in the sunlight.

Daniel hadn't believed that Charlie Palmer was a real police officer when they first met. He thought it was some sort of joke. Play tricks on the new guy. Team the skinny guy from the countryside with someone who looked like Henry bloody Cavill – hilarious. When Daniel had realised that he truly was partnered with the tall, charming man, who also happened to be intelligent and kind-hearted, he had felt inferior. He had been forced to push down his own numerous insecurities for fear that if he didn't, he'd be back in the countryside in no time. He had continued to do so ever since. It was hard enough moving to a position of more responsibility in a big, overwhelming city like London when he was used to small-town life. He couldn't let the fact that he looked like an underdeveloped teenager when standing next to Charlie get the better of him either. Knowing that this was not the time for an attack of self-doubt, he pushed down his jealousy at Charlie's stereotypically good looks.

'Do we think it's a body dump?' his partner asked as he joined Daniel and the anthropologist, who was now accompanied by a colleague also dressed in overalls and rubber gloves. The younger woman was collecting small pieces of bloodied grit with a fine pair of tweezers, dropping them into a clear plastic tube.

'I don't think so.' Daniel shook his head slowly. 'There's too much blood around the body. It looks like he was killed here. It's quite secluded in terms of passers-by – might have been a meeting, a deal of some sort. We're pretty much in the middle of the park so there are no houses close by, the athletics track would have been deserted at night, and as far as I can see there are no cameras around either. Would work well as a spot for a deal, although they would have had to climb the fence to get in.' Daniel pointed to the fence. Charlie nodded as he took a good look around.

Daniel cast his eyes back down over the dead man a few metres from his feet, trying not to focus on his injuries. The victim was white, wearing jeans, a grey checked shirt and brown boots, all smeared with blood. His sleeves were rolled up, showing tattoos on his right forearm, but they didn't immediately stand out as unusual. Not many people in the UK had gang-related tattoos these days; tattoo sleeves were far more common.

'He looks pretty ordinary.' Daniel huffed.

'Ordinary people still do drugs, still do stupid things,' Charlie pointed out. 'You can't tell much by just looking at someone. Do we know who he is?'

A nearby CSI overheard the question and joined the conversation. He held up his clipboard and read off the paper sheet. 'Rogan Simmons, thirty-six, lives in north London. He had his driving licence on him.'

'So whoever killed him either wasn't bothered about him being identified or was too stupid or panicked to try and hide the evidence,' Daniel said.

'Let's see what we can dig up on Mr Simmons here,' Charlie

said, nodding towards the body. 'I wonder if he's got a few skeletons lurking, given how gruesome his death was.'

Daniel glanced back at the body one more time, swallowing hard.

Charlie slapped him on the back. 'Aren't you glad you moved to London?' He grinned as he started off towards the entrance to the track, his hands outstretched, signalling for Daniel to take it all in. Daniel wrinkled his brow in a mock frown. He *was* glad he had moved; he didn't regret it for a second. His life had changed dramatically, but all for the good. Murder investigations were rare back in Derbyshire, and Daniel was extremely thankful he been able to transfer to the Met. He was starting to find a level of job satisfaction that he had only dreamed of before moving. It had given him a new lease of life. Nothing felt greater than the thought of putting a killer behind bars or giving a grieving family the answers they so desperately needed. This case was no different. He would find the person responsible and he would put him or her to justice. Superman Graves, he thought before following Charlie, his skin tingling with adrenaline.

What had started off as a hot-desk had evolved into Daniel's permanent station in the department. He slouched in the swivel chair, iced raspberry frappe in hand. Pushing folders and paperwork out of the way, Daniel logged onto the intranet and scanned his inbox. After reading his unread messages, he grabbed his drink and headed over to Charlie, who was standing talking to another officer.

'So where are we at with our victim?' Daniel asked, perching on the edge of a vacant desk. The other officer smiled and headed off across the office.

'According to driving licence records, our dead guy lived on Morley Avenue in Wood Green. He worked at a garage a few minutes from there. He was arrested for a drunk and disorderly two years back, but nothing else. Single, never married, no kids.'

'Okay. That doesn't give us much but at least we now know where he spent his days. Trip to the garage?' Daniel guessed.

His partner nodded. 'Yep, someone there must be able to tell us a bit more about him.'

'Hopefully they can tell us who gutted the poor guy!' Daniel pushed off the desk. He took a last slurp of the melting frappe, dumped the cup in the bin, and together they headed for the lifts. 'I'm driving.' Daniel patted the keys in his pocket.

Catherine Delamar's rented flat was small but bright. More importantly, it was close to the Thames, giving her the impression that she didn't live in a huge, smog-filled city. She had no view of the river but the scent of the water lingered in the breeze coming through the open window she sat next to. There was no time to linger in the moment, however, and after a few seconds she came back to reality and flipped the cover off her iPad to begin her daily routine.

Catherine was looking for something specific: a story, article or news piece that might fit into her line of work. Although sometimes opportunities were offered to her, being a freelance demonologist meant she often had to look for jobs. It was a career that required her to be proactive. After all, reports of demonic activity were not exactly the norm. Having spent twenty years in the business, though, she knew how to find the good stuff.

She had travelled all over the UK and Europe over the years, moving from case to case. She never chose huge jobs. No, the smaller, family-size opportunities were what paid her bills. Despite a fall in the number of real-life stories of the supernatural being reported in the news, there were still hundreds of official – and unofficial – reports of hauntings, possessions and pissed-off poltergeists that emerged every year across the UK and Europe. Catherine often had plenty to choose from. Very occasionally she would help two or three families in one place before moving on, but she never stayed anywhere too long. She liked the countryside and she loved to travel, given the opportunity – in fact, she needed to. She sometimes joked that she must have some gypsy blood in her from relatives long since departed.

London was the fourth place Catherine had stopped in this year, and she was loving it. After helping a single mother on a farmhouse near Satley in County Durham who had been convinced her son was the devil reborn, she had decided she would take a few days of holiday to release some stress. The boy, it turned out, had been severely autistic, but his school and doctor had failed to recognise his condition and his mother admitted that she herself had a penchant for the supernatural and, in hindsight, had perhaps been looking for something else to explain her son's behaviour.

A gang of teenagers in his school had begun to torment the boy every day. He'd eventually snapped, and anyone who got in his way felt his anger and violent nature, including his mother – and Catherine, numerous times over the few weeks she had worked with the family. Everyone involved was glad that the devil was in fact not walking the earth in County Durham, but it had taken a lot of Catherine's energy to prove this. Thankfully, the job had still paid. That was one of her conditions: whether or not she found a demon, her time was valuable and billable.

For the last three blissful days she had spent some of her

recently earned money being the ultimate tourist. She walked along the South Bank of the Thames to admire the London Eye, went shopping in Mayfair, and stayed for hours at Greenwich Observatory, looking out over the city of glass and metal rising up in front of her. Having grown up in rural North Yorkshire, Catherine didn't often get the chance to enjoy London, and she made the most of it.

Like all good things, however, her mini-vacation had come to an end. It was time to get to work again. Being a tourist didn't come cheap – and nor did moving every few months. Catherine needed a new job to sink her teeth into. Still unsure whether finding a case in London was a good idea or not, she nonetheless began her search.

As she tapped her iPad screen to load a video, she could feel her fingers fizz with excitement. Within seconds she knew she had found something worth pursuing.

She watched the video twice. That was all she needed. It all came down to the person: the look in their eyes, the genuine fear in their voice, the desperation emitting from them. People were sceptical by nature, always doubting her, and Catherine had found that people needed to reach a certain level of desperation before they would accept her help. They needed to be at their wits' end, their nerves shredded. She could tell from the news clip that Janine Morris had reached that stage.

The local news section of the BBC website that had picked up the story by a paranormal vlogger had handily left in enough information for Catherine to find out where the woman and her terrified family lived. She put down the iPad and reached for her phone on the glass coffee table. It would be a profitable case, she knew. The family might not be incredibly wealthy, but London wages were different to those in the rest of the UK. She bet they had a few more grand to spare than the average family elsewhere. But did that mitigate the risk of taking a job that had the potential to be so high-profile? So far she had done well to avoid the media circus that could follow a widely publicised report of paranormal activity. She chose her cases carefully, staying clear of any that seemed too risky or that might not pay off. It helped that the general public were hugely sceptical, but she did not want to see her photo in the newspapers.

But she needed the money. She had let herself enjoy London worry-free for a while, but she had spent more than she should have, and she didn't have that much to begin with. Her day-to-day living expenses were bad enough, even if she moved on quickly from the capital. That cemented it. With a deep breath, her mind made up, Catherine selected the number she wanted from her contacts and pressed call. After a few rings, a male voice answered.

'Marcus, dear? I found one. It's in north London. Do you know where Arnos Grove is?' Catherine asked, her mind blooming with the possibilities of what was to come as excitable butterflies danced in her stomach.

CHAPTER TWO

Janine was glad of the blissful mid-August weather. It was hot, but not overwhelming. More importantly, it meant that the children could be out of the house all day. She wished they weren't on summer holidays but were at school, safely away from the house. But since that was out of her hands, good weather was the next best thing. It made things a little easier. During the day, at least.

She watched Emma and Joe running around at the end of the garden, Joe brandishing a cheap water pistol that dripped more water down his front than it sprayed at his sister. They were as far as they could physically get from the house while still remaining on the property. Janine knew that was deliberate. They were both pretty vocal about not wanting to go in the house without their parents, scared that something would get them. She couldn't blame them. The thought made her shiver too. At six and nine, they were too young to play around the neighbourhood on their own, so the next best option, despite their complaints, was for Janine to let them stay outside all day, under her watch. Her eldest, Anna, was currently at a friend's house a few streets away. Given the circumstances, Janine would have preferred her to remain close by too, but there was something to be said for the girl being a safe distance from the house. Janine wished she had that option.

Standing on the patio, a glass of flat Pepsi in one hand, Janine turned and stepped back from her home. Sunlight beamed off the brickwork, highlighting cracks and chips. She squinted, her gaze flitting from the sliding doors to the kitchen window up to the end bedroom window. The sun was shining on the building but there was nothing warm about it, not any more. They had lived there for more than four years, but for the first time it felt cold and hostile. Nice weather could not change that.

She jolted when she realised she was looking for movement – the flutter of a curtain, a shadow withdrawing into the house, something – but all she saw in the window was the reflection of trees, fences and neighbouring houses. Still, a shiver rippled up her arms. The children's fear had been instilled in her, and now she was apparently looking for evidence to justify it. She stepped back into direct sunlight to get rid of the chill that crept over her skin.

With the children occupied and her husband at work, Janine decided to take the opportunity to recharge her batteries. She needed to shake off her fears and doubts for a while. She dropped down onto the browning grass and stretched her legs out in front of her before tilting her face up to the sun and closing her eyes. It was nice to hear Emma giggling rather than screaming or crying. Janine opened one eye a crack to see Joe chasing his little sister, water still spattering across the pair from the Super Soaker. Eyes closed once more, she forced herself to smile. It was the first smile to appear on her face in a week and she knew it would not linger, but she had to look for and acknowledge the happy moments, times deserving of a smile among all the uncertainty they faced. She'd go mad otherwise.

The past fortnight had been one of the most tiring and stressful times in her life. Everything had spurred from what she and Darrell had, possibly naively, assumed was simply Emma's imagination. At almost three in the morning a week ago, her daughter came running full speed into their bedroom. She had been shrieking and red-faced, tears streaming down her cheeks. She was utterly convinced there had been something in her room, standing behind the bedroom door, watching her and Joe sleep. This wasn't the first time one of the children had suffered a nightmare; after Darrell had checked the room to be sure there was no real cause for alarm, they let Emma sleep with them. An easy solution to a simple bout of night terrors. That was the Saturday.

On Sunday Emma had woken bright and early. Half asleep, Janine had heard her get up and run out of the bedroom. Within minutes, she was yelling for her father. Darrell had begrudgingly got up to check on her, to find her in the hallway outside her bedroom door, Joe watching her from his bed, confused, his eyes full of sleep and his short brown hair a mess of spikes and tufts. She had wanted a toy but refused to go into her room to get it, telling Darrell that the monster would get her if she did. That night she slept with them again.

After two days of this, Janine was already starting to lose her patience. By Wednesday afternoon she had resolved to put an end to this game her daughter was playing. Emma had asked Joe to get something for her from their room and he had refused. Within seconds they were screaming at each other. Then Emma lashed out and hit Joe in the face.

'That does it! Come here!' Janine snapped, swooping the girl into her arms as Joe whined behind her. 'I've had enough of this. There is nothing in your room and I'll prove it to you.' With Emma whimpering in her arms, Janine marched out of the sitting room and upstairs to the girl's bedroom. She took one step into the bedroom, then Emma went ballistic. The girl began to scream at the top of her lungs, hitting and kicking her mother, grabbing at the door frame, and Janine was forced to acknowledge something: this wasn't just a silly game. Her daughter was genuinely terrified. After that Joe refused to go into the bedroom either, claiming that he'd seen a shadowy figure too, following him around the house. Then things began to get stranger.

Two days later, it was Anna's turn. She shared her story with her mother later that day, sounding thoroughly shaken.

Janine had taken the two younger children out shopping, sick of hearing them complaining about the phantom monster. Anna was happy to be left behind to enjoy some peace and quiet. She had some school projects that she needed to complete so she decided to do some coursework – if nothing else, to get her mother off her back. Her books were in a pile on the desk in her room, and had been for the last two weeks, gathering dust as she enjoyed the summer holidays. But, when she switched off a rerun of *Friends* and trudged upstairs to get her books, they weren't there. She began to hunt around the house, checking her bag, the kitchen table where she often dumped things, by the television in the sitting room, but nothing. She wondered if maybe her mother had tidied her books away, but there were only so many places to look. After a lengthy search, the only room left to check was Emma and Joe's bedroom.

Anna was no baby, not like her little brother and sister. She didn't think they had seen something stalking them around the house, hiding behind their door or under their beds. Not really. Still, she had seen how scared they both were of the room now. When they went past it they pressed their little bodies flat against the hallway wall, holding their breath, watching the doorway closely as they shimmied sideways like nervous crabs waiting to be grabbed in the vicious beak of a seagull. Alone in the house, Anna couldn't help feeling a little anxious as she reached the top of the stairs and moved down the hall towards the room.

The air was silent, the outdoor sounds of birds, traffic, an ice-cream van jingle all hushed in the distance. Anna pricked her ears as she approached the closed door of the bedroom. Slowly she reached out a hand and gripped the handle, then stopped. The metal was surprisingly cold in her grip. A worrying thought occurred to her. What would she do if there *was* actually something in there? She was by herself. Her screams would go unheard. She could be left dead on the floor to be discovered by her little brother and sister hours later in a sticky puddle of her own blood, her heart wrenched out of her chest by something with fangs and claws like kitchen knives.

'Dickhead. Stop being so bloody stupid,' she admonished herself out loud, not quite laughing at how fast her imagination had got away from her. She twisted the handle and opened the door, to reveal exactly what she had expected: a messy room covered in toys. She stepped over the threshold and laughed, brushing her fringe out of her eyes and shaking off her nervous tension.

Settled, calmer again, she started to take a proper look around. She checked the open toy chest on one side of the room, pulled the covers off both beds, rummaged through the shelving unit, which was filled with colouring books and action figures, but found nothing. Irritated, she dropped to her knees next to Joe's bed. She crouched, then paused again. Hadn't Joe said that something had been under there a few days ago? Poking his mattress while he tried to sleep? Another icy chill rippled over her. *What if– No, you're being a dickhead again!*

Anna lowered her head and looked into the shadows beneath the bed. She saw a dinosaur toy, what looked like a pair of shorts, a dirty sock and a DVD of something with robots on it.

No school books, though. Her breath came out in a burst, adrenaline making her fingers tingle.

Anna twisted to look at Emma's bed on the opposite side of the room. She couldn't stop another shiver. Again she shook off her irrational trepidation and shuffled across the carpet, then lowered herself to look under the second bed. And there they were. A neat pile of five books, sitting conspicuously in the centre of the space, just out of reach. There were no toys, no clothes, just the books. Anna lay down. The carpet was rough on her cheek. She stuck her arm under the bed and reached for the books. Working the pile slowly with her fingers, she had got them close enough to grab when a sound stopped her dead. A scratching noise. She froze, lying on her stomach, listening. The house was silent, but she knew what she had heard. *Shit!* Grown-up logic forgotten, her mind whirring with horrible possibilities, she grabbed the books, pulled the pile into her arms and stood. As she made her way across the room to the door, the scratching came again. She spun, her skin crawling at the sound, which was like nails dragging down wood. It came from inside the wardrobe. It came again, louder, as though something was clawing at them from the other side, trying to get out. Anna shot out of the room and slammed the door behind her. With the books still in her arms, she grabbed her keys and left the house. She spent the rest of the evening at her friend Clara's, refusing to come home until her family were back. When they returned, they had found a rat's nest behind a hole in the plasterboard. They had never had rats in the house before. Not one.

After this, it hadn't taken long for Darrell and Janine to start noticing odd things too. Unfamiliar noises, rushes of cold air coming from nowhere, a smell of rotting meat in the hall near Emma and Joe's room. The feeling that someone was always just out of sight, but if they turned to look there was no one there. That was when Janine knew she had to do something.

They couldn't live like that, exhausted and jumpy at all hours of the day and night. She kept telling herself there was a logical explanation for everything, that their minds were playing tricks on them, but she didn't quite believe that.

Now, as the sun beat down on them, Janine opened her eyes again, not feeling even remotely relaxed. Emma and Joe continued to play. Janine jumped when Emma screamed when Joe poured water from the pistol down her back.

Janine prayed silently that someone had seen the news and would be able to help them.

———

Music blared out as Daniel and Charlie approached the small warehouse. Two metal shutters were raised to reveal the innards of the garage.

'Hello?' Daniel called out over the noise. 'Metropolitan Police.'

The men paused in the entrance to scan the interior, lit by fluorescent strip lights. A huge metal frame held three cars, stacked one above the other, each missing various vital parts. On the walls hung oil-slicked tools, spare tyres and exhaust pipes. Across the stained concrete space, a dented Ford rested half a metre off the floor on a blue lift. Two motorbikes leant against the wall in a corner. There was no one in sight.

'Well, there has to be someone here,' Charlie said, nodding to the laptop that had been hooked up to powerful speakers to blast out the music. 'I'll go right, you go left.' He entered the garage and headed towards an office cubicle with an open door and dirty windows that obscured what lay beyond them. Daniel walked over to the cars, which blocked his view of the back of the warehouse.

As he approached the frame holding the vehicles, Daniel

glanced at the cars, but saw nothing of interest. They had no reason to think that Rogan Simmons' death was connected to the garage, but it was somewhere to start. Daniel didn't want to rule anything out. There could be a car racket going on, for all he knew, or maybe a crime needing a getaway vehicle.

'Hello?' he called out again. 'My name's Detective Inspector Graves, from the London Metropolitan Police. Anyone around?'

Still no response. The music changed tracks, the vocals less shouty but the volume still loud enough to make the garage reverberate. If anyone was nearby they would struggle to hear his voice, unless they were right next to him.

'Anything?' he shouted to Charlie, who was peering into the office. Charlie turned and shook his head.

'Holy shit!'

Daniel spun round, one hand going to the baton on his hip.

'You scared the living shit out of me!' the man spat. He stood framed in the open doorway. Daniel relaxed as he took in the dirty overalls and oil-marked fingers of the man just metres from him.

'I did call out, but the music...' Daniel answered.

'Shit, sorry.' The mechanic winced before jogging around the car stack to silence the laptop. Daniel followed, and Charlie came over to join them. The relief of the sudden quiet was startling.

The mechanic turned back to them. 'I don't want to be rude, but why are you here?'

'Are you the business owner?' Charlie asked bluntly, ignoring the man's question.

'Yeah, I am. Jason Tagoe. What is this about?'

'Do you employ a guy called Rogan Simmons?' he asked.

'Yeah, I do. Has he done something wrong?' Tagoe glanced from Daniel to Charlie, rubbing his hands on his overalls.

'His body was found earlier this morning in Finsbury Park.'

Tagoe stumbled backwards. 'Fuck me,' he muttered, running a hand over his shaved head. 'How?'

'He was stabbed, probably sometime late last night. He was found at the athletics track in the middle of the park,' Daniel responded, careful not to divulge too much. He wanted to avoid influencing any information Tagoe gave them as much as possible – and he didn't think a press statement had been sent out yet.

'Fuck!' Tagoe said again, more emphatically. 'You know who did it?' Shock was visibly on his face.

'We don't currently have any suspects. We hoped you could help. Do you know anyone who might have something against Simmons? Anything drug-related, for example?' Daniel asked. The 'night-time drug deal gone wrong' theory still seemed most likely to him, given the little they knew. Tagoe simply shook his head, clearly still processing the information.

'What about gangs? Have you ever had any trouble here at the garage?'

The mechanic shot Charlie a dirty look. 'Gangs? Seriously? I'm Black, so your mind goes straight to gangs and drugs?'

'Calm down – I'm not implying, just asking,' he said, leaning closer to Tagoe. Tagoe shrank back. Daniel took note. It was something for him to work on. He wasn't exactly intimidating, while Charlie could get anyone on the back foot if he wanted to. Another pang of jealousy rose up through Daniel but he swallowed it down.

'Look, Jason,' Daniel said, 'we're not suggesting you have anything to do with this, but someone stabbed Rogan Simmons and left him to die in a park in the middle of the night. From what we know from the crime scene, it seems possible that Simmons had arranged to meet someone to make a deal of some sort. Since you're his employer, we figured you'd be a good place to start our investigation. Please, calm down and tell us what you know.'

'Okay, okay, sorry.' Tagoe rubbed a hand across his forehead, smudging a streak of grease above one eyebrow. 'I don't know much about Rogan – I mean, not his personal life. He is ... was a decent mechanic, that's why I hired him, but he was quiet. In his own head a lot.'

'Do you know if he was seeing someone? Did he have a girlfriend?' Daniel asked. They needed another lead, someone else to question about the man. They knew that Simmons had never married, but a girlfriend was a possibility. It was already evident to Daniel that Jason Tagoe didn't know much but he might know about a girlfriend.

'Actually, yeah, maybe. There's this bird who came round here a couple of times a few weeks back. Short thing, but fit, acted like she knew it. She had tattoos up one arm and I think she was Spanish,' Tagoe said. 'I never spoke to her other than a quick hi, but Rogan looked like he enjoyed her visits.'

'Any idea what they talked about?'

'Not really. Heard 'em chatting about him getting more ink soon. I think she might be a tattoo artist, so she could just have been trying to get his business, but she was properly flirting. Certainly wasn't here to get her car fixed up.'

Charlie nodded.

Tagoe looked happy that he was proving useful. 'There are a few tattoo studios near here,' he continued. 'Maybe she works at one of them?'

'That could be worth looking into, thank you. Anything else you can think of?' Daniel asked. Tagoe shook his head. Charlie pulled a card from his pocket and handed it to the mechanic.

'Okay, thanks for your time. If you do think of anything else, let us know. And if anyone comes around looking for Simmons, call us immediately.'

'Sure, no problem,' Tagoe answered, inspecting the card briefly before stuffing it into his back pocket.

Charlie and Daniel turned and headed out to their car.

'Okay, mystery Spanish girl with tattoos, where are you?' Charlie asked.

'I'll google studios.' Daniel smiled as they clambered back into their vehicle. 'Maybe I'll even get a little something while I'm there.' His grin widened when he saw his partner's jaw drop.

'You? Get a tattoo? Somehow I don't think you could handle the pain,' Charlie said as he started the engine. Daniel felt himself flush. He fought it back.

'Hey, don't judge a book. I'm not actually as pathetic as I look.'

'Mate, I didn't say you were, but I have seen you wince at a paper cut.'

'I'm not bothered by needles, though.' Daniel shrugged. 'Plus sometimes artists use that numbing foam, so...'

'Sod off ... no way, you have a tattoo? Where?' Charlie asked incredulously, looking Daniel up and down as if trying to see through his clothing.

'I'm not telling you!' Daniel responded, enjoying being deliberately secretive. In fact, he did have a tattoo, a meaningless six-inch tribal pattern between his shoulder blades, a symbol of his youth that he often forgot he had. He wasn't about to tell Charlie about it, though. These days, Daniel liked tattoos, but only when they represented something, and he knew Charlie would mock him for not remembering what his own meant. 'Right, first stop, Extreme Ink on Lordship Lane.'

Charlie pulled out and they went in search of the attractive Spaniard Jason Tagoe had described.

CHAPTER THREE

For one blissful moment Janine Morris had let herself be convinced that they might manage a day in the house without something weird happening. That wasn't too much to ask for, surely? But she was wrong.

She was busy in the kitchen, preparing lunch for herself, Joe and Emma. The air was filled with the sound of cartoons and the kitchen counter was piled with sandwich ingredients and condiments. The scream shattered the peace – and her nerves – instantly. In a heartbeat Janine was on edge. She leant against the counter, eyes closed. Hadn't enough happened already? Didn't she deserve one moment of peace? If it wasn't the kids claiming that a shadow man was following them or reporting voices in the walls, they were bickering and pinching. The whole family was wound tight and the children were starting to drive her crazy. She flinched when the scream came again.

'Shut up, Emma, I'm watching *Turtles*!' Joe bellowed from the sitting room as a third shrill cry came from the other side of the house. Janine admonished herself for bringing them indoors, but what could she do? They couldn't stay in the garden all day every day. She put a Nutella-covered knife down carefully on the edge of the sink and took a deep breath. It would be nothing. It had to be nothing. She simply could not take more demon talk.

'Coming, Emma,' she called, her energy already sapped. Just the thought of having to coax Emma into her own bedroom was too much to contemplate. The urge to bow to Emma's every demand was overwhelming, if only to put an end to her constant whining and tantrums, but Janine knew that would not work out well in the end. She couldn't set a precedent.

'Mum!' the girl yelled, the noise slicing through the walls. Something about that one drawn-out word cut straight through Janine, and she ran upstairs. As she turned into the bathroom and saw why Emma was screaming, she felt as though she had been sucker-punched.

The girl stood, stock-still, next to the bath, petrified and shaking. The front of her T-shirt and jeans were wet with blood. Spots of glistening red peppered the tiles around her. Child-sized fingerprints stained the edge of the sink and counter and the lid of the toilet. Wet lumps of bloodied toilet paper lay discarded on the floor.

'Oh God, Emma!' Janine swooped into the bathroom, wanting to pull the girl into her arms. She dropped to a crouch, frantically scanning the girl for the source of the blood, for a wound full of torn flesh and exposed bone. *What the hell did this?* an inner voice screamed in panic.

'Mum?' came a nervous mewl from behind Janine as Joe came to investigate.

'Keep back, sweetie,' she urged, not looking back at her son. She had to focus on Emma. The girl had blood all over her mouth – she looked like she had just killed an animal with her teeth.

'Did you cut yourself? What happened? Where hurts?' Janine asked, trying to keep her voice calm and steady.

Emma didn't answer. Her eyes were teary, her skin clammy. Then Emma coughed. A mist of blood sprayed out and dotted Janine's T-shirt. The girl's eyes widened in horror, and she sputtered an apology. Something in Janine's mind clicked.

'Joe, grab a fresh towel from the hamper in my bedroom, okay? Be quick,' she said, not calm exactly but relieved she now understood the situation.

'Emma, are you okay?' Joe asked, sounding unsure, as though he didn't quite trust his mother.

'She'll be fine. It's just a really bad nosebleed,' Janine answered, giving Emma a reassuring smile as Joe shot off down the hallway. 'How are you doing, baby? You okay? Just take some breaths, try to calm down. It's nothing to worry about,' Janine said to Emma, trying to soothe her daughter, brushing her blonde fringe, which was sticky with blood, from her daughter's eyes. 'I know it's scary, but it'll stop soon. Then we'll get you to the doctor, you can have a lollipop and that'll be that, good as new. Though you do need a wash first!' She forced another smile. Emma was taking steadier breaths already, and Janine was glad her words were of some comfort.

What Emma didn't realise was that the fear that bubbled in the pit of her mother's stomach had not actually gone away. It was slowly growing bigger, and a little voice in the back of Janine's brain was getting louder and louder. It was telling her that none of her children had ever had an unprompted nosebleed, and neither had she. It was telling her that this was too much blood. It was telling her that something was responsible for this happening to her baby girl. And it was telling her that whatever was doing this to her family was far from done.

Joe returned with a pistachio-coloured hand towel which

Janine handed to the girl. 'Emma, hold this under your nose, okay? We don't want to get blood all over the car. Joe, can you run the hot tap for me?' Her jovial voice told the children that everything was okay, that they would laugh at this in a few hours. She was relieved that they seemed to be buying it, but there was no convincing herself. After cleaning her daughter as best she could, not wanting to waste time getting her into the shower, Janine took Emma's hand and ushered the children into the hall and towards the front door.

'Right, let's go visit the doctor, shall we?' she said as they headed out of the door and into the sun.

None of them dared to glance at the house, for fear of seeing something looking back.

Daniel was surprised by the number of tattoo parlours in the area as they made their way into the fourth of the day. He had googled 'tattoo shops London' and dozens of red dots had appeared, covering the city. He was not surprised, however, that they were struggling to find the mystery woman who had supposedly visited and flirted with their murder victim recently. They had very little detail about her beyond a basic description, so it was like finding a tattoo needle in a haystack, a joke Charlie had cracked and Daniel had frowned at, apt as it was.

The bell above the door to Needlepoint Ink sang happily as they entered, contrasting starkly with the low throb of metal music and the buzz of tattoo machines inside. The shop, located on Finchley's bustling high street, was the most stylish they had been in so far. The windows on either side of the door featured displays of truly beautiful artwork in pencil and watercolour, surrounded by religious iconography, including a wooden statue of the Virgin Mary, a worn, leather-bound Bible with gold trimmings, and a silver cross that looked like it belonged on an altar. Inside, sunlight mingled with clean, fresh lighting. The walls were decorated like an art gallery and the front desk was a carefully crafted dark wooden counter with a fascia of intricate carvings of angels and devils winding and dancing around one another. Though unoriginal in its decision to reference religion, the place screamed of professionalism and promised nothing but the best quality of service.

Daniel made a mental note to remember the place in case he ever decided to add to his own ink. He had never felt inclined to get further designs, hadn't experienced the addictive feeling some people felt after getting tattooed. Having spent all morning traipsing from shop to shop, however, the thought of getting a new design had begun to form in the back of his mind. He mentally shook himself and brought his attention back to the matter at hand.

Leaning against the counter was an extremely pretty young woman with bright red hair tied up in a black paisley headscarf so she resembled a 1950s pin-up. She had small black plugs in her ears, fingers weighed down with a variety of oversized rings, and a colourful tattoo of a bluebird in flight across her upper chest. Daniel felt an immediate, startling wave of attraction wash over him as she smiled a greeting. His hopes deflated instantly as she gazed at Charlie for far longer than curiosity dictated. Charlie, however, had stopped to inspect a painting of a Japanese dragon winding its way through a mountainous landscape, not registering her amorous stare. She gazed at Daniel.

'Hi, guys, what can I help you with today? In for some fresh ink?'

Daniel glanced at Charlie. He couldn't help thinking his partner looked deeply uncomfortable again. Though he hadn't said anything, Daniel got the impression that Charlie was actually the one who was scared of needles. He had been jumpy in all three previous parlours whenever he heard the buzz of a machine, and Daniel thought he looked more pale than normal. Had he even flinched at the girl's question?

'I don't think this one could hack it, to be honest.' Daniel laughed, giving Charlie a pat on the back and earning himself a sharp glare in return. The girl grinned and Daniel could practically hear her saying 'bless'. 'Anyway, no, we're not here to get tattoos, unfortunately. I'm Detective Inspector Graves and this is my partner, Detective Inspector Palmer. We're looking for someone, and hopefully you can help...' He nodded at her, as if to indicate that was where she should say her name.

'Jenny – Jenny Cartwright,' she answered, her features growing serious.

'Jenny. Yes, we're looking for someone who might be able to give us some information on a case we're working on.' Daniel spoke more formally, and he could see it had the desired effect. The initial jovial atmosphere was gone and Jenny was giving him her undivided attention.

'I'll do my best to help,' Jenny said, seemingly willing to talk but clearly uneasy. She glanced over her shoulder to one of her colleagues, who gave her a 'what's going on?' frown. Jenny responded with a small headshake before looking back at the detectives. Daniel watched the man at the back of the studio, drawing something on a large piece of tracing paper. The guy didn't seem uncomfortable; he gave Daniel a polite smile before going back to his work.

'Great.' Charlie took over. 'We're looking for a Spanish woman, mid-twenties to early thirties, probably, quite short, with a tattoo sleeve on one arm.'

'And she may be a bit of a – well, let's say very flirtatious,' Daniel added. At that, Jenny's face lit up, though not with joy so much as uncomfortable realisation. She opened her mouth to speak, but quickly bit her tongue.

'You know who we're talking about, then.' Charlie's expression was stern, making it clear this was not a moment to lie or hide the truth. Jenny nodded and stole another glance at the man drawing behind her. He didn't notice. She turned back, leant forward and lowered her voice.

'Okay, yes, I'm pretty sure I do know who she is. Cassandra Salinas. She's – well, she had a thing with my manager a while back and it caused a lot of trouble. I don't know any details but, put it this way, it was a bit Jeremy Kyle.' She grimaced as she spoke.

'Jeremy Kyle?' Daniel asked.

'You know, where loads of people cheat and lie and want to hit each other with chairs.'

Both Charlie and Daniel nodded at this, instantly understanding what the woman meant. Homicide cases often started with issues that could easily feature on a show like that.

'Do you know where we can find her?' Charlie asked with an urgency that Daniel put down to Charlie's discomfort at being near buzzing needles as much as his desire to follow a lead. He seemed positively anxious – a world away from his usual suave, chilled-out self.

'I don't, actually.' Jenny frowned. 'But...' She bent down to retrieve something from a shelf under the wooden countertop. She pulled out a large red binder, dropped it onto the counter and started to flick through the hole-punched sheets of paper covered in names, numbers, notes and doodles. Daniel peered at the page she stopped at.

'There you go. We have her phone number and address. I think she got a tattoo here once.'

Daniel pulled out his phone and took a photo of the address before putting it into Google Maps.

'Well, would you look at that? She lives off Haringey Green Lanes.' He smiled at Charlie and waited for him to make the connection. It didn't take long.

'Haringey ... as in right next to Finsbury Park?' Charlie asked, one eyebrow raised. Daniel nodded and looked back at Jenny, trying hard to ignore how cute she looked with her brow wrinkled in confusion.

'So I was helpful?' she asked, her voice tinged with nerves still.

'Very, thank you,' Daniel answered with a smile. He was hoping it made him look confident and charming, but was afraid that it looked as awkward and stiff as it felt. 'Shall we?' he said to Charlie, breaking eye contact with Jenny. His shirt collar was suddenly tight and uncomfortable.

'Let's.' Charlie also thanked the woman and together they headed back out into the midday air. Charlie took a deep breath and his shoulders relaxed. He flashed a crisp white smile Daniel's way. 'Green Lanes, here we come!'

Daniel shot a quick glance back at the parlour, a wistful thought of Jenny and drinks flashing through his mind before he followed his partner to their car, all the while attempting to push away barbs of self-doubt.

Patience had never been one of his virtues, but since he had little choice other than to wait until Catherine Delamar deemed the time right, Marcus Spindler decided to try and relax. It wasn't going well. The day was warm, too hot for him, and as sweat beaded on his upper lip he took a gulp of his lemonade in a weak bid to cool down. It was flat and already warm, annoying him further. He brushed his damp fringe out of his eyes with a huff.

The pub he had chosen was nice enough, boasting a prime position just a minute or two from Regent's Park. The small terrace that encroached onto the pavement boasted tattered, but welcome, sun umbrellas on each of the picnic-style tables, which he was grateful for, and across the road attractive trees with rich green foliage danced gently in the mild breeze. A woman jogged past with her dog. A couple sat on a bench sharing a late lunch. It was an idyllic place to let an hour pass. Not for Marcus, though. Underneath the table, his leg bounced nervously – and not as a result of the overly sugary drink. The well-worn copy of *American Psycho* that he had read four times already sat on the table, untouched. He was not in the mood to relax.

As a child he had been in trouble continually, always finding himself the class troublemaker, the kid that teachers came to loathe. He had lost track of the number of times his mother had been dragged in to speak to the head teacher. It helped that he went to a new school every six months – his family never stayed in one place for long – but the teachers were always as happy to see the back of him as he was to be rid of them. No matter where they settled, it was the same story: detentions and fights and general truancy. By the time he was fourteen, his mother had given up trying to get him to go to school, something he was eternally grateful for.

As an adult he was much the same, minus the truancy. At forty-one he still found himself constantly distracted, his mind always racing with a million different thoughts. He got bored too easily and he couldn't stand waiting for things. In many ways, Catherine was his saviour. Marcus had tried a few times in his early years to hold down vaguely steady jobs but none had ever panned out, none lasting beyond a week or two. Working with Catherine was different. He had no regular schedule and, more importantly, the work was satisfying. He loved the subject matter of his job, if he could call it that.

While he had never considered himself as belonging in any type of social group, at school he had been a little too much into all things dark. The devil fascinated him, as did Salem, ghosts, demons, anything related to death, and anything creepy or morbid. He had tried not to stand out or draw attention, avoiding the stereotypes of black hair, tattoos, piercings, and a long leather coat teamed with biker boots. From his appearance alone, no one would have ever noticed anything particularly different about him. Anyone who spent five minutes with him, however, could tell he was different, and other children were often loathe to go anywhere near him. Adults too. Being the assistant to a demonologist therefore worked perfectly for him. He and Catherine knew everything there was to know about each other. Theirs was a symbiotic relationship.

Catherine could still irritate the hell out of him, though, and now was one of those times. She had called just a few hours ago with the exciting prospect of a new job on the horizon, only to leave him in limbo. Her energy had transferred to him like electricity and he had felt his adrenaline spike, yet here he was, agitated and uncomfortably warm, waiting for her to let him know she was ready. Catherine was the only person in the world he would even consider waiting for, but it was still a Herculean task. He yearned for instant gratification. Once he decided to do something, he had to do it there and then, had to dive right in.

Cold liquid running over the back of his hand shook him out of his thoughts. Marcus grimaced when he realised he'd spilled lemonade over the rim of his glass and over his wrist.

'Get it under control,' he muttered as he grabbed a napkin, praying for his phone to vibrate and let him know the show was on the road.

The early afternoon sun was pouring down when Charlie and Daniel reached Fairfax Road, a quiet street in Manor House lined with well-kept period properties. The address placed Cassandra Salinas's house halfway down. Charlie pulled up to the pavement and cut the engine.

'There it is – the white one with the brown roof tiles.' Charlie got out of the car. Daniel got out too, immediately feeling the heat and pulling at his shirt collar. The day seemed to be getting hotter, and he longed for air-con and a chilled drink. His was not a body built for sunshine.

'Let's hope she's in. I'm baking out here.'

They headed up to the front door. Daniel looked over at the bay window on the right, but the white slats and sunlight glinting off the glass meant he couldn't see inside. Charlie rang the doorbell, waited a few seconds, then knocked. There was movement inside, and the door opened a crack. A young boy eyed the men through the gap.

'What do you want?' he asked suspiciously. Daniel pegged him as around ten, but couldn't be sure from just half a face and a wisp of dark fringe. Daniel flashed a smile, bending down. 'We're looking for Cassandra Salinas. Is she home?'

'That's my mum. Who are you?' the boy asked, his brow furrowing further. The crack in the door got smaller.

'We're detectives. We'd like to speak with your mum to see if she can help us out with something we're working on.' Daniel kept his voice friendly, didn't see Charlie roll his eyes impatiently beside him.

'Is she in trouble?' came another suspicious question.

'Not at all.'

The boy remained silent for a second, clearly thinking

through his options. Then he yelled, 'Mum?' and closed the door on Daniel and Charlie.

'Charming,' Charlie muttered. They heard the boy yell again from inside the house and a few seconds later the front door opened once more, fully this time. The woman standing in front of them fit the description they had perfectly. She had a soft, glowing tan, a heart-shaped face that framed beautiful features, voluminous chestnut hair falling around her shoulders, and a tattoo sleeve on one arm. Her ankle-length cream skirt fluttered gently as a weak breeze sifted into the communal corridor behind her. She looked just as suspicious of the detective inspectors as her son had.

'Yes?' she spat, one hand on her hip, her beauty belying her attitude. Her voice retained a hint of her Spanish heritage, but she had clearly been living in England for some time.

'Mrs Salinas?' Daniel checked despite it being pretty obvious they had found who they were looking for.

'Miss,' she corrected, widening her eyes as if to say 'what of it?' Charlie huffed just loud enough to be heard and she threw a scalpel-sharp glare at him. It had no discernible effect on him.

'We're detective inspectors with the London Met. We understand you know a man called Rogan Simmons,' Charlie said, cutting to the chase. 'We need some information on him.'

'Why? What has he done?' Cassandra snarled back, suddenly on the defensive. Evidently she had no time for them.

'He got himself killed, that's what he did,' Charlie snapped, his blunt statement and tone surprising Daniel. 'We have a witness who says you have been pretty friendly with him recently, visiting him at work. Were you two an item?'

Cassandra stepped back, clearly reeling from the information. Her attitude changed in a flash, and she appeared more vulnerable. The transition was so instant, it was startling.

'Rogan's dead? How? What happened? How can he be

dead? I just saw him yesterday...' She put a hand over her mouth, her eyes tearing up. Daniel frowned at Charlie for being so harsh. Maybe they should have done this inside, not on her doorstep.

'It seems he was stabbed late last night in Finsbury Park,' Daniel told her, trying to keep his tone gentle. 'We're speaking with anyone who knew Simmons, to find out why someone would want to hurt him. You said you saw him yesterday?'

Cassandra took a deep breath in an attempt to regain some composure. She ran a finger under each eye, drying her tears.

'Yes, we went for a drink at a pub near his garage. We aren't ... weren't dating. He's just a friend. I can't...' Her voice cracked again and she put her hand up in silent apology.

'It's okay, Miss Salinas. Would you like to go inside?' Daniel asked but she shook her head.

'Do you know if Mr Simmons was in any kind of trouble?' Charlie pushed. 'Drugs, gangs? Someone obviously wanted to hurt him.'

Cassandra gave this some thought. 'I don't think so,' she said finally. Her tone was resolute, but Daniel noticed she wasn't looking at either of them when she spoke. He thought this was odd, given how direct she had been just minutes ago.

'You're sure about that?' he pushed gently. 'Anything you can think of may help our investigation.'

'No, Rogan is ... Shit, *was* a nice guy. I don't know why someone would do this to him.' She glanced at Daniel, but the look was fleeting. She looked like she wanted them gone. Daniel and Charlie were quiet for a moment to give her the opportunity to change her mind, but when she said nothing else Charlie offered her a card.

'Thank you for your time, Miss Salinas. Please let us know if you think of anything. We may be in touch again.'

With that Cassandra retreated into the house and the door clicked shut.

'She's lying,' Charlie stated as they turned back to the road. 'Let's get back to the office and see what we can dig up. And see if we can enlist Sergeant Harding. If anyone can dig up the truth, she can.'

CHAPTER FOUR

Daniel was glad to spend a few hours back at his desk, out of the sun. He couldn't think when he was uncomfortable, and the air-conditioning and cold drinks machine in the office were more conducive to a productive afternoon. He was therefore royally pissed off to have achieved very little.

Sergeant Amelia Harding, who had assisted him a few times since he had moved to London, had been assigned to the case, at Charlie's request. Daniel glanced at her as she worked, tapping away at her keyboard with a laser focus. She was a beautiful woman and he had been attracted to her immediately, his crush on her like that of a spotty fourteen-year-old kid infatuated with a hot girl in the sixth form, but of course he knew nothing would come of it. He had to stay professional. And he knew she was out of his league.

Amelia had been looking for personal, off-the-record details on Cassandra Salinas and Rogan Simmons for more than an hour, and was still coming up blank. Her frown and pout showed her frustration.

Charlie had been called away by Superintendent Peter

Hobbs to consult on a cold case that suddenly seemed less cold, leaving Daniel and Amelia to it. By six in the evening, Daniel had discovered very little to help them. Another thorough check of Simmons' criminal record and registered files had turned up nothing new, and Salinas seemed to have no record at all. She had reported a domestic disturbance eight months previously but it had been dropped the same day, with no further problems reported. Rogan Simmons was not mentioned in any of the paperwork. Daniel had found nothing that linked them, and nothing that would suggest a reason someone would want to kill Simmons. Their only connection was what Jason Tagoe had told them, which was just that Simmons and Salinas knew each other.

Two sergeants had spent much of the day talking to people who lived near the athletics centre in Finsbury Park, but had likewise turned up very little. One man who lived on Oakfield Road had recalled seeing an unmarked white van parked near the rear entrance to the park around three in the morning, which was something they could look into, but he could provide no more information. A few members of a running club that frequented the park said they often saw groups of teenagers hanging around in the area after the gates were closed, but Daniel doubted that a gang of pot-smoking skateboarders would gut a man and leave his body on a running track. Asking the drunks and junkies who broke into the park after hours would be a waste of time too.

'I take it you have haven't found anything,' Amelia said as Daniel raised his arms in a stretch, yawning. He broke the yawn when he realised she was looking at him, and tried to quickly regain his composure.

Amelia had recently had her hair cut and recoloured: it was a honey-kissed blonde bob that stopped just above her shoulders. He'd complimented her and left it at that, but he couldn't help noticing how well it suited her. Being caught yawning like he'd just come out of hibernation was not the image he wanted to portray. To her credit, Amelia did not react. He didn't know her well, but he had been impressed with her work. She was clever and capable and, as far as he knew, nothing but professional at all times. Annoyingly, this made her even more attractive.

'No, nothing of note,' he answered. 'You?'

Amelia shook her head. 'Not really. Simmons followed Salinas on Twitter, but he hadn't used his account in months. And Facebook shows they have a few mutual friends but that's about it. Mostly their connection seems to be tattoos, which makes sense. She works in a tattoo shop and he had plenty of tattoos. I did find one photo with both of them in it, with four others.' She twisted her screen and Daniel craned his neck to see the image.

'Could be worth checking who the other four are. It looks like it was taken at a convention, maybe, so these other people could be tattoo artists too.'

'Okay, will do.'

Daniel's phone vibrated in his pocket and he pulled it out, catching the time on the display. 'It's almost seven. Let's get on it tomorrow, okay?' He smiled at her before he took the call. 'Detective Inspector Graves.'

'Didn't you read the caller ID?' came a familiar, excited voice. He knew who it was immediately.

'I save my observational prowess for my cases these days, Rach.' He laughed. He caught Amelia frowning curiously at him, and decided to head into one of the vacant meeting rooms for privacy. 'How's it going?' he asked, pulling the glass door shut behind him and perching on the table edge.

'I'm great. Funny story – I'm in London.'

'What? Seriously? Since when?'

39

'Seriously, and since about two hours ago. I have a few days off and thought I'd visit my sister – and see if I could catch you too. Are you free tonight?' Rachel asked. Daniel said yes immediately. Even though he had moved from Derbyshire and no longer saw her at work every day, he counted Rachel Callahan as one of his best friends. They had become extremely close over the last few years. Apart from Charlie, he had yet to make any friends since relocating. He was too busy with work.

'I was going to stay in the office for another hour or so, but I need a break. Where are you? I'll come and meet you.'

'Well, I'm currently in Piccadilly Circus. It's a bloody nightmare, but I've never done the London tourist thing. Jenna always makes us do the real city stuff.' She laughed.

'Fair enough. You're only about fifteen minutes from me, so why don't we meet in the middle? Get the Tube to Holborn and head to the Princess Louise. It's a great pub I discovered near the Tube. Meet you there in half an hour?'

Rachel agreed and Daniel hung up, a buzz of excitement simmering in him. The day had been frustrating, to say the least, and a drink or two with a best friend was a welcome distraction.

He left the meeting room and said goodbye to Amelia, then headed for the stairwell, his thoughts on Rachel and their catch-up.

'Are you bloody kidding me?' Darrell snapped. She hissed at him to keep his voice down. He made a face. 'We're not moving the whole family into a hotel. I mean, are you insane?' he continued, his voice only slightly quieter.

Janine sat on the edge of their bed, her hands cupped over her face in a bid to keep calm. She glanced to the door to make sure it was shut. The last thing she wanted was for any of the children to hear them, though she suspected they had already heard something. Their voices were loud and the walls thin.

'You didn't see her, Darrell. There was so much blood,' she hissed at him, her voice quiet but loaded with emotion.

'Of course there was – it was a massive nosebleed!' he snapped. The ice in his whisky clinked against the glass. Janine glared at it. After a few drinks, he would argue that the earth was flat. This was his third.

'She was still bleeding when we got to the doctors. Even he said it was too much. If it hadn't stopped then, he would have sent her to hospital.' She reached for her phone on the bedside table and scrolled through her pictures. 'For Christ's sake, look at this! Are you telling me this is normal?' She thrust the phone into her husband's face so he could see the image of the blood-stained bathroom. He took it from her, squinting to get a better look, then looked surprised.

'Okay, yes, it looks bad. I get it – I would have been shaken up too. But a demon, Janine? Really?' He swallowed another mouthful of whisky as he gave her back the phone. 'You honestly think some supernatural ... thing is sneaking around our house intent on making our children bleed?'

Janine was silent, staring again at the glass as Darrell shook it, the half-melted ice now lonely.

'Don't you dare have another one...' she muttered. Darrell sighed, evidently irritated by the comment but willing to acquiesce. He put the glass down next to the vanity mirror opposite her.

'Seriously though, ghosts?' He came to sit down beside Janine. Her first instinct was to push him away, but already her fight was gone. She was drained, aching. When Darrell put an arm around her shoulders, she couldn't stop the tears from sliding down her cheeks.

'I know it's ridiculous. I'm pretty sure I'm going out of my mind, doubting every crazy thought, but there are too many things I can't explain.' She wiped her eyes and turned towards him. 'Can you? The way the kids are acting? Even Anna is freaked out. There's the weird smells, things moving around the house, the claw marks in the kids' wardrobe. The nosebleed is just the latest in a line of weird things. And I swear I've heard voices – coming from the walls, behind doors, like whispers where I couldn't quite make out the words. You tell me what it is.'

'I don't believe in ghosts and demons and monsters, Janine. And voices? I think it's caused by stress: the kids, the fact we've not been getting much sleep, it's all obviously having an effect on you,' Darrell said, though his words sounded hollow to Janine, as if he didn't believe what he had said.

'Maybe you're right. I don't normally buy into this stuff either, but...'

'But there's something, huh?' Darrell finished.

Janine nodded. She really didn't want to believe what was happening, what she had told the news crew. If she stopped to think about it for more than a few seconds her skin would turn to ice, her hair would stand on end, goose pimples would cover her arms. She had never seen anything supernatural before, never experienced anything, but she had also not outright rejected the possibility of other worlds, of ghosts and God knew what else. She was a believer in the theory that fire followed smoke, and she had seen far too many films, documentaries and news stories to think there was no truth behind them. Such stories had to originate somewhere. They couldn't all be made up, surely. Some of them had to be true. The thought only terrified her further.

'Okay, how about this? We see if we can find some ... expert or something to help us. To scope out the house and check what's what.' Darrell squeezed his wife's shoulder gently. 'Even if I don't believe in this sort of stuff, clearly it's affecting you and the kids. I've got to say I think it was a bad idea going on the morning news, but I get it. And maybe a professional will be able to put your mind at ease a little.'

At the realisation that Darrell was willing to consider bringing in help, Janine could feel a weight lift off her – not much, but enough to bring her ever so slightly out of the despair that was ready to consume her.

'Thank you, yes, I think that would help a lot. It's exactly what we need.'

Darrell leant across and kissed Janine gently, reassuring her after their argument.

The sound of the doorbell broke the moment. Darrell looked at his watch. 'Who could that be? It's past seven.' Together they stood, and Janine followed Darrell out of the bedroom. He headed for the front door while she went into the sitting room. The kids were remarkably quiet, and she wanted to know why. She found Anna engrossed in an episode of something on E4, Joe playing on Anna's phone, and Emma fast asleep in a pile of cushions on the sofa.

'You guys all right?' she asked, rubbing her forehead, feeling her temples throb. Anna turned and gave her a small nod and smile before going back to the television.

'Uh-huh,' Joe muttered, not looking up from the phone. Janine couldn't make out what Darrell was saying out by the front door and went to see who had come to visit, suspicious of anyone calling at this time.

She rounded the corner, pushing a rogue pair of Joe's trainers against the wall with her foot as she went. Coming up next to Darrell, she found herself face to face with a short woman who looked to be in her late fifties or early sixties, and a taller, chubby man she thought must be close to forty, although it was hard to tell. Both were well dressed: the woman in a pencil skirt, blouse and jacket, the man in an unflattering but pristine suit.

'Babe, this is Catherine Delamar and her colleague Marcus Spindler,' Darrell said. Catherine held out a hand and Janine shook it tentatively, unsure why she was shaking hands with these people. She was not a fan of unannounced guests, especially strangers.

'Hi, I'm Janine,' she said. There was a moment of silence as the four stood looking at each other. 'I'm sorry, who are you?' she continued.

'Oh, I'm sorry, of course, this must seem strange. Let me reassure you, Mrs Morris, you'll be glad we showed up. We're here to help.'

'Help?' Janine felt like she was missing something. She looked up at her husband, who was smiling – an odd, awkward smile, not happy but something else.

'Perfect timing, right?'

Then in a flash it clicked. Janine's mouth dropped open as she turned back to the visitors. 'Wait, so you're...'

'That's right. I saw you on the news, Mrs Morris, and I knew I had to come and speak with you. I'm a demonologist. Your case stood out to me immediately and I needed to see for myself. I came right away; I couldn't just sit idly by. I think your family may be in grave danger.'

The words took the wind out of Janine like a punch to the stomach.

CHAPTER FIVE

As Janine led Catherine and Marcus into their house, she felt horribly self-conscious, worried that the house was a mess and that the guests would think poorly of her. That was hardly what she should be concerned with, she knew, but she found it hard to shake the thought.

'Sorry for the chaos,' she stuttered, retrieving a Barbie and a handful of DVD cases from an armchair, signalling for Catherine to take a seat. Marcus looked over at the sofa, where Emma still slept, remarkably undisturbed.

'Darrell, would you mind?' Janine asked, her voice trembling as she nodded towards the girl. Her husband scooped up their daughter, tapped Joe on the shoulder and took them out of the room. 'You too, Anna.'

Anna went to complain but, clearly sensing the situation, opted to stay silent. She switched off the television and followed the others. Marcus took a seat on the now vacant sofa, pushing a worn maroon cushion out from behind him.

'Do you really think you can help?' Janine asked bluntly, eager to get started now that the children were out of earshot. 'I'm so relieved you're here. It's just been – well...'

'Awful?' Catherine answered. Janine nodded, noticing that, while Catherine watched her, Marcus scanned the room – for what, she wasn't sure.

'Mrs Morris, why don't you start by telling me about some of the things that have been going on, some more details of what you and your family have been experiencing?' Catherine rested her hands on her knees, leaning closer to Janine, who had taken the armchair next to the woman. As Janine attempted to explain some of what had happened Darrell returned, leaning against the door frame. She couldn't help noticing the fresh whisky in his hand but continued without mentioning it.

'Emma's nosebleed in particular – honestly, it terrified me. It was so ... extreme. The doctor couldn't believe it. Yet she's fine. Shaken, of course, but healthy, which is so strange. If you'd seen her! Everything combined, it's just...' Her voice trailed off.

'It's draining, isn't it?' Catherine stated more than asked. Both the Morrises nodded this time.

'Look, I won't lie to you. I can sense something in this house. I felt it the second I walked through the door. It's hard to tell if someone is being genuine on video, without meeting them or personally feeling the space they say is being targeted, but now I'm here I know I was right to come to you.' Catherine's face no longer seemed as soft; it seemed to become more severe as she spoke. The creases under her eyes, around her pursed lips, were suddenly more noticeable, and she was sitting up rigidly. Even her eyes looked different – colder, somehow. Janine shivered.

'I can't say what it is yet, but there is something ... and I'm afraid I'm fairly certain it's hostile. If we're dealing with a demon – well, this is always how it starts. With tricks, pranks, things to make you doubt yourself. You see, a demon wants to exhaust you, it wants to drain you. It feeds off desperation, enjoys your fear, and it will get nastier and more violent until it gets what it wants.'

'Which is?' Darrell asked, taking a gulp of whisky. Janine could see he was nervous, hiding behind the drink.

'One of you,' Marcus said, his voice cold. He was staring at Darrell with such intensity that Janine swore she felt the room chill.

'Like, to possess?' Darrell looked at Janine as he said the word, his eyebrows raised. Despite his outward cynicism she could tell he was increasingly uneasy, that he wasn't as able to dismiss these notions as easily as he might have wished to.

'Exactly, yes,' Catherine answered. 'A demon does not come from this world, from the living realm, so to speak, but it is desperate to cross over and will do anything it can to facilitate this. There are three stages to demoniacal activity: infestation, oppression and possession. The demon needs to make you weak so that when the time comes you won't fight back. It sounds as though it is already reaching the stage of oppression.' She spoke slowly, her words deliberate, and they hung in the air. Marcus stood up and began to pace around the room, his fingers tracing along surfaces. Janine and Darrell watched. He lingered in front of framed photos of the children, paying close attention to the various objects that decorated the room.

'Okay, hang on. You just said you don't know what it is, so couldn't it be something else? A ghost, maybe? Or, what are they, er, a poltergeist?' Darrell took a swig of whisky. Janine was surprised he was going along with the conversation, but found herself desperate to know the answer. She instantly looked back to Catherine.

'From what you've described, I think we can rule out a ghost. Ghosts are often seen, for a start, and none of you have witnessed a physical presence, correct?'

Janine shook her head.

'They are normally passive spirits, aiming to communicate,

often seeking help, but they are harmless, if a little creepy. And ghosts rarely move things.'

'Poltergeists do, though,' Darrell pointed out. 'I've seen the film. And aren't they ghosts?'

Catherine gave a thin smile, but there no warmth behind it. 'That is true: a poltergeist is a rather vengeful, aggressive spirit. And they like to frighten and cause trouble.'

'So it could be that?' Janine said, her eyes widening. 'Is that better or worse than a ... demon?' She was finding it hard to get her words out, not quite believing the conversation they were having.

'Better than a demon, worse than a ghost,' Marcus answered from across the room, his arms crossed. He made Janine nervous and she wished he would sit down.

'Well, let's just say there is something,' Darrell said, his scepticism clearer again. 'How would we tell the difference?' He glanced between Catherine and Marcus, his gaze stopping on the man when Marcus reached into his suit jacket.

'Simple.' Marcus took out a set of rosary beads. 'We will see if it hates God.' He grinned. Janine gagged at the expression on his face. There was nothing funny or enjoyable in the situation, in what they were going through.

'You mean using crosses and holy water? Like an exorcism?' she asked, panic seeping into her voice.

Once more Catherine nodded. 'Demons hate God – they hate religion, vindictively so, in fact. Faith in God, an exorcism by a true believer, is hugely threatening to a demonic entity. It is the one thing that can truly banish them and prevent them from crossing over. Are you religious, Mrs Morris?'

'Not really, no. I mean, not officially. Darrell doesn't believe at all, and I suppose I don't really know.' She looked to her husband and he frowned.

'It's always seemed ridiculous to me,' he said, his tone just short of dismissive. Catherine latched on to it immediately. In a second she had shifted in her seat and locked her focus on him.

'Let me tell you now, Mr Morris, God is very real. Demons are very real. I have first-hand experience. Trust me when I say that if you don't start believing pretty damn quickly, and we don't fight to get rid of whatever has its sights set on your family, things will get worse very quickly. Demons want to possess, to come over to this realm. What if it wants one of your children, Mr Morris? Tries to take one of them? Will you believe then?'

As though her voice was ice, Darrell looked as if all the heat had been stolen from his body. His face was noticeably pale. The ice in his whisky trembled quietly in the glass as his hand fought to stay steady. Janine had rarely seen her husband stunned into silence, but he did not answer Catherine. Rather he looked down at his feet as though in acquiescence.

'Can you help us then?' Janine asked. She needed a definitive answer. Just as Catherine's warning had lanced through Darrell, its barb was firmly in her too. Her three beautiful children were in this house, just one floor above them, where even now something could be watching them, waiting, ready to pounce when the right moment came. It was almost too much to comprehend, but her body ached with the need to do something about it. She had to protect her family, and if that meant placing trust in these strangers, that's what she would do.

Catherine glanced back and forth between her and Darrell, then moved her attention to Marcus. Something passed between them, Janine could feel it. When Catherine turned back to her, Janine knew what her answer would be.

'Yes, I believe we can. And we will. But we need to talk terms.'

Janine swallowed a painful lump, terrified of what was to come but knowing she had to go through with it. Darrell came to her armchair and perched on the side, taking his wife's hand.

'Tell us what we need to do,' he said, his voice solemn but determined. Janine held back a tear as she felt him squeeze her fingers gently.

'So London life suits you, then?' Rachel Callahan asked, finishing her cherry lager.

'You mean, apart from all the bodies?' Daniel smiled, arching one eyebrow, and Rachel laughed. He wasn't sure whether it was the drinks or having one of his best friends sitting opposite him that made him so happy. She'd already picked apart his lack of a love life, but he had missed the gentle ribbing, the jokes, the comfort and familiarity she brought with her. Since he had moved from Buxton he hadn't put much effort into his social life, which consisted of occasional drinks with colleagues or a rare Chinese takeaway and poker at Charlie's Bethnal Green bachelor pad. He enjoyed being in London, but outside work he was pretty much on his own. Rachel had been his confidante for a good few years, almost his therapist at times. Her insights were second to none.

'Yeah, about that – how are you, of all people, coping with being a homicide detective inspector? You faint at the sight of a scratched knee. I still can't believe you've overcome everything – you know, what happened with Amanda.'

Rachel was one of the few people, family aside, who knew what Daniel had gone through over a decade ago, what he had done for his sister. She was well aware that he would always bear a deep emotional scar, one that affected almost everything he did.

'Honestly, I'm as surprised as you are. The most recent victim? The killer was bloody vicious. And any time I see a body that's even slightly cut up, I can't help having flashbacks.

It's hard, I won't deny that, but the satisfaction of solving cases outweighs it all, for the most part. After all, what happened to Amanda made me want to join the police force – it was bloody good motivation. And working with Charlie helps. He's a brilliant partner, a bit of a lifesaver in general. Stops me feeling so adrift, even if he does cause a few bouts of jealousy every now and then.'

'Has anyone taken the piss out of your surname yet? I bet a few people haven't been able to resist.'

'Charlie did, naturally, but no, mostly people just frown, as though they have misheard, then ignore it and move on.'

'I get that – might seem a bit juvenile to laugh at. And I know what you mean: I love the feeling, the satisfaction of actually helping. It's what kept me in homicide for so long. I don't envy the stress levels, though. I'm glad I switched to community work,' Rachel said. 'I still get to help people without having to worry about bodies turning up.'

'You saying I look stressed?'

Rachel nodded, her ponytail shaking. The trace of a smirk lined her lips. 'All I'm saying is, I swear you've gone more grey since last time I saw you.'

'You know I'm only thirty-four. Full grey is a bit off just yet! Anyway, have you got time for another drink? I'm not ready to let you go yet. It's so good to see you, even if you do take the piss out of me.'

'I don't have to get up early,' Rachel said with a wide grin, as he got up and headed towards the generously stocked bar.

'I do, but one last one, okay?' His head wasn't exactly spinning, but too much more would surely make him fuzzy the next day. The mechanic case was bugging him, and he was not about to lose a day to a hangover. They still had next to nothing to go on, and frustration and alcohol-induced exhaustion did not mix well. He hoped that the coroner would turn up something useful. The thought of standing in a morgue while fighting off a hangover made him feel queasy.

'Do you believe in this stuff?' Rachel asked as he sat back down and pushed her drink across the table. She held out her phone to him, but he couldn't read it properly from where he was sitting.

'What is it?'

'It's on the *Metro* online. I was having a quick browse while you were at the bar. Some woman saying there's a demon in her house. Creepy.'

Daniel rolled his eyes and took a sip of his pint. 'Come on, you know I don't buy into all that supernatural crap. Don't you think there'd be proof by now if ghosts and goblins existed?'

'What do you call this, then?' Rachel challenged, holding the phone out to him again. He took it and had a quick scan through the piece, not watching the video clip that accompanied it.

'Not evidence, that's for sure. An overactive imagination, though, I'll give you that.'

The noise level in the bar rose briefly as a conversation started to get heated. Daniel and Rachel looked over instinctively, ready to intervene, but the issue dissipated as quickly as it had arisen. The small group were already laughing and clinking pints again, and didn't seem like they would cause any trouble.

'I think ghosts exist,' Rachel continued as they turned their attention back to each other. 'At least in some capacity. Maybe not like dead people haunting places, but I heard this interesting theory once that they could be people in a parallel universe who accidentally cross over a line sometimes and that's why we only get blurry or see-through glimpses of them. And why they often don't react to people or things on this side.'

'So now you believe in multiple universes?' Daniel frowned.

'How strong is that drink?' They laughed, but Rachel didn't drop the subject.

'I'm serious. Don't you think it's weird that there are so many stories about ghosts and demons and monsters, from even hundreds of years ago? And new ones all the time? They have to be based on something.'

'Maybe. Or they're a result of humans constantly having to find justification for things they don't know how to explain.'

'Mr Cynical, party of one.' Rachel smirked.

'You know me. I like to go on facts.'

'And how's that going?'

'Right now, not very well.' Daniel had explained the basics of the case to her – what he was able to share, at least.

'You remember back in Buxton when that body turned up in the old dairy warehouse and you beat yourself up for days because we didn't instantly find out what happened? You need to allow the facts to come into view organically. You can't just force them to appear.'

'Okay, point taken.'

They sipped their drinks.

'Let's just hope you don't have a serial killer on your hands,' Rachel added. Daniel gulped another mouthful of his pint, shivering from her comment.

The smell of chemicals in the air was mild from outside the small building that was Haringey Mortuary, but it still overwhelmed Daniel and he was glad he'd limited his alcohol consumption the night before. He hated mortuaries with a passion. This one was surrounded by trees, on a pleasant leafy road, but still he felt sick. The thought of dead bodies, ones sliced and picked apart no less, made him feel nauseous, and he longed to be anywhere else. That was not an option, however, and he tapped his foot as he waited for the coroner dealing with their case to arrive.

Charlie was silent too. Daniel knew his partner wasn't as bothered as he was to be around the dead. Charlie didn't look uncomfortable, but he was unusually quiet, jumping when a man in a crisp white lab coat bounded into the small waiting area.

'I'm sorry I'm late, I got held up on an important call,' the man said, his tone unapologetic despite his words.

'Hi, Samson,' Charlie said. 'This is my partner, Detective Inspector Graves.' Daniel stood and shook the doctor's hand. It was warmer than Daniel expected, as though Samson should be as cold and slick as the bodies he examined.

'Graves ... you new?' Samson asked, his lips curled into a grin. His eyes were hyperactive behind his glasses, and Daniel could tell what he was thinking. *With a name like that, maybe it should be you working here!*

'Relatively, I suppose. And I make a point of not visiting mortuaries if I don't have to,' Daniel answered, glancing through the glass door to the shiny steel and white tiles of the examination room beyond. He couldn't help noticing the unmistakable shape of a body on a shiny metal table. Whoever was unfortunate enough to be lying there was covered with a white sheet, but he assumed it was Rogan Simmons.

'I'm Samson Lepard – good to meet you. Shall we?' Samson said. Without waiting for a response, he led them into the examining room. Daniel felt his stomach flutter, but ignored it, following the doctor and Charlie. Without ceremony Samson stopped by the body and pulled the sheet back to reveal the pallid form of their murder victim. The man's abdomen had been opened up entirely, the skin peeled back around the ribs and his internal organs removed. Bile bubbled in Daniel's throat and he turned away instinctively.

'You could have warned us,' he muttered as he leant against a nearby counter, trying to stay on his feet, fighting the urge to pass out.

'What did you expect?' Charlie smirked from behind him. 'Want some water?'

'There's a drinks fridge in the back,' Samson said, indicating a small office space in the corner of the room, a room only slightly more inviting than the morgue proper. 'Take what you want. And I'll have a Red Bull. Just please don't spill anything.'

Samson waited while Daniel retrieved two cans of the energy drink and took a gulp before carefully placing the can well out of the way. Daniel was glad of the drink. The sugary liquid covered up the bitter taste of bile. He stood a few metres from the body, more out of a wish to keep away from the body than a fear of contaminating the area by spilling his drink.

Samson put on blue latex gloves. He pointed to the left side of Simmons's ribcage. 'See the nicks along the costochondral and the costal cartilage here? How they stripe?'

Charlie leant in to get a better look.

'Caused by a serrated blade of some kind?'

Samson nodded.

'Do you know what kind?' Daniel asked. He was keeping his gaze off the body, taking regular sips of his drink.

'I struggled at first, but luckily for me the weapon hadn't been cleaned before the killer used it. It left a few particulates behind.' Samson stepped back and took another drink, as though deliberately building the suspense.

'Of?' Charlie urged, raising his eyebrows in expectation. Samson lowered the can and set it down. 'Motor oil.' Daniel and Charlie looked at each other, both thinking the same thing.

'Looks like we'll be paying another visit to our mechanic

friend then,' Charlie stated. Daniel was not convinced that Jason Tagoe, the owner of the garage Simmons had worked at, seemed a likely suspect. That didn't mean that Jason hadn't divulged other details, however. And of course he could have just been a very good actor.

'So did you narrow down the possible weapon?' he asked, eager to have something more concrete to take to Tagoe.

'After I found the oil traces I did a search of widely used mechanics' tools, but that turned up nothing that would cause these marks, so I spread the net wider. A variety of options came up, but after a few digital comparisons with the striations, it seems a hunting knife of some sort is our culprit. One with a large, very sturdy blade – a serious piece of outdoor equipment. The blade would be about thirty millimetres wide and probably over fifteen centimetres long.'

'Which explains why this chap was so cut up,' Charlie added. Daniel had a flashback to the previous morning: the body starting to bake on the red rubber of the athletics track. Someone had really gone at Simmons – a savage attack by anyone's standards. Certainly a large blade would be capable of doing that kind of damage, but the person wielding the weapon must have been holding on to some boiling anger. Again, Tagoe didn't seem to emit that kind of energy when they had questioned him, and he wasn't a suspect. It was possible that Cassandra Salinas was still linked somehow, but she was petite compared to Simmons. Did the angles match? Was she strong enough to overpower Simmons and inflict such mutilation? And if so, why?

Daniel shook his Red Bull and found it empty. As though his surroundings were sentient and had been waiting to pump pungent preservatives into the air, he could feel nausea ready to come back with a vengeance.

'Anything else you can tell us?' he asked Samson, wanting to be done, to get out into the relatively fresh air of the city, even if it was still hot outside.

'I can't be certain, but I think the knife would have been held like this.' Samson retrieved a scalpel from a metal drawer unit and held it by the handle, the blade pointed down. He did a stabbing downwards motion, then switched to lashing out and up to the side. 'It seems that the killer sliced rather than thrust the blade, to have a stronger grip on the handle. Those areas of the ribs aren't as tough, but still, to leave such clear marks there means some real strength behind the blow, and real animosity. I reckon the killer is right-handed and not that tall, but they could have been crouching slightly, which would make their stance more solid and allow more force behind the blade.' Again he mimed in slow motion how he suspected the attack had occurred.

'Okay, so the height might not be exact – could be someone short or tall – but we have a right-handed killer who may be into hunting and has some connection to cars.' Charlie thrust his hands in his jeans pockets. 'Thanks, Samson. I would shake your hand but – well, you know.' Samson smiled. His eyes still seemed a little manic, possibly exacerbated by the caffeine, though Daniel suspected the man was always like that.

'No problem, gentlemen. You know the way out?'

'Keep going until we smell fresh air?' Daniel answered. Samson gave him a jovial frown and Charlie laughed. Daniel was only half joking. He practically counted the seconds until they were back outside in the sunshine.

CHAPTER SIX

Janine was staring uneasily at the half-empty bottle of whisky in her grip when Anna's voice made her jump. She narrowly avoided dropping the bottle.

'So what the hell was that last night?' her daughter demanded, having entered the kitchen with ninja-like stealth. Janine would normally have scolded her for her tone, but not this time. She simply didn't have the energy. There were more important issues vying for her attention. Janine placed the bottle back in the wooden rack on the counter and turned slowly to Anna, not entirely sure what to say.

Anna was standing with her hands on her hips, her perfectly styled wavy brown hair falling over her shoulders. Her neon Katy Perry concert T-shirt was an ironic contrast to the ripped denim shorts and black biker boots she had teamed it with. Her lips were pursed with disdain and irritation. She was no longer a kid who could be fobbed off with a vague answer and a kiss on the head.

'Can you please dial down the angst a bit, Anna?'

That got a tut and an eyebrow raise but Anna's posture relaxed a touch.

'They were here about the...' Janine found that she couldn't bring herself to finish the sentence, but Anna did it for her.

'Freaky demon that's ruining our lives?'

Janine nodded, flinching at the word she dreaded. 'Yes. It seems they saw the news piece and think they can help.'

'Oh my God, really? That's amazing, I can't take much more. I still think we should just move, though.'

Janine would have laughed at the blissful ignorance of the comment if she hadn't partially agreed with it. In some ways, she thought it might actually be easier to move.

Catherine Delamar had emailed Janine a quote for her services barely an hour after leaving the night before. The numbers made Janine want to cry. Her husband, on the other hand, was successful in drawing tears from her. They argued about whether they were being conned, about manipulative people preying on the weak and defeated, and how Janine let her emotions and paranoia get in the way of the truth. Darrell followed it with another jab at her stupidity at appearing on the local news site. The real problem was that Darrell could not offer up another explanation when Janine put him on the spot, tears streaming down her reddened cheeks. A few thousand pounds was a big gamble – an insane one, in fact, given what it was for. She was well aware of that. But if it meant that her family felt safe and secure in their home again, if they regained control over their lives, surely it was worth it.

'It's only money,' she pleaded, to be rewarded with a groan and an eye roll.

'Only money we don't have, you mean,' Darrell pointed out, throwing his arms out in exasperation, his voice sharp, verging on aggressive.

'Yes, we do – we're not totally poor, you know. We could–'

'What, dip into the kids' college funds, not have any sort of holiday this year? I thought you wanted to take the kids to Florida?'

'I want the kids to be safe in their own fucking house!' Janine fired back, fresh tears coming with the anger. A seemingly endless silence followed.

Eventually Darrell agreed to pay Catherine and her colleague, but Janine didn't feel like it was a win, not in the least. She felt neurotic, paranoid, and couldn't shake the thought that maybe Darrell was right and they were being swindled. More than that, she was starting to feel alone in all of this. Sure, the kids believed that there was something supernatural disturbing them, but she needed an adult on her side. The few friends she had told had been supportive but highly sceptical, and they weren't close by. She needed Darrell, her husband, the father of her beautiful children, the man she shared her house and her life with, to be on her side. She felt as though he was thinking it was worth paying more to get her off his case than to ensure the safety of their family, and that only upset her further. Janine hated herself for thinking it, but it was a barbed thorn of a thought that she couldn't quite pull out.

Naturally, she said none of this to Anna, who was now working through a tube of Pringles so fast it was like she'd not eaten in a week.

'So are they doing it, then? They're going to get rid of it?' Anna asked through crunching mouthfuls, flicking crumbs off her chin, her eyes wide as she waited for an answer. Janine realised she had been lost in her thoughts and nodded.

'Yes. Your dad and I don't really see any other choice. They're coming this evening. We felt ... well, there's no point waiting.' She put her hand out for a few crisps, but when she put one in her mouth she realised she didn't want it. She wasn't hungry in the least. Her appetite had been dwindling for days.

For all of her complaining, Anna seemed instantly better

and bounced out of the kitchen. As Janine found herself alone once more, the weight of the situation pressed down on her and it felt as if something was watching her again. Something just out of sight, enjoying the pain and misery it was inflicting, relishing her suffering. What if that was all it needed? Catherine and Marcus had warned them clearly. Demons fed on misery, actively looked to weaken the spirit. She shivered. Suddenly, paying a demonologist didn't seem quite so absurd. Janine left the kitchen too, eager for the company of her children.

As they approached the garage, Daniel's hope of getting fresh information sank. When they spoke to Jason Tagoe the previous day, the place had been thumping with music, car parts spilling out over the tarmac out front, open for all the world to see. This was not the case now. Daniel was irritated. They had a personal address for Tagoe, but he'd been hoping for the easy route. If the guy had done a runner it would make things a lot more difficult. Charlie remained by the pavement, scanning the empty street as Daniel approached the garage, also markedly quiet.

The two large metal shutters were pulled down, heavy padlocks bolting them shut, but Daniel noticed that the person-sized blue door to the left was ajar. A shiver kissed the back of his neck. As he reached the door he slowed his breathing and craned his head, listening intently. Somewhere nearby the jingle of an ice-cream van rang out, but the garage was silent. He glanced back to his partner, who was keeping one eye on him and one on the street. Charlie nodded. Daniel pulled out his baton and gripped it tightly, his knuckles going white.

'Hello? Mr Tagoe? This is Detective Inspector Graves. I spoke to you yesterday,' he called out from beside the door.

There was no response. He shifted to the opposite side and leant in, peering through the gap. The garage interior was dark, with only the sunlight providing any illumination. Dust shimmered in ethereal clouds in the sunbeam, hiding what was beyond.

'Mr Tagoe, are you there?' Daniel called out again. 'I'm here to speak to you about Rogan Simmons.' Motionless, he waited for an answer. Again none came.

'I don't like this. What small business owner would leave his property open and unattended? Think he's bolted?'

Charlie joined him by the door and leant in to listen, just as Daniel had. 'Let's check it out,' he said, his voice low, caution filtering into his tone. Daniel nodded and pushed the door inwards with his free hand.

'I'm coming in, Mr Tagoe,' Daniel warned, eager not to surprise anyone who had somehow not heard his previous calls. The door squealed as he pushed it open. Light spilled into the space, forming a skewed rectangle across the oil-stained concrete floor, silhouetting Daniel's figure. Small stars of sunshine reflected off the tools hanging along the walls. A good proportion of the garage remained in shadow. Daniel looked around near the door, spotted a heavy industrial power unit on his left and flicked the first switch in a line of four. An overhead fluorescent strip-light blinked noisily to life above them. Daniel pushed the rest of the switches up and the garage slowly filled with a dirty yellow light. Everything looked much the same as the previous day, though marginally tidier, with no tools left on counters and no dirty rags lying around.

'I'm getting the impression that Tagoe didn't open up today,' Daniel said, his voice low. 'I really don't like that the door was unlocked.'

Charlie turned back to the blue door and pushed it shut. He took his hand away. There was a quiet click and the door opened a crack. He pushed shut again, and again the door opened.

'Someone likely pulled this shut behind them and it just swung back on its own,' he said, looking at Daniel.

'Someone who didn't know it would do that. Surely Tagoe would have been aware it would reopen. He'd have locked it.'

'Yup,' Charlie muttered. 'Think that someone's still here?' He also unclipped his baton, holding it ready at his side. He signalled to Daniel to go left while he went right, heading towards the walled-off office space. Daniel took a long breath and crept along the left wall, following the counter. His gaze flicked from side to side, looked for anywhere someone might hide. Then he spotted the two doors on the left. Tagoe had appeared from one of those on their visit yesterday. Keeping his footsteps as soft as possible, he reached the first door. Both were closed. He listened hard, tuning out the noises made by his partner, but heard nothing else.

Door one proved to be unlocked. Daniel entered the room quickly. His gaze swept over the space. It was a stockroom. Light filtered in from two grimy windows high on the opposite wall, revealing three aisles of floor-to-ceiling metal shelving containing boxes of parts stacked in an orderly fashion. A few files gathered dust on a separate shelf nailed to the wall next to the door, and a mop and bucket sat beneath it. Tagoe was not there. Confident there was nowhere someone could hide, no other exit, Daniel turned back to the garage proper and shut the door behind him.

Through the yellowing rippled glass of the office he could see Charlie inspecting something. Another scan of the garage found no other movement. Time for door number two. Daniel reached for the handle. This one was not locked either.

Inside it was dark. Daniel fumbled for a light switch, found one and pressed it. Light blossomed. He was in a two-stall bathroom with a miniature sink and equally tiny mirror squeezed in one corner. A pungent smell crept into Daniel's nostrils and his skin crawled instantly.

He looked down at the concrete floor and saw exactly what he didn't want to see. A spatter of blood spots led to the second stall, the door of which was shut. Using the tip of his baton, Daniel pushed the door.

Jason Tagoe sat, fully dressed, on the toilet seat, slumped back. His eyes were open, shiny, and his face was slack and pallid in the places it wasn't covered in blood. As Daniel leant towards him, holding his breath and trying not to gag, the cause of death was immediately clear. A nasty wound on the right side of his skull revealed a mixture of bone chips and flesh glistening among the clotting blood. Daniel stumbled backward, vomit rising up his throat.

'Fuck! Charlie!' he yelled.

There were running footsteps, then Charlie came in to see what had caused such a reaction.

'Fuck,' he echoed.

CHAPTER SEVEN

The garage hummed with life. Daniel was trying to keep his nerves from showing on his face. He hadn't eaten in hours. Though he was most definitely hungry, he knew he wouldn't be able to keep down anything for a while. He was still in shock: first from the fact that their only genuine suspect in the Rogan Simmons case was now dead, and second due to the brutal nature of his murder.

Now not only did they have no suspects, but they were no closer to having any clue about the killer's motive either. A feeling of helplessness often threatened to overshadow his determination to solve a case, and Daniel could sense that struggle building. He prayed that the squad around him would turn up something he and Charlie could work with. His faith in his own abilities had grown substantially since he had moved to London, but he was no miracle-worker, no Sherlock-Holmes-style genius. He knew he wasn't about to spot a minuscule clue no one else had registered, and solve the case with a witty piece of exposition to a dumbfounded audience before receiving rapturous applause.

Three crime scene investigators, a medical examiner and a

forensic anthropologist had already worked up some significant analysis. It was ruled that Jason Tagoe had been killed the night before, just a few hours after Daniel and Charlie had questioned him.

'Whoever killed him was not particularly careful,' the forensic anthropologist, Stephanie Mitchum, informed them. 'From the pattern of damage on the victim's body, I'd say this was a quick, violent attack, and probably quite opportunistic.' Her auburn hair was pulled back into a tight ponytail, the taut skin on her face emphasising her severe tone. When not speaking, her mouth was a thin line that appeared unable to form a smile.

'Another quick, nasty attack ... spur of the moment. Sounds like the same MO as with Simmons,' Charlie summed up. They were standing in the garage, outside the small bathroom where the body was still propped. Daniel glanced at the metal shutters, one of which had been opened to allow easier access. A sergeant was forcing back a journalist.

'That didn't take long.' Daniel nodded as the police officer pushed the young man and his huge microphone back to the street. His cameraman stumbled in a bid to get out of the way.

'Anyway, Charlie is right: it seems likely we're dealing with the same killer. Maybe he killed Tagoe because we questioned him about Simmons, to shut him up. Shit.' He sighed, his sentiment echoed by Charlie's forlorn expression.

'Whoever did this did it quickly,' Stephanie elaborated. 'The back of the victim's left knee was smashed in with a solid, likely metal weapon, which I believe is also what did the damage to the skull. Though I've yet to do a thorough examination, it would seem that blunt force trauma killed the victim almost immediately.'

'So our killer came up behind Tagoe, incapacitated him by taking out one leg, then finished the job with the head wound?'

Daniel asked, loosely miming the attack movements. Stephanie nodded.

'And followed up with another blow to make sure,' she added. 'He would have died very quickly. One of the CSIs checked the bathroom and found traces of bleach mixed with blood, on the floor and one wall. The room was cleaned but hastily, hence blood spots remaining.'

'So they stuck around just long enough to clean up, but didn't do a great job. Maybe they were panicking,' Charlie muttered, as much to himself as to Daniel and Stephanie.

'We're checking the sink and toilets for fibres and DNA samples now,' Stephanie said, picking up Charlie's train of thought. 'The killer may have cleaned themselves up too. The wound to the back of Tagoe's head would have caused blood, and possibly hair or bone fragments, to spray out backwards, pretty much directly at the attacker. I doubt they would have avoided getting any of that on them.'

'That could help us. Being bloodied and dishevelled would certainly make someone stand out. Any idea about the weapon?' Daniel asked, though he suspected he knew the answer.

'Given the injuries and the attack scenario, a tool from the garage. It would have been heavy, with a large, probably fairly rounded end. Some kind of wrench, maybe. I'll inspect the bones in the lab when everything here is wrapped up but I suggest you start looking for a missing tool around here.' Stephanie gestured towards the wall that was covered in equipment before bidding them a temporary farewell and headed back into the bathroom.

'Well, that will be easy.' Charlie groaned.

The day dragged for Amelia Harding. She found herself working on numerous cases, supporting a handful of senior colleagues, but the tasks were routine, with nothing to sink her teeth into. Chasing a security firm on a minor jewellery store robbery. Filing statements from a break-in.

Until Detective Inspector Graves called. Amelia was surprised that they'd found another body, one seemingly linked to the murder of Rogan Simmons, and she was more than ready to help out.

Amelia had found that she had a natural affinity for homicide cases, and made sure she manoeuvred herself into a role where she would get to assist on them. She loved watching crime shows on TV – she watched so many she sometimes had trouble keeping track of the episodes she'd seen. She also devoured crime novels, though less than she would have liked.

A double murder with no suspects and no motives got her blood buzzing, and she put her investigative skills to work the second she hung up the phone.

Having already tried to find a motive through the known but shallow connections between Rogan Simmons and Cassandra Salinas, it was time to see how Jason Tagoe slotted into the picture. Daniel told Amelia that he suspected Tagoe had known something that the killer wanted to be kept a secret, since he had been killed shortly after being questioned. They were going to talk to Salinas again, and needed Amelia to see if she could find a connection between Salinas and Tagoe.

Amelia started with some simple online stalking of Tagoe's Facebook page and Instagram accounts, and business registration details. Cassandra Salinas did not appear once, and Simmons only showed up as an employee at the garage in some official paperwork, with no social or personal connection to Tagoe beyond that.

Frustrated by her lack of progress, Amelia changed lanes

and started down another route. Opening the files on Rogan Simmons, she scrolled through the photos until she found the shots she was looking for. Her screen filled with hi-res images taken in the mortuary, detailing every tattoo the man had. Neither Charlie nor Daniel suspected that his murder had been gang-related, but Simmons had ink, Salinas had ink and worked at a tattoo studio, and Amelia had seen from Tagoe's social media that he was a fan too, with a few pieces of art himself. There were also the photos of Salinas and Simmons at what seemed to be a tattoo convention. Daniel suggested it could be worth a look. Although she was not convinced anything would come of it, it was somewhere to start.

She started with known gang tattoos, particularly any known to feature prominently among Greater London's criminal database. Unlike in the USA, however, little attention was paid to tattoos in the UK prison system, and there was not much to go on. Simmons had a cross on one arm, and playing cards splayed out in a design that included a skull and roses, but Amelia couldn't link either to any criminal activity. The symbols were pretty familiar in the world of tattoo iconography, though perhaps the cards were a reference to gambling. She made a note to see if Simmons had ever had a problem with that.

She was scrolling through the photos of the dead man's ink for the fourth time. The images were starting to blur together when something caught Amelia's eye. It was a symbol around the size of a £2 coin, blended in so well with the surrounding design that she had barely noticed it. It was nothing special. It was in the shape of a bird, like a crow, solid black with a small star in the centre. As she zoomed in on the image, she became certain of something. She had seen it before.

With a new resolve she started to sift through all the tabs open on her browser. Fingers singing across her keyboard, she raced through pages, scrolled through images – and then there it was. Amelia clicked on the second image and it popped out larger on the screen, giving her a clearer view.

Jason Tagoe had posted a photo on Instagram six months ago of a tattoo on his left shoulder. It was an all-black design, showing what Amelia thought was an old American muscle car of some sort, driving out of an explosion of flame, smoke and car parts. It was clearly referencing the garage – maybe it was Tagoe's favourite car? To the top right of the design was the bird, flying out of the chaos. Amelia pulled up the photo of Simmons and positioned the two images side by side. The birds were almost exactly the same, both solid black with the same negative space star in the centre.

'Same artist?' she muttered to herself. She had an inkling that someone else connected to the case would have the very same mark branded on their skin too. Amelia opened up a new tab, searched Cassandra Salinas on Facebook and clicked on the woman's profile. Looking through the photos took a while – Salinas had posted more than three thousand – but after a few minutes Amelia had what she needed.

The design on Salinas's ankle consisted of intricate vines, leaves and blossoms, winding their way up the side of her calf. Two bird silhouettes topped off the artwork. One featured a star.

'Bingo.' Amelia grinned, picking up the phone to call Daniel.

CHAPTER EIGHT

Sitting in a line on the sofa, Anna, Emma and Joe Morris reminded their mother of the three wise monkeys, but the thought failed to bring a smile to Janine's face. Her stomach was barely allowing her to keep down the paltry lunch she had forced herself to eat, and her throat felt rough, as though coated in sand.

The quietly ticking clock on the wall said it was almost five. Catherine and Marcus were twenty minutes late. Anticipation was working its way through every nerve in Janine's body and she could not sit still. She was wound as tight as a spring, and it was making her feel sick.

'Are you okay, Mummy?' Emma asked. Emma didn't know what was about to happen; Janine thought it easier to explain that they were waiting for some friends to come round. At least she was sitting still – a minor miracle given her normal state of hyperactivity. A soft toy of Olaf, the snowman from *Frozen*, sat on her lap, his fixed cheery expression at odds with Janine's own. In a bid to mimic the happy character Janine willed her lips to show a morsel of positivity, an attempt to reassure her daughter if not herself. She picked up her wine glass from the coffee table and took a small sip, then another. A few seconds of calm came over her as she closed her eyes and savoured the flavour, but all too quickly the moment was over. Her mind was unable to stop turning over what was about to happen.

Across the room, Darrell stood against a bookcase, whisky in hand. Janine wanted to berate him. She was beginning to feel genuinely worried by how much he was drinking. Proving that she was a massive hypocrite didn't seem like the best idea, however, and she needed her wine. He looked just as tense as she was, and an argument would whip up in seconds given the atmosphere. Still, she put her glass back down, as though to set an example.

'Do we really have to be here?' Anna said when no one had spoken for a few minutes. Unlike her little sister, she was fully aware of what was going on and had already said that she did not want to be around to witness a demonologist in action, did not want to witness a demon materialise and cause havoc right in front of their eyes.

'Yes, you do,' Janine answered a little too sharply, then regretted it immediately. She was keenly aware of the effect this whole ordeal was having on Anna, on all of them, and she softened her tone as she continued. 'Catherine said that the whole family needs to be here. Whatever we're going through, it's important that we're together for this.'

'What if something horrible happens, though?' Anna complained. 'I saw *Insidious*. You're not supposed to communicate with demons. If some nasty red and black monster shows up, I'm out of here.' The girl spoke with utter sincerity, and Janine fought a wave of dizziness at the mention of monsters, not sure what to say. She doubted a physical being would be summoned into their sitting room – the very notion was ridiculous – but surely something would happen. After everything they had been through so far, surely they would hear things, see things. It scared her not knowing what. The weight of the unknown pulled at her nerves.

'That's why we're bringing in the experts,' her father answered. 'It'll be fine. I'm sure they know what they're doing. And this isn't a film, Anna. I don't think a monster will appear.'

Janine thought she could sense a bite of sarcasm in Darrell's words, but again she chose to ignore it, rather than confront it. Maybe he was covering up nerves, maybe not, but it didn't matter. It was too late; they had paid up. The demonologists would arrive any minute. Janine was beyond caring whether or not it would prove to be a con. She needed to get past whatever was going on. If Catherine could help, then she'd be crazy not to let her.

'What if they do summon something, though? It could latch on to one of us. I don't want to be possessed!' Anna continued anxiously.

Emma looked at her big sister with confusion. 'What's coming?' she asked. Anna went to respond but Janine stopped her.

'Don't,' she warned, glaring at the teenager. Anna folded her arms and slumped back on the sofa, scowling but heeding the warning nonetheless. She muttered something under her breath, but Janine chose to ignore it. She wanted an argument with her daughter even less than one with her husband. Overall, Anna was turning into a pretty decent young woman, but she could well and truly flip when she wanted to, and Janine needed all of her energy to focus on the issue at hand.

The doorbell rang. Joe jumped up as though rocket-propelled.

'I'll get it,' he squealed, clearly the only one in the room who was excited about the visit. Janine followed him swiftly. She wished she too still enjoyed the blissful ignorance of childhood, where things were an adventure, full of intrigue and fun, not tainted with a constant fear of what was to come.

As she walked along the hall towards the front door, a chill washed over her and she paused. Without even thinking, she angled her gaze to look up at the ceiling, at Joe's and Emma's room above her. Her brain told her that something had moved up there, that she had heard footsteps even though the whole family were downstairs.

'Enough,' she chastised herself in a whisper, before realising she wasn't just aiming that at herself. 'Whatever you are, your time is up.' Her words bristled with venom, hissed from between gritted teeth. Maybe nothing had been up there; maybe her nerves had played tricks on her. But then again... She found it easier and easier to believe that something was harassing them, and she wanted it to know that its time was up. She was done letting it mess around with her family.

'Mrs Morris, good to see you again,' came the unmistakable voice of Catherine Delamar. Joe was standing next to her, still grinning, and behind them was Marcus Spindler, wearing a rather more grim expression. He had a large black leather bag in one hand. With no greeting beyond a nod, he pushed past Catherine and headed for the sitting room.

'No time to waste,' he said as Darrell came forward to shake his hand, which he took briefly but firmly.

Janine swallowed, flexed her fingers at her sides, and flinched when Catherine took one hand in hers.

'It's going to be okay, Janine, I promise. We're going to get rid of this thing. I won't leave until we do. Come, now. Marcus is right, we need to get started.'

Janine nodded and was about to follow Catherine when Joe tugged at her top, pulling her back.

'Did you see him, Mum? He was at the top of the stairs again. Are they here to make him go away? I hope so. I can't stand it anymore.' He stared up at her, his big green eyes frightened, and his fingers found hers. For a second, Janine thought she was about to throw up. She glanced back towards the stairs. *Nothing there, Janine, nothing there.* She ushered Joe to the sitting room to join the others, then pulled the sitting-room door shut behind her.

'Are we ready?' Catherine asked.

Janine grabbed her wine off the coffee table and gulped back a mouthful, nodding. 'Yes, let's get this over with.'

It wasn't long before the sitting room began to take on a new form. With the sun starting to lower and the blinds shut, an eerie, sallow orange light tried and failed to break through. Dust-speckled beams lanced in through gaps in the slats, piercing the space but achieving little. Janine couldn't help thinking it was a sign that the light was failing to combat the darkness. The room felt cold, almost hostile. It was unnerving. How could her own home suddenly seem so unwelcoming?

There was some light, however, coming from numerous candles. Catherine and Marcus had laid them out all over the room, and tiny flames danced on the coffee table, the fireplace and on all three bookshelves. They failed to add warmth. The black wax felt threatening, only adding to the dour sense of gloom that was taking over.

Janine watched as Marcus moved around the back of the sofa, feeling unsteady at the sight of the small wooden crosses he held in both hands. He began to place them around the room, just like the candles, six in all. They were just over twelve centimetres in height, simply manufactured and lacking any real detail, yet with every one Marcus set down, the tension in Janine's gut tightened further. Marcus caught her gaze.

'They piss off demons,' he explained. 'Any religious iconography does, really, but they particularly hate crosses.' His lips turned up in a thin smile, as though he was genuinely amused by the idea, but Janine could not smile back. Unlike him, she found no joy in what they were doing.

Emma giggled at the curse word. Anna tapped her gently on the head, frowning. Joe tried to tap Emma too, but missed. He stuck his tongue out at her instead, a gesture she dutifully returned.

'Be quiet and play with Olaf,' Anna muttered before she turned her attention back to the visitors to watch with cautious fascination.

'Demons have a long history of animosity against all forms of religion,' Catherine stated. 'They can't resist reacting. The crosses should help with that.'

'Hang on, you want this ... demon ... you actually want it mad?' Darrell asked. He sat on the arm of the sofa next to his son. He had been quiet for a while, but Janine could tell he was starting to get worked up. How could he not? With every minute that passed, the idea of a manic demon targeting them seemed to feel even more real to Janine, harder to brush off as paranoia or imagination.

'It's a necessity, I'm afraid, Mr Morris. You see, we need to know what this is. We need its name. In order to find that out, we have to engage with it, distract it. The more agitated it gets, the more forthcoming it will be. Only once I have its name will I have any power over it, and a chance of casting it out.'

'Is it dangerous?' Janine asked, not liking how weak her voice sounded. She had not topped up her wine and was now longing for more. The pressure in the room was unbearable.

'I won't lie. Yes, yes, it could be.' Catherine's voice was low, sincere. It bit right into Janine, who sagged against her husband at the response. 'The more angry this presence gets, the more risk there is.'

'That's why we wanted you all together,' Marcus chimed in, leaning against the fireplace, having evidently finished his set-up. 'There's strength in the family unit, something in our favour, but it could go after any one of you, should you be apart when we contact it.' Marcus's expression was more stern and his eyes darker. Though he had one hand in his pocket and his stance was casual, he did not look relaxed.

As one, the candles flickered. Shadows bloomed around the room, hoops of light swirling across the ceiling to cast twisted shadows off ornaments and light fixtures. Everyone fell silent. No windows were open and no breeze had fluttered in. Just as quickly as they had begun to flicker, the flames fell still again and the shadows calmed.

'We're not alone,' Catherine announced. Janine felt her heart skip. Anna whimpered, and Catherine put her finger to her lips. The teenager kept quiet but took her little sister's hand, her eyes wide. Emma used her other hand to angle her soft toy out at the room, as though letting the snowman see for himself what was going on.

'Everyone, stay very still,' Catherine whispered, holding one hand out as she surveyed the room. Marcus retrieved another wooden cross from his bag on the floor but kept hold of it instead of setting it down like the others.

Janine watched Catherine closely, studying her body language. The woman was elegant, almost regal, in the flickering light, but there was something unsettling about her that Janine couldn't name.

Then Catherine spun so quickly towards the door that Janine jumped.

'Did anyone hear that?' Catherine asked, her voice a murmur. No one nodded, as though they were scared to move. 'Marcus, could you check? We need it here but it seems ... hesitant.'

'Or it's messing with us,' he responded. He walked across the room nonetheless and slowly opened the door to the hallway, still holding the cross. Janine swallowed as Marcus headed out of sight. She felt like she might pass out, and was fighting the urge to grab her children and flee.

'I need to establish dominance. It needs to come to me, not me to it,' Catherine explained, not turning to the family but surveying the ceiling, the edges of the room, the darkening corners.

'What's that gross smell?' Joe asked. His voice dripped with disgust as he wriggled around on the sofa, his nostrils flaring.

'I don't smell–' Darrell started, but the words stopped in his mouth. He sniffed.

'I can – it's, like, rotten or something. Oh God, it's here, isn't it?' Anna squealed.

'Marcus!' Catherine called, her voice startlingly loud in contrast to the previous hush. 'It's here!'

Marcus bounded back into the sitting room, cross still in hand. On the shelving unit next to him a photo frame fell over with the sound of cracking glass.

'Did you do that?' Janine asked, her pulse starting to pound. Marcus shook his head, the cross held to his chest.

'Demon!' Catherine called out. 'Your time here is up! You have been tormenting this family for too long, and you need to leave!' Her voice bellowed, deep and resonating. Janine put one hand up to her mouth, glancing at her husband to check his reaction. He looked as scared as she felt, his mouth slightly open, as though not quite believing the situation. The children huddled closer together.

'The strength of this family is better than you, their love is stronger than you. You will not find what you need here. Leave!' Catherine yelled. Then she fell quiet. The Morrises stared at her, not sure what to expect. The candles continued to flicker, but Janine thought it was getting darker. She looked from flame to flame.

'Have they...' she mumbled. Darrell followed her finger, which pointed around the room. The flames had died down to almost nothing, minuscule buds where there had been healthy golden tongues.

'Shit,' Darrell muttered. Emma didn't giggle at this curse, only gripped her soft toy tighter.

'Dad?' Anna moaned.

'Ssh,' Catherine whispered, again putting her hand out to silence them. They fell quiet, waited. Then they all heard it: a rattling, like an object being moved. Catherine flicked her gaze around the room, then so did the others. All searched for the source of the sound. Anna yelped when the cross on the mantelpiece fell on its side. Everyone stared at it – everyone except Catherine, that is. She pulled a necklace out from under the collar of her blouse to reveal a small silver cross, then she held it up and out to the room.

'What is your name, demon?' she asked, not yelling any more. The rattling was back. They all stared around the room.

'Oh God,' Janine whimpered when the cross on the coffee table trembled and fell over, just like the first. Darrell stood up, sweat starting to bead on his forehead. He pulled at his collar, taking deep breaths before swigging the last of his whisky. Janine had walked past Catherine to grab his hand when a guttural whine froze her on the spot. Her heart lurched in her chest at the unnatural sound.

'Catherine?' Marcus said, concern spearing his tone, tilting his head, his eyes wide. Janine turned slowly, not wanting to see the woman but needing to more than anything. She couldn't help gasping. Catherine stood bolt upright, her arms flat at her side, her legs tight together, but her head was tilted back and she was staring at the ceiling. Everyone went quiet as broken, scratchy words started to tumble from Catherine's mouth.

'Scarruss ... adraam ... pracasaasiss...' The words stretched out from Catherine's mouth slowly, hissing and rough, reverberating around the room as they got louder.

'Adramelech!' Catherine yelled in a deep voice that was booming and alien. Emma screamed and burrowed into Anna's side. Janine wanted to grab her family and run, overwhelmed by the need to get them out of the house and away. Darrell moved closer to the hallway door. Janine thought he had the same idea. His eyes were wide in horror. She met his stare for just a second. *Do you believe me now?*

'Adramelech? Is that your name?' Marcus asked the room, closing in on Catherine but looking up and around him. The woman fell silent. Then her head began to turn, ever so slowly, until she was looking at Marcus, her eyes open yet glassy. As one, the three crosses on the shelves toppled over. Without a word, Darrell bolted out of the room into the hallway.

'Darrell!' Janine went to follow him but Marcus blocked her way, an arm stretched out in front of her.

'Stay with the children!' he snapped. She jumped backwards, shocked at his aggression.

'Demon, I know your name. I have dominion here; you have no power.' He began to speak in what sounded like Latin, holding out his cross towards Catherine. As he spoke, the words came faster, spilling over his lips, spittle sprayed and his voice got louder until he was shouting. Janine grabbed for her children, who were bunched up behind her, terrified of what was happening yet utterly unable to act.

Marcus shouted one last word, then touched the cross to Catherine's forehead. She dropped to the floor, her body limp. The silence was so sudden that Janine thought for a second she had gone deaf. The kids didn't move. Marcus didn't either, except to look down at the woman. The whole room was still, the candles not even flickering.

'Look,' Joe whispered after a few seconds, pointing to

Catherine, whose hand was twitching, fingers tapping softly on the carpet. Like life returning to a corpse, she gasped and sat up, her eyes wide, her hands behind her to steady her.

'What ... what happened?' she asked, her voice dry. She pushed her hair back from her face, breathing deeply. All eyes were on her. Then the unmistakable sound of glass shattering from somewhere else in the house pulled everyone's gaze towards the hallway. The door was still open, shadows pooling beyond.

'Darrell?' Janine called, her voice barely a whisper. She took a step towards the door, a hand held behind her, signalling the children to stay put. She called out again, then paused. She had heard something – a shuffling sound, or feet scuffing across the floor. A dark silhouette burst into the hallway, slamming against the wall.

She screamed. 'Oh God, Darrell!' She went to grab hold of him, but something stopped her. Darrell stumbled forward, sliding against the wall, and light fell on his face. His eyes were rolled back, the whites exposed. Saliva frothed around his mouth and dribbled down onto his shirt. A painful growl came from deep in his throat. As Janine stood there, terror-stricken, wanting to take him in her arms but unable to move, Darrell dropped to the floor.

Her head pounding so much she feared she would pass out, Janine lowered herself, one hand steadying herself, the other touching her husband's chest. It was still. As the tears broke and her mind screamed out silently, she heard someone behind her. Not turning, her body shaking as she fought to understand what had happened, Janine felt a touch on her shoulder.

'I'm so sorry,' Catherine whispered.

CHAPTER NINE

The search for a weapon in the garage was a bust – not that anyone was surprised. Even though it was relatively tidy, the place was brimming with tools, some in their rightful place, many not, and it was impossible to work out what might have been missing. A small lead had been found, in the form of a box, with an indentation in its fabric lining that suggested maybe a knife was meant to be kept inside it. Daniel and Charlie hoped it would prove to be the same knife that had been used to kill Rogan Simmons, but without the weapon itself it was of little use. Daniel suggested that Cassandra could have taken the knife on one of her visits to the garage to see Simmons, but it was just a guess. He had no way of proving this.

UV lights provided a glimpse of the path Jason Tagoe's killer took to leave the crime scene. A few drops of wiped-up blood led towards the main door to the building, but no spots had shown up on any of the equipment. The CSIs agreed that whoever had killed Tagoe had most likely taken the weapon with them, no doubt ditching it somewhere later. A perimeter search had been ordered, taking in the streets surrounding the garage, but nothing had been found.

The body had been taken to the mortuary in Haringey. There was no need for an autopsy, as it was obvious how Tagoe had died. They hoped to find trace fibres, cells or marks – anything to illuminate the case.

When he left the garage, Daniel found himself even more frustrated than when he had looked down at Rogan Simmons' body. There was simply nothing solid to go on. Without any suspects, and two victims with no obvious ties to anything nefarious, finding a motive for the deaths was nigh-on impossible, though they would canvass the area and check CCTV. That could give them something.

After leaving the crime scene, Charlie Palmer was called away to meet another inspector on an unrelated case. That meant Daniel took ownership of the tattoo lead uncovered by Sergeant Amelia Harding. He was not convinced it would lead to anything, but it was currently all they had. He was outside the Costa on Finchley high street a few minutes down from the studio, an iced coffee in hand, enjoying the late afternoon sun that warmed his face, when he heard Amelia call out to him.

'Wake up,' she said with a grin, pulling her sunglasses up to rest on her head as she came to a stop next to him.

'I'm awake, promise.' Daniel smiled, shaking the drink at her. 'Nice and caffeinated.'

'Long day?' Amelia asked.

'Naturally. And Charlie being called away isn't exactly helping. Let's keep this short. If we can find out anything about the tattoo connection, I'll count it as a win. After you.' He gestured towards the shop before binning the remains of his drink.

Amelia nodded and led the way to the entrance of Needlepoint Ink where Charlie and Daniel had been the day before. As Amelia pushed the door open and the bell above it jingled, butterflies flew a loop in Daniel's stomach. The redhead with the magnetic smile once again sat behind the counter. Her face lit up when she saw him.

'Come for that tattoo after all then, Inspector?' She grinned. Daniel flushed instantly and Amelia looked confused, raising one eyebrow. He struggled to regain his composure, would have laughed at the thought of being caught in between two women he fancied, were it not for how awkward he was feeling. He paused to calm himself and brought his attention back to the matter at hand.

'I'm afraid not. Jenny, right?' he asked, though he did not need to check her name.

'Yep.'

'And I'm Sergeant Harding,' Amelia added, still watching Daniel.

'We were hoping that someone here might be able to help us out with the investigation we mentioned yesterday.' He pulled his phone from his pocket and found an image of the bird silhouette tattoo Amelia had discovered. 'Do you recognise this?'

Jenny took the phone and tapped the image to zoom in. Her smile vanished. Daniel felt a knot start to form in his stomach. Her expression was the type that never came with good news.

'Yeah, actually, I do.' She grimaced. 'It's a signature, only...'

'What is it?' Daniel urged as Jenny struggled to find the right words. His schoolboy feelings were completely forgotten as Jenny bit her bottom lip. Were they about to strike gold?

'Well, the, er, the artist who did this, Glint, he's ... kind of ... dead.' The words hung heavy in the air, the buzz of the needles in the parlour heightening their impact. Daniel licked his lips, which felt dry and irritated. Their only new lead, and it was literally a dead one?

'Can you elaborate?' he asked slowly.

'Okay, you know Banksy?' Jenny said. 'Who got famous

from doing all those street art murals? There's one not far from here, on the North Circular.'

Amelia nodded. Daniel narrowed his eyes, not sure where this was headed.

'Well, he got famous because he's good, obviously, but also because no one actually knows who he is. The mystery of it all makes Banksy super-popular.'

'Surely someone getting a tattoo can see who is doing it,' Amelia interrupted. Jenny nodded and continued.

'Of course, normally. But Glint did all the work with a curtain in the way, from loads of different studios. And anyone who got a tattoo by Glint would be forced to sign a non-disclosure agreement, whether they actually saw him or not, and his tattoos always came with a signature – that bird. He became pretty well known over the past few years, as much for all the dramatics as being a good artist.'

'And now he's dead.' Daniel frowned, still unsure how this could be useful. A dead artist as a link between two murder victims and a weak-at-best suspect was hardly the light at the end of the current gloomy tunnel he felt stuck in.

'I'm surprised you didn't hear about it.' Jenny swivelled in her chair to type something into the computer on the counter. A few seconds later she invited them to come around the counter and see the screen, which showed a news report. 'See? There was a fire at a convention in Manchester. Seven people died. Apparently Glint was among them, though it's never been proven. I mean, how could they? But since then no one has seen Glint. It's pretty weird, if you ask me, kind of pretentious.'

Daniel got the sense that Jenny thought the idea of a mystery tattoo artist ridiculous. Her tone seemed more dismissive than before. She was about to close the page when he spotted something in the article.

'Wait, can you scroll down one second?' he asked. Amelia

leant in closer next to him, curious about what he had spotted. He could smell perfume: he wasn't sure if it was hers or Jenny's, but he did his best to ignore it. Now was not the time.

As the article went into more detail about Glint, who was described as a minor celebrity in the tattoo world, Daniel spotted the word 'fortune'. It seemed that when the enigmatic Glint disappeared, what had happened to his fortune became shrouded in as much mystery as the artist himself. The article eventually dismissed most of the drama and secrecy that surrounded Glint as wild theories, even stating that the tattooist may have used the fire as an excuse to retire, but that no one would probably ever find out the truth. Still, Daniel felt more positive. It may be nothing, but it was interesting nonetheless. Money was always a good motive for murder. They would be on to something if they could connect Glint more solidly to the victims.

'Jenny, thank you, that's really useful. Amelia, shall we?' He indicated towards the door. Amelia and Jenny frowned, surprised by the sudden resolution to the conversation.

'That's it?' Jenny asked. 'What did I say?' She leant forward on the counter and Daniel smiled at her.

'I think you may have found us a possible lead.'

'No way! That's ace. Glad I could help,' she answered, her own smile stretching. She was looking directly at him and he swore for a second that they were having a moment, their eyes connected in that extra-special way. Then Amelia tapped him on the shoulder and the bubble popped.

'Detective Inspector?' she said, before thanking Jenny and heading to the door, the bell chiming above when she pulled it open.

'Thanks again, Jenny,' Daniel said as he followed his colleague, his head still turned towards Jenny.

'No probs. Hope to see you again soon, maybe for that

tattoo? I'm a pretty good artist myself, you know.' This time her grin was undeniable. When she winked, Daniel had to try hard to stop himself stumbling out of the studio. As the door closed behind him, he glanced back. Jenny gave a little wave through the glass.

'So, we have a motive?'

The bubble burst a second time as Daniel turned to see Amelia standing, her hands on her hips, eagerly waiting to hear what Daniel had stumbled upon. The afternoon traffic clogged up the road behind her, a double-decker bus throwing up exhaust fumes as it chugged past. She had the hint of a smirk on her face, her lips curving, but Daniel pretended he hadn't noticed. He didn't want to be teased, especially by her.

'Not necessarily, but it could be something. According to that article, Glint was loaded but the money is unaccounted for – at least, publicly. It's possible that whoever killed Tagoe and Simmons knows about the cash, and presumably Tagoe and Simmons did too. Hence why they're dead. Obviously, it's just a theory at this point, but it's a start.'

He saw the logic click for Amelia.

'Interesting... I mean, it's hundreds of thousands, right? Maybe more. And whether Glint is actually dead or not–'

'Someone with knowledge and a desperate need for money could have gone after it,' Daniel finished her thought. 'We need to find out as much as we can about Glint. Client lists, contacts, known associates. Did he actually die in this fire? And let's question Cassandra Salinas about him too. I still think she was hiding something from us, and she does have a Glint tattoo after all.'

With a sense of hope, Daniel was about to part ways with Amelia when his phone went off.

'One sec,' he said, answering the call. 'Detective Inspector Graves.'

As he listened to the voice at the other end of the line, all feelings of joy began to flee and he felt his shoulders sag. 'I'm sorry, can you say that again? A demon?' He couldn't quite believe what he was being told. It didn't make any sense. Amelia was watching him, unable to hear the other end of the conversation. Her eyes went wide at the word 'demon' and she mouthed it at him, her eyes narrowing.

'Can't you send someone else? I'm following up on another lead as we speak.' He frowned, his free hand rubbing at his temples and then his afternoon stubble as it sank in that his evening off had just gone out the window.

'Okay, sure. Have you called Palmer? Can you get him to meet me there? Thanks.' He ended the call and shoved the phone back in his pocket, sighing as he did.

'What the hell was that about?' Amelia asked immediately. 'I did hear you say demon, right?'

Daniel nodded. He took a breath and looked back at Amelia. 'We have another body on our hands. Crazy as it sounds, the woman who called it in claimed to be a demonologist, said something about an exorcism gone wrong. She said a demon killed someone.'

'Which is clearly bollocks.' Amelia frowned, though she pulled her jacket closer around her.

'Of course. Someone needs to go and look into it, though, and guess who got the call. Apparently everyone else is busy.' Realising he was moaning to a junior colleague, Daniel gave a thin smile and shrugged.

'Well, do you need any help?' Amelia said, clearly willing.

Daniel shook his head. 'No, thank you. Palmer is going to meet me there. If you could go back to the office for the last hour or two of the day and look into Glint some more, that would be a great start. I might need your help on this too, though. Keep your calendar free, okay?'

Amelia nodded and said goodbye, heading back to the Tube station where she had parked, in the opposite direction to him. She promised to call if she found anything, and Daniel silently thanked his lucky stars to have such a reliable sergeant. Amelia was a real asset to the department – and Daniel felt like he was going to need all the help he could get.

He strode back to his own car. His stomach was already churning with the prospect of what he was about to face, the word 'demon' spinning in his mind.

Aware that any case with an unusual twist would prove popular, Daniel had expected a certain amount of activity. What met him as he turned into Whitmore Close, which was in Arnos Grove, gave him a headache before he had even parked.

As daylight gave in and started to creep towards night, the silent lights of ambulances and police vehicles threw impossible patterns across the block. Faces lit up in a wash of colours as the crowd stood, watching the spectacle that was taking place, some simply curious and others jostling to get near the cameras that accompanied the small army of journalists. Smartphones recorded everything.

Daniel pulled in to the kerb as close to the house as he could, switched off the engine and took a deep breath before stepping out into the chaos. He headed for the perimeter being maintained by three weary constables and flashed his badge as he crossed the line. From somewhere behind him he heard voices call out, wanting statements, but he ignored them.

'Is Detective Inspector Palmer here yet?' he asked the closest uniform, who nodded and pointed to the front of the house where two paramedics were deep in conversation, their faces confused. He had to speak with them at some point, but wanted to catch up with Charlie first, so he headed up the path to the open front door. Light bloomed out across the small step. Inside, he heard his partner's voice. Daniel pulled blue plastic bags over his feet and moved down the short hallway, then took a left. He had to stop immediately.

'Oh good, you're here. This is … insane,' Charlie announced with a nervous laugh. Between him and Daniel lay the body, although an opaque plastic sheet kept it hidden, for which Daniel was thankful. Next to Charlie was another paramedic and the same CSI Daniel had met in Finsbury Park. He nodded a grim greeting. Daniel thought everyone looked a bit dumbstruck.

'Tell me,' he responded, crouching to take in the scene. Spots of something recently dried dotted the laminate hall floor, and beyond Charlie he could see a sitting room in mild disarray, but neither told him much.

'I'll try. I imagine you know that the call about the death came in from a woman claiming to be a demonologist? Catherine Delamar. She's outside waiting to give a proper statement. Apparently the family who live here claimed that something was haunting them. They called in her and a colleague to basically perform an exorcism of the house.'

Charlie signalled for Daniel to follow him and turned round in the hallway, heading into the sitting room. Daniel stepped past the other men, careful not to nudge the body in the narrow, crowded space.

'They really were,' he mumbled as he took in the room: the crosses and candles that littered every surface, the rosary beads on the coffee table. Some of the candles were still burning, and their flames added a strange motion to the light from overhead bulbs. A soft toy lay discarded on the floor and the sofa cushions were messy, one hanging off the edge.

'Delamar has claimed that, during a confrontation with the

demon accosting the family, the victim, Darrell Morris, stormed out of this room before stumbling back again moments later, foaming at the mouth and with his eyes rolling back in his head. He died right there in the hallway. The kids witnessed everything.'

Daniel couldn't help groaning. So there were children involved? That made everything so much worse. 'Where are they now?'

'The wife is outside with one of the paramedics. She's in shock, naturally. We'll have to wait until she's more lucid to question her. As for the kids, they're with a friend of the family a few streets away. We'll need statements from them too. We have a social worker on standby, but I wanted to get them away from the circus outside. Their faces will already be on the news. I don't want reporters thrusting microphones at them too.'

'Yeah – what is with that outside? I figured there would be some attention, but that's ridiculous,' Daniel said, even now aware of the constantly flashing lights trying to break through the blinds.

'It's mainly because of the mother, Janine Morris. She was interviewed by the *Haringey Advertiser* for a news piece just a few days ago about this supposed demon. In fact, the woman who interviewed her tried to do a follow-up piece with me when I got here. The original video is already going viral.'

'Shit, I know which one you mean. Rachel showed me the article last night. It's all nonsense though, right? I mean, this is not the work of the supernatural.' Daniel squinted at the closest cross, lying on its side on the fake oak bookcase next to him.

'You might want to hold on to your doubts for a while longer,' Charlie said, pulling a face as he spoke.

'What exactly does that mean?' Daniel asked, although he got the feeling he did not want to know. He had meant what he had said to Rachel. He firmly believed that the supernatural was folklore and stories dreamed up by people desperate to find explanations for things they could not understand. In his eyes, the very notion of ghosts and goblins was laughable. This was not why he had joined the police force. Still, Charlie's expression unnerved him. Not because he thought for one second that this case was really delving into the realm of demons and devils. Rather, it meant that, just like the case he was already on, this one was going to get complicated, the last thing he wanted. *One confusing murder case at a time, please!*

Charlie waited a second for Daniel's response, clearly not sure how to phrase what he wanted to say. He ran a hand through his blond fringe, pushing it off his forehead, and perched on the arm of the sofa.

'Sounds like he was poisoned,' Daniel interrupted, already thinking the story was a cover.

'Let me finish. We all thought the same thing as you. Problem is, the paramedics did a pretty thorough examination of the body and they agreed there was no sign that the man had been poisoned. They'll need to run a tox screen, of course, but they were pretty certain. And there were no traces of anything in his spittle. It appears that his heart stopped, just like that.' Charlie clicked his fingers.

'Come on, seriously? There must be hundreds of poisons that could have this effect on someone. And people have sudden heart attacks all the time. Nothing you said sounds like the work of a demon. Has the house been searched?' He looked around the sitting room, searching for anything else odd – apart from it looking like a set from *The Exorcist*.

'A preliminary sweep. There was a smashed glass on the floor, minute traces of whisky. All of the alcohol bottles have been catalogued and taken for testing.'

'Well, there you are, then.' Daniel shrugged. 'Sounds like you're getting sucked into all this demonic crap. The question we should be asking is who poisoned him.' Daniel went to leave and Charlie stood up straight.

'*If* he was poisoned. And if I were you, I wouldn't discount anything yet. I don't think it's that straightforward.'

'And here I was thinking you were a rational, intelligent man,' Daniel commented, only half joking. He was surprised that his partner was being so open to other possibilities. No, they didn't know who was responsible, but it was pretty obvious that Darrell Morris had simply been poisoned. All this demonic fluff was just an outlandish cover story. It had to be. The alternative was ridiculous. And Daniel could not claim to know everything about his partner, having only been working with him for a few months, but he was pretty certain that Charlie didn't really believe a demon was responsible for the dead man.

As they stepped past the body, heading for the front of the house, a chill came over Daniel. It snaked down the nape of his neck. He hesitated. Despite all the noise outside, he felt as if everything had gone quiet. It was an unsettling sensation.

'What?' Charlie asked. Daniel shook his head and pulled open the front door, bracing himself for the chaos outside.

Ridiculous, he thought again. *Demons aren't real.* He believed that, he really did. Shaking himself mentally and circling his shoulders to loosen them, he aimed for the two paramedics still in conversation by the ambulance, but the chill hadn't left him. He could feel it in his bones.

CHAPTER TEN

'She doesn't really look like a murderer,' Charlie muttered as they watched Catherine Delamar through the one-way mirrored glass. They had made the decision to take her in to headquarters at Scotland Yard and were now monitoring her. They wanted to get a sense of her before they questioned her and took her official statement. The woman did not seem fazed by her surroundings and sat with her hands in her lap, prim and upright. Her style was simple and smart. Her pressed skirt, white blouse and well-cut jacket gave her an air of trustworthiness, which Daniel thought ironic.

'Not really, but we both know that doesn't necessarily mean anything,' Daniel said. 'Is there anyone who doesn't know this is one-way glass these days?' He sighed as Catherine glanced in their direction, her emotions hard to read. He knew she could not hear them, but he still felt like she was eavesdropping.

'Blame crime shows.' Charlie smirked. 'You take her and I'll take Mr Spindler. Tag team if we need to?'

Daniel nodded and Charlie left the room. Alone, Daniel moved closer to the window and focused on the woman on the other side. He wasn't sure exactly what to expect from her, but at least she seemed fairly co-operative so far.

'Hi, Mrs Delamar, my name is Detective Inspector Daniel Graves.' He greeted her warmly as he entered the interview room, holding out a hand. She stood and took his hand. Her hand felt weightless in his. Daniel wondered if she was really as innocent as she seemed.

'It's Miss, actually,' she answered calmly before sitting back down, her movements smooth and proper. It struck him that they had made that mistake with Cassandra Salinas as well, but he let the thought pass.

'I read your statement. It's ... quite a wild story,' Daniel started. 'Hard to swallow.' He wanted to tell her it was ridiculous and she should just come out with the truth, but he needed to hear it from her, to see how genuine she was. Her smile faded as she brought her hands up to rest on the metal table between them, though she kept eye contact with him.

'Such a horrible ordeal. My heart truly goes out to the Morris family. It is not at all what was intended.' Her voice was soft. She reminded Daniel of a kind old relative, someone who would always be there for you with words of wisdom and a cup of hot tea. Her mannerisms and voice only heightened this impression, and it was worryingly disarming. Daniel mentally shook himself, aware that he needed to look past all that.

'Intended? What exactly did you intend? Not for someone to die?' he asked, trying to maintain an edge to his voice. He wanted to needle her, push her, pick at the story until she revealed it was nonsense. Catherine's eyes widened and she looked genuinely taken back.

'Detective, you must understand that Darrell Morris's death was the exact opposite of what Marcus and I intended. We were there to help that family, and I am devastated that we failed so spectacularly.'

'"Failed" is an interesting choice of word. Most people would say you succeeded. The Morris family bought into the pretence of a being haunted by a demon, and you used it to your advantage.' Daniel knew that would get a reaction. Sure enough, Catherine's face tensed.

'And here comes the part where you tell me that demons and devils don't exist, I suppose, that you think my story is just a convoluted narrative to cover up the truth.' Her voice was still calm but her features had hardened.

Daniel nodded. 'You said it. How about we cut to the chase? You and I both know that demons aren't real. And we all therefore know that a demon did not kill Darrell Morris. So tell me, Miss Delamar. Who did?'

Across from him, Catherine swallowed. She looked down at her hands, as though searching for answers there. For the first time her composure seemed to have slipped. Not by much, but enough for Daniel to feel confident that he would resolve this in no time.

Janine Morris was just about aware of the room around her, but she was struggling. Moments after waking, she was doing her best to piece together familiar sights among the blur. She figured she was in a hospital bed, but her vision refused to crystallise and her thoughts remained muddy.

She blinked and rubbed her eyes, which helped clear things up – visually, at least. The world outside was dark, the city lights twinkling. Janine wondered what time it was. The last thing she remembered was being at her house, with her family, and... *Oh God.* A tsunami of events flooded over her and she started to shake. The demonologist, the exorcism, how scared the kids had been...

Darrell.

Wiping her face with a sleeve, Janine tried her hardest to get her breathing under control. Slowly she steadied herself. She needed to take stock, to figure out what had happened, how she had ended up in hospital.

What do I remember?

Collapsing. She remembered falling to the floor, someone helping her. Dirt and gravel under her hands. She checked her palms, inspected the grazes that had just begun to scab over.

An ambulance. She had been sitting in the back of an ambulance with someone talking to her, though she didn't remember the conversation. Had the woman been a paramedic? Probably. It was all hazy, patchy, like remembering a heavy night through next day's hangover.

The kids!

For a split second her heart filled with panic, but her gut knew they were safe. Alison – they were with Alison. And a police officer. She took a deep breath, her pulse slowing again. The children were safe. Alison wouldn't let anything happen to them.

Janine realised that she must have succumbed to shock and been brought in for observation. The image of Darrell stumbling towards her, his eyes white and his mouth full of spittle, flashed in front of her. She held back bile even as she wept. Once more she fought to calm herself, her chest heaving between sobs. She reached out and gripped the cold metal bar at the side of the bed to ground herself.

Eventually her tears slowed, then stopped. Janine's breathing became steady. She noticed for the first time how quiet the hospital was. No one shared her room. She stayed motionless, listening. From somewhere she could hear a phone ringing, and a snippet of a conversation by someone on the move – perhaps a nurse on her rounds. Other than that, the world was still. Not even traffic noise from outside penetrated the silence. She guessed that she was too high up.

For a while Janine simply sat there, the bed sheet rumpled around her knees, not sure what to do with herself. She wasn't attached to anything, no drips or other equipment. Perhaps she had just zoned out so completely that the paramedics wanted to make sure she hadn't gone catatonic, and she was resting where a nurse could keep an eye on her. I feel fine, she told herself, before realising that actually she felt a bit too fine. Sure, she had just cried her guts out, but a feeling of numbness had crept in around the edges.

'Perhaps I'm still in shock,' she said out loud, and clapped a hand to her mouth when her voice splintered the quiet.

After another minute, Janine had had enough. She was filled with too many questions. How long she would be in hospital? When she could be back with her children? What had happened to Darrell? Who had taken her husband from her?

Footsteps outside the room got her attention. She swung her legs off the bed, then realised she was in a hospital gown. Her own clothes were not in sight, probably stowed away by a nurse, and she shivered when her bare feet met the cold floor. She made her unsteady way to the door and peered out into the long white corridor, which gleamed under fluorescent strip lights that hummed gently. At the far end of the corridor two doctors were talking over a flipchart, but otherwise it was quiet. She jumped when a door opposite her swung open, revealing a short, rather plump nurse with a kind smile and an immaculate uniform.

'Mrs Morris, what are you doing up? You need your rest. What you went through today ... well, it takes a toll on your energy.' The nurse spoke with a soft Lancashire accent. Janine calmed as the woman ushered her back towards her own room, before questions burst out of her.

'I'm afraid I don't have all the answers yet, Mrs Morris, but how about I call up one of the police officers? I think they went for a coffee, but I'm sure they'd be happy to answer anything they can.'

'That would be brilliant, thank you,' Janine said as the nurse tucked her back into bed. She still felt oddly numb, but the reassurance the nurse gave was welcome.

'Now, get some rest. I'm sure one of the officers will be up shortly. And my name is Nurse Grantham, in case you need me.' The woman shone another kind smile at Janine and then she was gone.

Rest, Janine told herself, *good idea.* She lay back and closed her eyes but her brain would not stop chattering and she soon gave up, sitting back up in bed.

The room seemed darker now, and Janine rubbed her eyes. Had Nurse Grantham turned the lights down? She couldn't remember. Maybe she had turned off one or two. It was late, after all. Janine couldn't remember her doing so, but she was hardly in a clear state of mind.

Not yet ready to sleep again, she got out of bed, moving over to stand in front of the window so she could look out at the city. She could just make out the tip of the Shard, a few Canary Wharf skyscrapers in the distance. She took in the vista slowly, appreciating the view despite what she feared the city held. Out there life was moving on, people unaware of what had happened to her family on Whitmore Close. She sought to find her house, at least the area, in the city, but she wasn't sure where she was. It dawned on her that she didn't even know which hospital she was in. Her room had no signs to indicate its name.

Shifting her focus, she stared at her own reflection in the window, appalled by what she saw. She thought she looked worse even than when she had been interviewed; that morning seemed like aeons ago. The weary woman who looked back at her was pale and hollow, a barely-there shell of a person. Her body seemed to have shrunk, as though she were slowly collapsing in on herself from the stress of all she had been through.

She let out a low sob, surprised that she could see her breath as it steamed up the glass, hiding the city under an opaque oval for a second or two. Had her room grown colder too? She put her hand to the window to feel its chilled surface, gasping when something whipped past her reflection. She spun round.

The room was empty, silent.

She became horribly aware of how vulnerable she was in the hospital gown. Her heart began to thump.

With her back to the window Janine stood, frozen. She had seen something, she knew it, and she shivered as her brain began to process things again: everything that had happened to them in the house, what Catherine had warned her about, the image of her husband in his last moments. Demons targeted people, they messed with them, weakened them emotionally and physically.

It followed you, a voice in her head whispered. The thought chewed into her mind as her knees threatened to buckle. *It never wanted Darrell or the children. It used them to get to you. And now it's here. And you're all alone.*

Her pulse throbbed, blood pumping painfully through her temples, and she felt as if she might faint. She gripped the window sill at the small of her back, desperate to steady herself. She knew she couldn't stay where she was. It wasn't safe. She couldn't let what had happened to Darrell happen to her. She didn't care about herself, but she couldn't leave the kids. She was not about to let them lose both parents in one day.

Janine took a step towards the door, then paused, her gaze flitting around the room, searching for anything out of the ordinary. Nothing happened. A quick breath, and she dared to take another foot forward. The lights flickered off and on, a hissing buzz above her, and she froze again.

'Shit,' she gasped. Her voice was a tremble, muffled by tears and fear, her body shaking. She was petrified, yet she knew she couldn't stop. Mustering all her willpower, she took another step across the room, then a second, a third, edging past the end of the bed. She whimpered when a metallic clanking began. Eyes wide, she slowly turned her head to find the source of the sound, at once needing to know what was making the noise and dreading what she would see.

High on one wall, a metal vent cover rattled in its brackets. As she watched the screws began to twist, one by one. The rattling was getting louder as the cover banged against its frame, the sound echoing around the room. Unable to move even as her mind screamed at her to run, Janine listened as one drawn-out word, guttural and laced with intent, came from the thick darkness inside the vent.

'Aaaadddddrraammmmeelleeeccccccchhh...'

The vent cover creaked and fell off the wall, slamming onto the floor. It skidded towards her, coming to a stop next to her foot, the screws bouncing away into the shadows.

Janine screamed and ran towards the door. She threw herself into the corridor, shrieking when a shadow loomed in front of her from nowhere, wrapping strong arms around her to pull her to it. She hit at the form, fighting to get free as its grip tightened.

'Mrs Morris!' Nurse Grantham shouted. The human voice was like a beacon. Twisting towards it, Janine tripped over her own feet. As the officer holding her caught her weight before she hit the floor, she sagged and burst into tears.

'Oh goodness, Mrs Morris, what happened?' Nurse Grantham asked, gently taking her hand. Janine could not answer. Her body shook uncontrollably, the horror and distress too much for her to overcome.

'So she never broke character? Not once?' Charlie asked Daniel.

Daniel shook his head.

'Bugger. Spindler was the same. He didn't slip once. Frankly, it was weird.'

'That they seem to believe every word of the crap they're telling us, you mean?' Daniel frowned, then took a swig of the thick black coffee he was gripping as though it were a genuine life force. 'After the day I've had, I was hoping for simple, not crazy. And they were a full-on serving of whack job.'

They stood in the small kitchen unit a few corridors away from the interview rooms, both yawning and frustrated. Charlie poured a coffee for himself, then sat at the only table and blew on his drink before sipping carefully. Daniel joined him, sitting opposite.

'I really thought that at least one of them would admit how stupid this all is, and that they poisoned Darrell Morris.' He shook his head, sighing as he tried to drum up some energy. His irritation was palpable.

'Me too. But what I don't get is why. Let's assume they're responsible and they did kill Morris. What exactly are they getting out of it? They're our lead suspects instantly, they must know we wouldn't buy into the demon story, and they've effectively terrorised a family. Why?'

'Money? Fame? God only knows. To me, it looks like a con gone wrong. They trick this family into thinking there's a demon in their house, charge them a shitload of money to get rid of it, then they make a big song and dance of it all. A wave of some rosary beads, the demon is gone, and out they frolic with a bank account full of cash.'

'But that doesn't explain the victim. Was it an accident? A coincidence that he died when they were there? Or did they actually plan to kill Darrell Morris?'

'Coincidence? Yeah, right,' Daniel scoffed, shrugging when Charlie frowned at him. He was exhausted, and knew that he was not in the right frame of mind to explore the logic behind this case. The cheap plastic wall clock above the countertop fridge said it was past ten. He had no idea where the hours had gone but he needed sleep badly, having woken before five that morning.

'We need to speak to the medical examiner, get the toxicology report. That could be key.'

'If we can find out how he died, we can fill in some of the pieces. And don't forget we still need to get statements from the wife and children. Their accounts could prove invaluable. We need something that will let us pick apart Spindler and Delamar's story.'

'It pisses me off that we couldn't charge them with anything,' Charlie snarled, pulling a face at the bitter taste of his coffee. 'This tastes like absolute shit.'

'Death by demon isn't exactly in the books. We're going to have to find out the how, then move on to the why before we can go after them again. And yes, it does.' Daniel put his own half-empty mug on the table. Charlie took the mugs and poured the remnants of both drinks into the sink before rinsing the mugs and stacking them on the drying rack. He turned back to Daniel, who was still sitting.

Charlie looked far less put together than normal, Daniel thought. His skin was bleached out from a combination of unflattering lighting and exhaustion. Better than me on a good day, but still... They needed to rest and step back for a while. He knew before Charlie spoke what he was about to ask, but let him speak anyway.

'What if they didn't do it?' Charlie said, his words tentative. It was the question they didn't want to answer – and, in fact, one they couldn't. Daniel batted it aside, not willing to tackle it in his current state.

'Then we need to find out how we arrest a demon,' Daniel answered as he stood. 'I need to go home and get some sleep. I'm worried I might actually start listening to you, start believing all this supernatural bull myself. And it'll be a dark day if that happens.' He laughed as they headed out into the quiet halls of the building, which was empty due to the late hour.

As Charlie headed back up to their department to grab his belongings, Daniel made his way outside to the car park. He walked fast, eager to get home. His eyes felt heavy and his brain had had enough. Yet, as he walked towards Westminster Tube station, light from the streetlights washing over him from above, Catherine Delamar's face filled his mind. Either the woman was crazy, which meant a difficult case, or she was telling what she thought was the truth, which meant an impossible case. He couldn't for one second believe that a demon had killed Darrell Morris, but Delamar had been convinced. Having Spindler back up her preposterous story only made things worse.

With two cases now on his desk, neither with an easy resolution in sight, he prayed for a good night's sleep. He knew he would need all the rest he could get. As he headed down the steps into the Tube station he felt a weight settle on his shoulders – a weight he feared would not lighten any time soon.

CHAPTER ELEVEN

The next morning, Daniel was disturbed from a vaguely peaceful slumber by an early morning phone call. One of the constables watching over Janine Morris had called in an incident at the hospital overnight. His department had allowed the most unsociable hours of the night to pass, but homicide cases waited for no man and the superintendent was up and working by six. That meant Daniel was too.

Apparently Morris was having full-blown hallucinations, claiming that the demon that had killed her husband was now after her. Daniel had hoped to get a statement from her, but her doctor didn't think she was stable enough to undergo any questioning; she feared it might trigger more hallucinations. She was apparently close to catatonic, and sedatives and a night's rest had not alleviated the issue. It seemed possible that she had suffered a total mental breakdown and would be of no use to the case any time soon.

So Daniel went to see the Morris children, who were still being looked after by a family friend. He took Amelia with him, hoping she might help to settle the children. He had never been great with kids but Amelia was an aunt twice over. He prayed that she was better at talking to kids than he was.

Sitting in Alison Taylor's cosy semi-detached house on Ravenscraig Road, not two minutes away from the Morrises' house, Daniel found himself faced with a devastated teenager and two confused younger siblings, none of whom were happy to be out of bed. Even though Alison and a counsellor were present, getting information out of the three Morris children was proving difficult.

'Anna, you said that you experienced things in the house yourself. Could you talk us through them?'

The girl glared at them out of reddened, sorrowful eyes, then gave a vague account of things moving, strange noises, odd smells, but nothing very concrete to go on. She sounded insane. Daniel got the impression that she'd seen too many horror movies, which she referenced numerous times. To make matters worse, she either burst into tears or tuned out every five minutes, making her stories difficult to make sense of.

As for the younger children, Joe and Emma, the girl didn't seem to understand what had happened and the boy came up with some weird theories. They agreed that weird things had happened in the house, that they had seen something in their room, and Anna backed up their stories, but their accounts of the demonologists' visit were less consistent.

Emma seemed to think that the previous night's events were some sort of scary magic show. She was adamant that she had not enjoyed it one bit and that it had upset her, but she was either not aware that her father had died or was in denial. Alison pulled Amelia to one side at that point, explaining that Emma had been told what had happened but that she seemed unable to understand it. She kept asking after both her parents.

Joe, on the other hand, knew full well what had happened.

'It was like a zombie demon! It flew in and attacked the

strange woman, and made loads of things float and fall over, then it screamed at us, and then it stole Daddy's soul and took him down under the earth!'

Anna scolded Joe, calling him a stupid baby. She told him that he was making things worse, at which point he too burst into tears.

After twenty minutes of tears and tantrums, the counsellor called time on the session. She rather bluntly informed Daniel and Amelia that the children were simply not ready to talk about everything and that they would need some time before being questioned again. She was not sure what was going to happen to them, and was worried about Janine's condition. Luckily Alison was more than willing to have the children for the short term, which they seemed okay with. Certainly none of them wanted to go back to the house on Whitmore Close.

Amelia and Daniel left the house feeling a mixture of relief and frustration. They were silent as Daniel drove to a nearby drive-through McDonald's for coffee, but when they were waiting for their drinks, they could not hold in their thoughts.

'I know they're kids, but I was hoping for at least something sensible,' Amelia complained. 'I mean, what the hell do we do with all that?' She frowned as she heard her unintentional pun.

'What I'm concerned with is that they all seemed pretty certain that something had targeted them. Flying demon aside, they all agreed that they had experienced strange things in the house ... where does that get us? I don't believe that something was visiting them in the night, and I reckon things moving around can easily be explained away. I also doubt that someone has been breaking in to terrorise them for the last fortnight by hiding behind doors and making strange noises, but that's an entire family – and two suspects – adamant that there was a supernatural presence in the house.'

A smiling teenager wearing a cap and apron called 'Latte?'

out of the delivery window. Daniel nodded, taking the drink to pass to Amelia.

'So it has to be a case of mutual imagination, right?' Amelia asked, lifting the lid to blow on the hot drink. 'If the younger ones decided they had seen something, real or not, and kept at the game, they could certainly start to convince themselves of what they had made up. After long enough it could start introducing doubt into the rest of the family. How many times can something be denied without evidence to back up that it's false before it seems possible that maybe it's actually true? Throw in sleep exhaustion and the fact that it's a pretty small house for a family of five, and who knows? Anna said her brother and sister had been sleeping with their parents, in their bed. That can't have been good for anyone.'

'So you think we're dealing with shared paranoid disorder?' Daniel tapped his fingers on the steering wheel, wishing his drink would come too. He had only had one coffee so far today. A number of friends and colleagues had commented on his caffeine addiction. He knew it wasn't healthy but he disregarded their advice, figuring that in his line of work he was far more likely to be stabbed or involved in a high-speed car crash than to die from overexposure to coffee and energy drinks.

'It's certainly possible. I mean, look at what's just happened with Janine Morris. It sounds like the shared idea of a demon may have turned into a shared psychosis for her – probably triggered when her husband died. If we can find any evidence that contradicts the demon theory, then maybe we can break the paranoia the Morrises are sharing and get the truth out of them.'

'Large black coffee?' the same server called, holding a drink out. Daniel smiled gratefully, taking the coffee too quickly and almost spilling it. He pulled away from the window, then parked in the car park.

'Let's say for a moment that we're right. Shared paranoid

disorder. All we need to do is prove that two demonologists with no motives killed a man, prove how they did it, and show Janine Morris and her children that there is no such thing as demons so they can regain their sanity and continue with their lives. Simple...' It sounded to him like an impossible mountain of tasks, a mountain with no clear route to the top and probably full of traps. He took a sip of the coffee, swearing when he burned his tongue.

'Not forgetting that we also need to find out who killed Jason Tagoe and Rogan Simmons, and if that mysterious tattoo artist Glint is real. And if so, if he's connected to the murders,' Amelia pointed out, smirking. 'I haven't got very far with my research yet.'

'Fill me in while I drive us to the mortuary. We're meeting Palmer there.'

'It's going to be a busy day,' Amelia said. Daniel simply nodded and sighed. They sat in silence for a few minutes while they finished their drinks: a brief peaceful oasis in their day.

A familiar but entirely unwelcome feeling rippled through Catherine Delamar as she stood at her sitting-room window. The fresh blue sky outside failed to inspire any inner peace. Holding her breath, she peeled back the white cotton curtains to get a better look, then dropped the fabric back in place.

'How long do you think they'll be out there?' Marcus asked from across the room. He sat on the sun-faded grey sofa, his legs outstretched, boots resting on the coffee table. His leather jacket was draped over the arm of the sofa. Catherine looked at his feet and frowned. He made a dramatic show of lifting his legs and putting his feet on the floor.

'I don't know, but I'm really not happy about it. They

actually woke me up, can you believe that? Not that I slept much anyway.' She brushed an invisible crease from her blouse, a nervous gesture, before taking a seat opposite Marcus and retrieving her glass of water. For a second she wished it was something stronger, even though it wasn't even midday.

'They tried to swamp me when I came in. Animals, the lot of them,' Marcus growled, glancing in the direction of the front door, which was triple locked and had the chain on.

'I know. I had to let you in!' Catherine snapped, before mouthing a silent apology for her tone. She had been preparing herself for something like this to happen. After all, it had before. But this was more extreme than she had expected. One woman with a Dictaphone and some friends with placards in a tiny town near Inverness didn't cause much fuss. In London, it had caused a stampede. Competing news crews, angry parents, self-proclaimed Satan worshippers, all shouting and vying for attention outside the flat she was renting. Even a police car had turned up to keep an eye on the crowd.

When the ambulances had shown up at the Morris house the night before, it had not taken long for the neighbourhood to pay attention. People living on the street had begun to gather first, then those from the next roads down. Catherine presumed that someone must have overheard either the police or the paramedics talking soon after because, like ants to the picnic, the press vans had shown up, everyone eager to get a glimpse of the demonologists.

As officers led her and Marcus out of the house, as they were checked by a paramedic, as they were bundled into a police vehicle, cameras had flashed non-stop. Journalists shouted out to them, other randoms tried to start vile chants. Back at her flat after being questioned by the police, an enthusiastic reporter with a cameraman had jumped out of an unmarked van and tried to get an interview with her. The sergeant who had driven her had warned the man to back off, and for a while he did, but at just past seven in the morning Catherine had been woken to fresh chaos on her doorstep. She had spotted the same reporter still there among the crowd.

'They're just so determined. Like vultures hovering over my almost dead corpse, waiting for their next big story.'

'Which we need to make sure does not feature us,' Marcus mumbled. He had the look of a sullen teenager, but Catherine empathised. She felt like hibernating, going into hiding and waiting until everyone had moved on, Scotland Yard included. She felt bad for the Morris family, particularly the children, but she cared far more about her own well-being.

With a tremble in her fingers, Catherine took her iPad off the table and opened the cover.

'Are you sure you want to do that?' Marcus asked. He had been working cases with Catherine for years, and she knew instantly what he meant. Did she want to open herself up to the wider world? Where human beings were just as terrifying as the demons they exorcised? She shook her head but opened the internet app regardless.

'We need to know what we're dealing with so we can protect ourselves.'

Google showed her instantly. Nearly every national press outlet had something on the story already. She scrolled through them, her heart sinking with every new piece.

'Oh God...' she whispered, dropping the tablet into her lap. She wiped a tear from her cheek. Marcus leant forward and she passed the iPad to him.

'You have to be kidding!'

The headline said it all.

THE REAL DEVILS OF LONDON TOWN

Beneath the bold text was a shot of Catherine, Marcus just behind her, being led towards a police car. The front drive of the Morris house was lit up with stark, aggressive lighting, swathes of blue striking across Catherine. It was a nightmare moment, caught in time for all to see.

'I didn't think it was going to be this bad. We need to do something,' Catherine said. Marcus greeted her words with a 'no shit' glare.

'And what would that be?'

'I don't know, but with those people camped outside, these articles... they will all blame us! I don't want to have to up and run, not again,' Catherine heard her voice rise and she swallowed panic. Her pulse sped up, and she could feel a nasty headache brewing. 'The police don't have any evidence they can use to pin this on us, but with all this press attention, they'll find something – anything – that they can use against us. I never expected them to believe us, but with this kind of public interest, they'll be under pressure to find evidence. We need people on our side.'

Her mind swelled with memories of cases when locals had become hostile. She closed her eyes for a second, hearing the splintering of the glass the time a mob had attacked her car, feeling the vehicle shaking as though she were still in it. The police were one thing, but sometimes those who took matters into their own hands could be much more dangerous.

'So let's convince them,' Marcus said. His eyes had widened, and Catherine thought she could see the wheels turning as he finally came to life.

'How?'

'They don't believe our story, sure, but what if they hear from someone else? Someone they're more likely to believe? I think it's time we gave Reverend Newman a call.'

At the mention of the name, Catherine shivered. They only

ever used that option when they had to. It made Catherine nervous. It had only been necessary twice before, and both times it had been a risky move. Religion and the legal system had never been the best of friends. Marcus was right, though. It had come to that already. And while she couldn't yet tell how things would play out, if anyone might help swing things in their favour, it was Reverend Newman. She nodded, and Marcus pulled out his phone.

CHAPTER TWELVE

'How am I back here already?' Daniel complained, shifting uncomfortably in the plastic waiting-room seat. 'I feel like I'm being punished, and I don't know why.'

'That's a little dramatic.' Amelia smirked, an eyebrow raised. 'At least it's not you lying on that cold metal table.'

'You know, as someone working on my cases I thought you'd be more supportive.' Daniel groaned, though he gave a little smile to show he was not being serious.

As always, the mortuary building smelled of chemicals and was cold and unwelcoming. *Couldn't they at least put some flowers in here? Maybe some nice art on the walls?*

'And I bet he's going to be late again,' Daniel continued, referring to the coroner Samson Lepard. 'While we wait, how's the tattoo case research going? You said you weren't having much luck.'

'Honestly, I've struggled to get anything useful. The internet is full of information about Glint, but it's all really vague. Makes it difficult to find anything that will help us. I did find a phone number for a guy who represented Glint in terms of press, though, so I'll give him a call. Maybe he can tell me who Glint is and if he's actually dead. But that's it so far.'

'Let's hope he co-operates. The Tattoo Killer could already have a new victim lined up, especially if they're as desperate as the evidence suggests.'

'Is that what we're calling him? The Tattoo Killer?' Amelia said. Daniel laughed, feeling glad to have a distraction from their surroundings – not that the new subject was any less morbid.

'Not bad, huh? The Tattoo Killer and the Demon of Arnos Grove.'

'Shall I release those to the press as the official case names? DI Graves versus the Tattoo Killer...' Amelia drawled dramatically, batting Daniel on the arm gently. He chuckled, feeling his cheeks flush before reminding himself not to read anything into it. *Friendly banter, not flirtation.* He had found that it was all too easy to invent meaning behind something to try and suit a fantasy, good or bad.

'How about no. I think the less we say to the press about it at the moment, the better. We already have one high-profile case. I don't think I want my name publicly attached to two unsolved investigations. I'll start getting a reputation I'd really rather not have.'

'You mean that's not what you're aiming for?' Charlie Palmer barrelled in through the door to the waiting room, Samson Lepard right behind him. He grinned at Daniel, who threw a glare his way.

'Hilarious, Charlie. Samson, not really good to see you again. Can you help us solve at least one of these cases, please?'

Samson nodded enthusiastically. He was dishevelled, in a stained, creased lab coat. Daniel hoped the stains were coffee or burger sauce. He didn't want to think about the alternative.

'Sorry I'm late. It's getting kind of busy in here at the

moment,' Samson chattered on as he led them into the room Daniel hated most. 'You're not the only ones bringing in the bodies.'

Daniel narrowed his eyes, telling Samson not to go into the details.

'But on the topic of *our* cases...' Daniel led in.

Samson signalled for them to follow him across the cold, sterile space to a wall of metal doors. He stopped at a body drawer and pulled the handle. The drawer slid out.

'So this is Darrell Morris?' Amelia asked. The strip lighting cast a strange dirty colour across the face of the dead man in front of them.

'Yep, it sure is. Unfortunately for you, he's not telling us much.' Samson giggled, but when no one took the bait he carried on. 'I'm sure you all know that the paramedics at the scene did a preliminary check. It seemed that poison was the likely cause of death. So I did a tox screen to confirm this.' Samson grabbed a file from a stack on a nearby table and flicked through to find the page he was looking for. He handed it to Charlie, who glanced over it, frowning.

'I don't know what all this means. Anything useful in here? Topline stuff?' Charlie asked in an attempt to speed the coroner along.

'Well, no drugs were found, other than minor traces of ibuprofen and aspirin. Alcohol though, quite a bit, which is how I think he was poisoned.'

'So he did die from poisoning? And alcohol was how it was administered?' Daniel asked. He had expected the answer to be more complex, and was glad that a cause of death had been found already.

'I'll be honest. I found very little evidence of what could have poisoned him but I would guess that the toxin of choice was hydrofluoric acid. There were no traces of the acid itself, suggesting that it was neutralised by the time I ran the screening, but the damage fits and the pH level in the body was lower than normal.'

'That sounds horrible.' Amelia winced.

'And it would have been. While external symptoms are easier to recognise – we have all seen the damage that occurs when acid comes into contact with skin – internal ones are not. The paramedics at the scene probably didn't know what they were dealing with, since most of the injuries sustained are internal. The acid would have caused major organ damage, which in itself is enough to die from, and the pain would be pretty extreme depending on the amount he had swallowed. Any bile or vomit produced as a result of the body trying to purge would have caused more damage to the GI tract, increasing absorption rates and more quickly leading to cardiac arrest. So there you have it, internal damage and heart failure, your cause of death, ladies and gentlemen.' Samson wiggled his fingers as though he had just performed a magic trick, his grin a little too broad for Daniel's liking.

He pulled a face and the man dropped the smile. 'So let's assume that hydrofluoric acid was ingested, and killed him as a result. How easy is it to administer? Would it mix easily with a drink without being noticed?' he asked. Samson, Charlie and Amelia looked interested. Daniel knew that if they proved how Morris had been poisoned, then they would know what evidence to look for, and they'd be far more likely to find out who the murderer was. It was the start they needed to put an end to this outlandish case.

'Very easy. It's colourless and mixes easily with other liquids. Spike a drink and there you have it.'

Daniel leant closer to Darrell Morris, as close as his churning stomach would allow, glad that the body looked pretty normal. A sheet covered the victim up to the top of his chest.

His throat and lips were discoloured, the skin raw and cracked in places as though burnt. A memory from the scene of the crime hit him. There had been a smashed glass with traces of whisky in the kitchen, and he recalled seeing a bottle or two on the side.

'Did you test the whisky?' Daniel asked as he straightened up.

'Yep, and that's the kicker. It was fine. In fact, the CSIs took every beverage bottle from the house and found no traces of hydrofluoric acid in any of them.'

'Could it have come from somewhere else in the house? Maybe it was in a different drink to the one the victim dropped?' Charlie asked.

'Maybe,' Samson conceded. 'He'd have needed to be drinking pretty quickly, but I suppose it could have been one he had before the one he dropped. You can buy the acid in quite a few places. It would never normally be kept near food and drink, so I suggest checking the garage. '

'I'll call this in, get some bodies over to the house to do another thorough search.' Amelia jumped into action.

'Get everything finger-printed too,' Daniel told her. 'Even the bottles that have been tested already. One could have been swapped out so the prints would be different.'

He was starting to build a picture in his mind. Assuming that Catherine Delamar was behind the death, she could easily have swapped a bottle. She'd had ample opportunity to do so. He just needed the proof.

Amelia nodded as she headed out of the morgue, phone in hand.

'So now we need to link the cause of death to our demonologist friends. Somehow I don't think a demon would use acid in a drink,' Daniel said. 'Thanks, Samson.' He went to shake the man's hand, then had second thoughts and pulled back.

'One day maybe you'll get over your fears, Detective Inspector,' Samson said, turning to offer a hand to Charlie, which he took. 'I do wear gloves, you know. And I wash my hands after touching the bodies.' He waved his fingers in the air. Charlie let out a deep roll of laughter as Daniel grimaced.

'Sure, one day,' Daniel answered through gritted teeth, knowing that day would never come. No matter how many bodies he saw, there was no way he would ever get used to them.

As they left the coroner to his gruesome business, Daniel prayed that they could wrap up the Morris case quickly. He was concerned that he was being spread too thin. The thought of more bodies turning up, either demon- or tattoo-related, made him feel sicker than the body he had just seen. He felt as if he was spinning plates in the air and that at some point soon they would come crashing down around him, causing damage that he would not be able to repair.

While Amelia got started on the hunt for evidence at the Morris house, for something to link Catherine Delamar and Marcus Spindler to the death of Darrell Morris, Daniel knew he needed to revisit the other case. Divide and conquer. Maybe the internet didn't know anything concrete about Glint, but he bet that Cassandra Salinas did.

He was glad he had Charlie with him. Together they came up with a plan of attack as they headed back towards Finsbury Park and Salinas's house.

Second time's the charm, Daniel thought, trying to ignore the anxious feeling in his gut.

'Yeah, I have a Glint tattoo. What of it?' Cassandra Salinas asked as she turned to give Daniel and Charlie a better look at the intricate design on her ankle. Her voice was filled with attitude, but she clearly enjoyed showing off her ink.

They were sitting on the threadbare sofa in her modest home off Haringey Green Lanes. Daniel felt his stomach rumble and swallowed, hoping no one had heard. He had recovered from the earlier 'dead body proximity' moment on the drive over and he was craving lunch, having been unable to stomach much breakfast.

Charlie stood to get a better look at the tattoo, but Daniel had already seen it in the image Amelia Harding had found. As Salinas let Charlie inspect it, a frown painted on her already overly made-up face, Daniel glanced around the house.

The ground-floor flat was simply decorated and would have benefited from a makeover, but otherwise was fairly well maintained. The furniture looked cheap and nothing matched, but it still kind of worked. He could tell that Salinas took some pride in her home, despite lacking the wealth to make it a real standout. Even the variety of kids' toys on display were tidy, kept in a neat pile next to the television.

Daniel wondered if Salinas fit the bill of a person desperate enough to murder. She was evidently not well off, but she didn't seem to be on the brink of financial collapse. She had a child – would she risk losing her child, and her freedom? But her attitude was what kept him suspicious. She had been reluctant to let them in to talk to her and so far had said very little, instead watching them intently.

Daniel looked at Charlie, asking him to explain their interest in Glint. His colleague did so, but only in brief, not mentioning the missing money. They were eager to see what Salinas knew about the mysterious artist, and if she was aware of the missing money.

'Both Rogan Simmons and Jason Tagoe had Glint tattoos, you do too, and we want to find out the level of connection between the three of you. We also need some more detail on Glint, if you happen to know anything.'

Salinas had not shown any real emotion on finding out Tagoe had been killed, but she was now starting to look uncomfortable, shifting position in her chair as she looked between the detective inspectors.

'Like I told you, I was friends with Rogan, kind of, but I only met Jason once or twice. That's it. You know, lots of people must have Glint tattoos. Maybe Rogan told his boss he should get one. I know I didn't.' She crossed her arms over her chest and sat back in her chair. She was continuing to be cagey, clearly waiting to see what they would say. Her answer gave nothing away but, just like the last time he had spoken to her, he got the distinct impression that she knew more than she was letting on.

'What can you tell us about Glint? Did you ever meet him?' he asked. Charlie held a notepad and pen ready, which Salinas glanced at. Her eyes narrowed and one eyebrow rose, though she did not comment. Instead she looked back to Daniel.

'I can tell you he's dead, so he's not your killer. But I bet you already know that.'

Both men nodded and said nothing, forcing her to continue.

'He was a brilliant artist. It sucks that he died. I wanted another Glint tattoo. A lot of people did.'

'And what about Glint as a person? Did you ever meet him, see him face to face?'

'Of course not. No one did,' Salinas answered, her tone blunt. 'That was the whole point. It was supposed to be a mystery. That's why people cared.'

'And about the mystery – do you know anything about it? Like, who he was, or how he died? There's a lot of theories out there. Maybe you know one that's more truth than fiction?'

Charlie readied his pen, but Salinas said nothing. It looked to Daniel like she was choosing her words carefully, though he couldn't be sure. She was proving very difficult to read.

'Detectives, I'm one of hundreds of people with a Glint tattoo, and I probably know just as much as they all do. I never met him, never even heard his voice. I read he died in a fire or something. That's it. And I bet you already knew that too.'

'Miss Salinas, I'm going to be frank,' Daniel said, lacing his fingers together and leaning towards her. He was getting annoyed at the woman, and decided it was time to cut to the chase. She certainly couldn't say any less than she already had. Baiting her seemed to be worth a shot. 'We're here because two people we can connect you with are dead. You are the only person alive and in the picture that links these murders to any sort of motive. We have spoken to staff at Needlepoint Ink. I think Glint and tattoos has something to do with this murder, and I think you are deliberately withholding information from us. If you don't start talking, I'm going to charge you with obstruction.' He locked his gaze on hers and was surprised to find she held it, not breaking contact. The threat was an empty one, and it was possible that she knew it. He had nothing to charge her with, but he was hoping she would react anyway.

'Look, I didn't kill either of those men. I'm a mother. I wouldn't put my son in trouble like that. I told you what I know, and if you don't want to accept it that's your problem. Maybe you should go back to Needlepoint if they seem to know so much.' Her tone had shifted from calm and collected to defensive and sharp in a heartbeat. She was leaning forward, her posture rigid.

'What do you mean by that? Do you think someone at Needlepoint is responsible?'

'I mean you could do worse than look into the people who

work there. They aren't all clean-cut angels. Maybe throw some accusations at some of the crooks there instead of hassling me.'

Charlie was scrawling a few notes when Salinas stood up abruptly. 'Now, I have to go collect my son from his friend's house. Are we done here?'

Daniel knew that he had nothing more to use against her; she had effectively shut down the conversation. Sure, he could pry a bit more, pick at her, but something told him that Cassandra Salinas had some experience of how the police worked, and the last thing he needed was an harassment complaint. It hadn't been entirely useless, however. A finger had been pointed squarely at Needlepoint Ink, and Daniel had an inkling that it would prove to be a pretty fruitful lead. Maybe she knew something she feared would get her in trouble, maybe she didn't want to be seen talking to the cops, but she had squealed just enough. They hadn't looked into anyone else from the shop yet – and who knew what they might turn up once they did?

'Silver lining,' Charlie said as they headed out into the cool day. 'You get to see that girl again.'

Daniel stopped in his tracks to throw an icy stare at his partner but couldn't help smiling when Charlie grinned openly.

'Not exactly the way I like to meet women. Hi again, are you a murderer or do you know someone who is?' he said in a snarky voice.

'Hey, sometimes unorthodox is the best approach.' Charlie smiled and patted Daniel on the back. 'Let's go find out.'

Daniel flushed as he followed Charlie to the car, a kernel of hope growing inside him. *Maybe*, he thought. *Crazier things have happened.*

The day flew after Daniel and Charlie had left Cassandra Salinas. Daniel had asked Rachel over for a meal at his flat. She brought the wine, and over some overcooked beef and a delicious but very rich cheesecake he picked his friend's brain as best he could. It was her last night in London and he couldn't miss the opportunity.

Rachel Callahan had always been his sanity-check, his barometer for normality. Once again he wished she was still his colleague as well as his friend. Charlie was proving to be a great partner and budding friend, but Rachel had a gift for the logical, the practical, that Daniel felt he sometimes lacked.

She waited patiently while he filled her in on the details of both cases that he was allowed to share, topping up their drinks as he spoke.

Amelia Harding and a crime scene team had gone back to the Morris house and searched for any evidence of hydrofluoric acid. They found nothing. They had also looked for signs that anything in the house had been tampered with, anything that could have resulted in Darrell Morris coming into contact with the acid, either deliberately or accidentally. Again, they found nothing. Amelia had been tasked with looking into the pasts of Catherine Delamar and Marcus Spindler the next day, with help from another officer. They needed more dirt on the duo if they were going to rule out the poisoning being a freak accident.

The body of Darrell Morris had undergone a second post-mortem by another coroner. She had said that Samson Lepard was probably correct in thinking that the victim had ingested acid, but she was less certain of the type. She had found no other injuries though either, which got them no further along.

The sergeant monitoring Janine Morris had stayed in the hospital all day, waiting for any developments, but Janine's nurse said that she was still not fit to make any statement. She was simply not mentally sound enough. She was also being regularly sedated as a precaution against her hurting herself or anyone else.

'Have you spoken to any experts on the subject?' Rachel had asked as she mulled over having another slice of dessert.

'No, why would I? We know we're not dealing with the supernatural.'

'Process of elimination. To rule it out.'

'I don't need to rule it out, Rach, it's nonsense. I'm not in some cheesy exorcism film where the cop seeks out a guru only to find out it was true all along,' Daniel had answered, irritated. He had been surprised she had even entertained the option. It was not what he expected from her.

'Well, look what you're dealing with. You have basically no evidence pointing to the demonologist woman or her colleague, the coroner can only be ninety-five per cent sure how the victim was murdered, and the press are already having a field day. Of course, most of the general public is unlikely to believe in demons, but they are normally also far less vocal than the ones who *do* believe in stuff like this. If you get the facts from an expert, maybe you can use that in a statement to stop some of the public hype about the case.'

'I suppose, maybe.' Daniel wasn't convinced, though, and he couldn't place why. With a raised eyebrow, Rachel worked it out for him.

'You're nervous, aren't you? That maybe you'll find something you don't want to find, something that you can't explain. Just like the police always do in horror films.' She gulped a mouthful of wine but pushed the cheesecake away. Daniel looked up from his own dessert.

'No. I know all that stuff isn't real.' He meant to sound confident, but even he could hear the uncertainty in his voice. He found he wanted to move on from the subject, but he knew that Rachel wouldn't let him.

'But that's the point, isn't it? No one knows for sure, not completely. Remember the Latoya Ammon case? That woman in America who claimed her kids were possessed? There were hundreds of pages of official reports filed that seemingly backed up her claims. And that's not the only one. Hell, google demonic cases. The internet is full of them. And the Enfield haunting, the most famous case of demonic activity in England. You really think every single one is fake?'

Daniel didn't answer. He didn't know what to say. He knew exactly what Rachel was getting at, and she was right. He didn't want to give that minuscule doubt in his mind any power.

'I suppose it wouldn't hurt to speak to someone. Maybe at one of the universities.'

Rachel gave a self-satisfied smile. Daniel frowned. Maybe the demon argument wasn't logical, but as usual, his friend was. He hated when she was right – only because she always knew it too. He really didn't believe in demons and ghosts and all that nonsense, but then again, there were plenty of other things he would not believe in were it not for scientific evidence.

They moved on to the second case giving Daniel grief, but this time Rachel was not able to offer much advice. She vaguely remembered reading about Glint, but could do little more than to agree with the way Daniel and Charlie were proceeding.

That day they had gone back to Needlepoint Ink. They had spoken to the manager of the parlour, a few other staff, even a regular customer, and could find nothing obviously out of the ordinary. The manager had been open about his time in jail a decade ago, and had shown them all the paperwork detailing the legitimacy of the business. All of the employees had heard of Glint, though none claimed to have met the artist, and none of them had a Glint tattoo. They had found nothing to justify why Cassandra Salinas had fingered the shop, and were left with yet more inconclusive information. It upped Daniel's suspicion of

Salinas slightly. Why had she pointed to the shop? To take attention off her? He didn't know why she would do that. Maybe she was still keeping information from them, but that was only a hunch. All they had achieved was to muddy the water further.

Rachel locked on to the mention of Jenny in Daniel's account of the day. She knew about him liking Amelia too, and had found his awkward crush sandwich inside the tattoo shop hilarious. She had been Daniel's confidante in romance since he had found out she was gay. Daniel had thought he was being subtle when he told her about Jenny, but evidently he had failed. She insisted on updates, big or small, and he had promised to oblige.

After Daniel had promised to visit her in Derbyshire and catch up around their old haunts when he had some free time, Rachel bid him farewell. Her parting shot was to tell him to call his sister. He was genuinely sad that she was heading back home so quickly. He was glad that she had taken the time to catch up with him, since she had primarily been in town to see her sister, but it had gone way too quickly.

Rachel leaving only emphasised the lack of balance in his work–life balance. His too-small flat somehow suddenly felt huge, a hollow, empty space with no soul. Daniel shivered, the dark night emphasising the emotional shadow falling over him.

CHAPTER THIRTEEN

Daniel Graves was startled awake so suddenly that his heart was still thudding when his brain realised it was only the innocent honking of a truck that had broken his sleep. He rolled onto his side and checked the time on his phone, which was charging on the bedside table, as he listened to the truck continuing its journey through the night.

He sighed at being awake yet again in the small hours, frustrated that he had been woken from a deep slumber. He had never been the best sleeper, even as a teenager often waking in the early hours, then groaning as his parents forced him out of the house to school still half asleep. He'd lost count of the number of times he'd been kicked off the morning bus by the driver at the terminus, having slept past his stop. Then of course there had been years filled with nightmares, in which he relived over and over the moment that had changed his life. His sister could have died that night, and thanks to him someone else had. He had become good at shutting the memory out, the image of what he had done getting easier to push away with time.

This incident kick-started his caffeine addiction, after he discovered rich blends of foreign coffees at seventeen. His body had long since adapted to functioning on significantly less sleep than the prescribed eight hours, but he was still annoyed to be awake. He had been dreaming about something nice for once, something calm and welcoming, but the memory faded away fast. As his brain got into gear, the real world came back to him. A virtual storyboard of bodies and tattoos and fictional demons and news vans flashed through his mind and had him fully alert in a way that caffeine never could. With a depressingly familiar feeling of resignation he got out of bed. He had slept in just a pair of boxers and he searched the floor next to his bed until he found some shorts and an old Abercrombie T-shirt, bought back when he was convinced that his gym trips would have some effect. He had never gained the muscular build the brand was known for advocating, but he'd kept the shirt nonetheless. He only wore it indoors though, not eager to show the world how skinny he looked in it. It occurred to him that Charlie would probably look great in the T-shirt, and he cursed silently before pushing the thought away. He had far more important things to worry about. Besides, he could not allow his jealousy of his partner to build into anything. It would be toxic for their working relationship, and he liked working with Charlie. He knew that he could have been teamed with someone much worse.

As Daniel stepped out into the open-plan living room/kitchen, a mixture of streetlights and moonlight cast thick bars of shadow across the ceiling and kitchen cabinets. He felt the mild fuzz of the bottle and a half of wine he and Rachel had shared. He grabbed a clean mug from beside the sink and filled it with water, then took a gulp.

From across the flat, there was a click. Daniel turned, looking towards the dark sofa, the shadowed outline of the television, the small glass table he'd bought on the cheap and hated. He couldn't place the sound, couldn't tell where it had come from. He stood still, waiting to hear it again, but the night was quiet. Then, just as he was rinsing out the mug, he heard it again. Confused, he flicked on the light, illuminating the space where he stood.

Leaving his mug drying on the rack, he headed around the breakfast counter and into the living area, searching it but not seeing anything out of the ordinary. More annoyed at being awake than at not finding the source of the mysterious noise, Daniel slumped onto the sofa, raking a hand through his hair. A newspaper sat on the table. He was reaching for it when the click came again, louder this time. He leaped to his feet and moved round the table to the window. Something had ricocheted off the glass, and he had to see what it was.

Parting the slats in the blind, he looked out at the quiet street below. His neighbourhood seemed like a ghost town. Streetlamps threw down cold ovals of sickly yellow and white, spotlighting bins, parked cars and patches of front gardens, but everywhere else was shrouded in dark secrets.

Scanning the houses opposite, Daniel looked for what could have caused the clicking against the window, half-expecting kids up way past their curfew to be on the pavement below, out to cause grief. He saw nothing, however, and stifled a yawn, thinking that perhaps he had imagined the sound, that he was not as awake as he had thought.

His blood chilled when he saw the figure below, standing just outside the pool of light cast by a streetlight, next to a tall hedge that lined a driveway. The figure was looking directly at his window.

Instinctively, Daniel stumbled back, catching his leg on the corner of the coffee table and swearing.

'Thanks,' Jenny Cartwright said to the taxi driver as she stumbled out of the car and onto the pavement, giggling to herself when she almost dropped her purse.

'Stay safe, okay, miss?' the driver called before pulling away from the kerb, leaving Jenny alone.

She didn't feel too bad, considering, but she was looking forward to her bed. The concrete paving slabs felt too hard under her feet through the soles of her well-worn Nikes and she longed to collapse into sleep, wrapped up in her covers. She had gone for drinks with the guys from the tattoo shop to bid a fond farewell to Damon, their most recent guest artist, and had got a little carried away. She realised after the fourth tequila shot that she was getting too drunk, and had switched to water – and a few swigs of other people's drinks. The water had dulled the effects of the liquor just enough to maintain the buzz but keep her upright.

Hearing a car backfire a few roads away, she jumped. She couldn't help letting out a nervous laugh, feeling stupid for being jumpy. As her laugh and the distant car faded away, she became aware of how silent the neighbourhood was. She lived in a small estate off Finland Street in the Canada Water area. At four in the morning, there was no one around and no lights at any of the windows.

In minutes she had reached the entrance path to the flats. She was relieved to see the familiar surroundings, but it was far too dark for her liking. Only the occasional streetlight and a few small wall-mounted lamps illuminated the route towards the central area the apartments wrapped around. She could just make out the edge of the water that connected to the bigger quays and the Surrey Docks water sports centre a road away. Moonlight shimmered off its surface.

Jenny stopped and leant against the wall under one of the wall-mounted lamps. Angling her handbag so that she could see inside, she rummaged around until she found her phone. Squinting to focus on the screen, she finally succeeded in turning on the torch feature. Taking unsteady steps, she made her way down the path towards her flat.

The place was, of course, deserted. Normally there were dog walkers, joggers, and that irritating kid in the building two down from her who was always chucking stones at the ducks.

Jenny really wanted to move, like the Graces, who had found a three-bed house in Greenwich after Steve Grace had inherited money. But she wasn't exactly flush, so for the time being she was stuck where she was. She didn't hate the place, but she had moved to London with a much bigger vision in her head than the reality she had so far achieved – a studio flat she rented from a friend.

Artistic from an early age but with little academic focus, it wasn't until she turned nineteen that Jenny found her calling. Her cousin had decided to get a tattoo to commemorate the loss of a close friend and, knowing how good an artist Jenny was, had asked her to create a design. When Katy had finally got the tattoo done, Jenny was blown away with the results and with pride at her artistry. Seeing how good it looked and how happy her cousin was gave her a sense of elation. With her parents' support, Jenny quit her job as an office assistant at a stationery supplier and got an apprenticeship at a tattoo shop in Lincoln so she could learn the ropes. She outgrew the tattoo shop, and Lincoln, after spending three years working there. As a direct result of watching *L.A. Ink* one summer, she knew what she wanted to do next. She wanted to move to London and become the English version of Kat Von D.

As Jenny headed up the exterior stairs to her third-floor flat, she scolded herself for not yet getting close to her dream.

'Got a way to go yet, Jen,' she muttered as she fumbled her key into the lock, succeeding on the third try. The door opened more quickly than she expected and she fell into the flat, dropping her bag. It hit the floor, spilling its contents.

'Fuck it,' Jenny muttered, her voice loud enough to startle her. She pushed the door shut with one foot, then, on her knees, began to feel around for whatever had fallen out of her bag.

Then, as though a blindfold had been taken off her, she could suddenly see. Her compact mirror, lip gloss, a half-eaten pack of Polos, random coins lay scattered on the floor in front of her. The free-standing lamp next to the door had come on.

'What the...'

She caught a movement out of the corner of her eye. Her breath caught painfully in her throat. Before she could stand up, the intruder charged towards her.

Daniel sat for a second, rubbing his ankle. Had he really seen what he thought he saw? He shook his head. It was preposterous. He must have imagined the figure looking up at his window, the unmistakable shape of ... of horns. God, he felt stupid even thinking the word. *This case is really getting to you, Danny. Snap out of it.*

He felt a shiver run over him. Maybe his imagination had added the horns, but he knew he hadn't invented the figure, the clicks against the glass.

'Shit,' he whispered into the darkness, slowly moving into a crouch. He had to know, had to check again for his own sanity. Daniel edged to the window, then stopped. That seed of doubt was back again. Why couldn't he shake it? He didn't believe in the supernatural. It was Rachel's fault – clearly what she had said had got under his skin. Slowly he reached up with both hands, gripping the wooden sill. He took a deep breath.

He craned his head to look out between the slats of the

blind. The figure was gone. His breath burst out, steaming up the glass, and he pulled two slats apart to get a better view of the street. His gaze shot from house to house, garden to garden. Nothing moved.

'Fuck... Danny boy, you're going nuts.' A shimmer of anger tinged with self-loathing washing over him. He turned back to the kitchen. The flashing green timer on his microwave said it was just past four. He knew he wouldn't get back to sleep, so he headed into the kitchen. 'May as well make some breakfast.' He pulled a bagel out of the bread bin and cut it in half. His mind raced. He couldn't believe this case was getting to him so much.

When the bagel was in the toaster, Daniel made a pot of coffee, thinking about the day ahead. He felt that he should tell Charlie about what he'd seen, then had second thoughts. He still got the impression that sometimes Charlie doubted him, doubted his abilities. Deep down Daniel suspected he was simply projecting his own feelings onto his partner. After all, Charlie had told him a few times what a great detective inspector he thought Daniel made. Telling a new colleague he was imagining demons, though? That was never going to look good. Charlie would think the stress was getting too much for him, maybe suggest he take some time off. Four months in and on leave for stress – not the best option.

'And maybe it is stress,' Daniel conceded out loud as the bagel popped out. He was buttering it when his phone rang.

Who the hell is calling at this time?

His stomach lurched at the thought of another body. He dropped the bagel on the counter and jogged into his bedroom, where his phone was buzzing frantically on the bedside table. Before he grabbed it, he hesitated. Unknown number. He didn't like answering the phone when he didn't know who was calling, but a sense of responsibility took over. He knew the call might be important.

'Detective Inspector Graves,' he said. The line was silent, with just a hint of a crackle to say it was connected.

'Hello, DI Graves. Who is this?'

The line hissed. 'Aaaaaddrreeeemmellleeecccchhhhh...'

Daniel's blood ran cold. There was a dull thud as his phone hit the floor.

Jenny tried to scream as she pushed herself backwards, instinct fighting the haze of alcohol in her system. Her voice was a whimper. She winced as her back caught the sharp edge of the table she dumped her post on. The intruder dodged past the sofa and Jenny spun around, reaching up for the vase that sat on the table. With all her strength Jenny threw it. It flew over her attacker's shoulder and smashed. She cursed.

Get out! her mind bellowed at her. Jenny scrambled across the floor towards the front door. She just had to get outside, grab the handle, pull it down and get outside. There she could yell, she could wake the neighbours. It was easy, she knew it. She just had to be fast. Safety was close – she just had to grasp it.

Jenny pushed up off her knees, launching herself at the door. A hand grabbed her ankle and dragged her backwards. Her left elbow slammed onto the floor and pain shot through her. She choked as her attacker pulled her backwards again. Her assailant was suddenly on top of her, their weight pinning her down. She spat strands of hair out of her mouth, gasping for breath.

A hunting knife sliced down, embedding itself into the floor next to her face. Her eyes widened with horror. Her attacker did not wait; she saw their leather-gloved hand pulling at the knife. Chips of the cheap wood flooring came up as the weapon was freed. She knew her attacker would strike again, knew they would not miss the second time. She shoved her right hand under her and with a grunt pushed upwards and sideways with all her strength. Her assailant fell off her and the knife skittered across the floor, hitting the skirting board with a thunk.

Now! Jenny shot forward again. In an awkward half crouch she gripped the handle and pulled it. The door swung open. Cold air blasted her face but she took no notice. Her legs unsteady under her, she raced out of the flat. Agony burning through her, Jenny risked a glance back at her house, knowing she shouldn't but unable to resist. The figure charged towards her. Jenny ran. Her hair whipped behind her as she sprinted down the steps, her footsteps echoing around. She could hear her attacker behind her, could feel their presence, and took the steps two at a time.

'Help!' she screamed as her voice came back to her, croaky but loud. 'Help me!'

Her lungs ached with exertion. She jumped the last few steps, her ankle twisting as she hit the path that edged the water. She stumbled forward, pain lancing up her leg, and her pursuer careened into her. The knife blade hit its mark, slicing through her thin jacket to find skin. She opened her mouth to scream even as she fell. The water enveloped her, filling her mouth, ice-cold tendrils snaking into her.

Frantically Jenny tried to turn herself the right way up, looking for the surface as the dark, dirty water did its best to make her its own. Her feet found the muddy bottom of the pond and she pushed herself up, gasping as she burst out of the water.

'Jenny!' someone yelled. 'Oh shit, Jenny, what happened?'

Her mouth full of water, Jenny swam towards the edge. An arm came down, grabbed her hand, and she could feel herself being pulled out onto land, the concrete siding scratching her ribcage through her top. She sagged against the hard ground, coughing for air.

'Jenny, did you fall?' It was one of her neighbours, Mr Kerswell, his deep voice full of panic. 'What are you doing out here alone?'

'Alone?' She sat up, her body complaining at the movement.

A startled duck was paddling away towards an island of spiky plants across the pond. There was no one else there. Whoever had attacked her had gone.

CHAPTER FOURTEEN

'Well, you look like shit,' Charlie said bluntly as he circled Daniel's desk and pulled up a chair. He looked at the parade of empty coffee mugs and tilted his wrist to check his watch. 'How long have you been here? I thought I was in early.'

'Since just after five. I was the first one in. Gave the cleaner a scare.' Daniel smiled, feeling the exhaustion in his facial muscles. He had been sifting through emails, checking a few loose ends on other case files, and researching demons and demonology. Now his eyes stung. He rubbed them as he tried to look alert. He felt heavy, his body struggling to stay awake.

'Er, why?' Charlie asked. His eyes narrowed at the vintage sketch of a dancing demon that filled Daniel's screen. 'And I thought you didn't believe in all that stuff,' he continued, pointing at the image. 'Had a revelation?'

Daniel went to respond but found himself at a loss for words. He was still thinking about the events of that morning, trying to make them make sense. Over and over again he had remembered the figure watching him, the phone call, that voice...

'What?' Charlie asked. 'You went to say something and stopped. Spill.'

Daniel sat still, attempting to formulate a sentence that would not make him sound like he was ready to be admitted to a hospital bed one down from Janine Morris.

'I ... experienced something, something I can't entirely explain. I didn't get much sleep.'

Charlie leant forward and raised his eyebrows encouragingly.

'Something ... someone, maybe ... was outside my house last night. Well, this morning. A truck horn woke me up and when I went to get some water I heard something. A clicking. It sounded like something pinging against the window so I took a look, and there it was. This figure. It was standing there in the shadows across the street, looking up at my flat, right at me.' Daniel slumped forward, running his fingers through his hair. He could hear the office strip lights humming gently above him, the clatter of someone typing across the department. He straightened when he noticed that Charlie had not said anything. Instead his partner seemed to be lost in thought. Daniel clicked his fingers in front of Charlie's face to get his attention.

'Sorry. So, someone was watching you? Did you see who?'

'No, they were like a shadow, all black, but it was weird. It was like they were *made* of shadow, not just simply wearing black clothing and standing out of the light. It was really weird. But that's not all. They had ... well, horns.' As Daniel uttered the last word he winced. He had been holding on to the thin hope that verbalising things would make him feel less insane, but instantly he had proven that hope to be wrong. 'Shit, just listen to me. I sound like I should be institutionalised.' He expected Charlie to burst out laughing, especially given how adamant Daniel had been that there was no such thing as the supernatural. Instead Charlie was still quiet. Daniel could see the cogs turning.

If someone were to look at Charlie Palmer, it would be easy to dismiss him as someone who was superficial. He was effortlessly good-looking, always impeccably presented, and he had one of those perfect smiles that often came with a shallow mind and a fake veneer hiding a dull or obnoxious personality. Daniel had briefly thought the exact thing when he had first met his partner despite himself, intimidated more than impressed by the handsome bravado that emanated from the man like pheromones. But as soon as Daniel had given Charlie more than a cursory glance, had heard the man speak and witnessed the way he thought and acted, he'd been forced to admit that he had judged Charlie unfairly.

Despite this, Daniel was relieved that Charlie was not simply dismissing his story, not throwing out some sarcastic comment.

'There was one more thing. After I saw the figure, someone rang me. It was this horrible voice, deep and scratchy. Really freaked me out. I dropped my phone.'

'What did it say?' Charlie asked, his brow furrowed.

'You remember the name of the demon that Catherine Delamar said was harassing the Morrises? It was that.'

'Aldrama something? What did it say?'

'Yeah. Adramelech. And that's all it said, in this really bloody creepy drawn-out growl. I was so surprised, I dropped my phone, and when I picked it up the caller had gone.'

'Strange,' Charlie mumbled, almost to himself.

'Palmer, look, I've got to ask, how come you aren't ribbing me for this? Even I'm struggling to believe myself.'

'Because I got a phone call too. At around the same time. I was asleep. It didn't wake me, but it was an unknown number.'

Daniel felt his heart jump. Charlie had also received a call? What could that mean? He instantly felt less crazy. 'Well, if you got a call too … we need to get them traced.'

Charlie nodded, and said that he would contact Patrick Marsden, an IT specialist who contracted for Scotland Yard.

'I don't think a demon was outside your house, but I'm thinking we're being played. It's as if someone is actively trying to make us doubt ourselves, you in particular, but we need to be able to prove it. We seem to have clues piling up around us that all link to this case and somehow point to a reasonable scenario, yet there's no proof of anything. The death, the poison, the crackpot demonologists – and now odd phone calls and creepy weirdos in the middle of the night. Delamar has to be behind this. We just need to find the proof to nail her for it.'

'Well, the alternative is ridiculous. But if you did believe in demons, then it doesn't bear thinking about. I did some research into the history of Adramelech, and it made me feel queasy.' His mind flashed back to the image of the figure outside his flat and he shivered. 'According to various online stories, he was a sun god or king originally but later became linked to the concept of child sacrifice. One writer on demonology even said he became known as the Chancellor of Hell. He also features as a fallen angel in *Paradise Lost*. It all makes super-creepy reading, but what worried me the most was the child sacrifice element.'

'The Morrises have three children … shit, are you thinking that maybe Delamar was after the children for some reason?'

'I don't know. Given how Darrell Morris died, I'm not sure.'

Charlie sat back in his chair and folded his arms over his chest. 'Woman goes after the kids, father finds out what she's planning, father is killed, bye-bye witness. Sure, she'd still have to get away with it from an evidence angle, but then we're struggling.'

'Wait, so if this is true, then ... I mean, this is pretty complex. She would have known there would be an investigation, she would have known about the press, all the attention. You can't have someone die from a supposed demonic attack and expect no one to notice. And if she was responsible for the figure I saw, the calls, then maybe–'

Daniel didn't get to finish his sentence. His colleague was on the same wavelength instantly. 'Like she may have done this before? Fuck! We need to find out who Catherine Delamar and Marcus Spindler really are.'

Jenny Cartwright pushed through the heavy entrance doors to the reception at Scotland Yard and headed for the main desk. She was a woman on a mission. Behind her, her friend Calvin struggled to keep up.

'Hi, I need to see Detective Inspector Daniel Graves immediately. It's extremely important. I got attacked last night in my own home. Some crazy arsehole with a knife. My shoulder is killing where I got stabbed. Can you believe it? Stabbed in my own bloody flat! They broke in – it was terrifying. I must talk to him.'

The receptionist looked taken aback. 'That's terrible, I'm sorry to hear that, but I'm afraid this station is not for reporting a crime. Did you call 999?'

'Of course I did – I'm not stupid. Two sergeants and a paramedic came but they didn't find anything. The attacker had already legged it. I think one said they would patrol the apartment building, but I'm not sure. They took down some details, but what else could they do? It was almost five in the bloody morning. I've had no sleep – I mean, could you if you got stabbed? Anyway, I don't care about them, I want to talk to

Detective Inspector Graves. I think I was attacked because I helped him on a case he's working on. Someone is pissed off, I'm sure of it. Is he here? Can you call him?' Jenny could feel herself getting worked up as she spoke, her voice getting higher, but she couldn't stop it. She scanned left and right, looking through the glass panels in the doors leading off the reception area. She jumped when Calvin put a hand on her shoulder.

'Jen, calm down. Take a breath. Try not to get worked up again. You don't want to have a panic attack.'

'I know, I know!' she snapped before apologising. Calvin simply smiled understandingly. She was glad he was there to support her. Even though she was obviously safe at that moment, she found that she couldn't shake off the fear. She'd only had a few hours of nightmare-riddled sleep, and it was all she could do to stop herself from huddling in a corner. She was aware of how she must look: a bedraggled, sleep-deprived woman, gabbling a story about being knifed in her home. She knew her hair looked wild and traces of last night's make-up were still smudged around her eyes.

Should have kept my mouth shut, she thought as a memory of the vicious shadowed figure charging towards her played in her mind. *I put myself in the fucking crosshairs.* Her stomach clenched as she thought yet again of how close she had come to dying in the pond. She thought of the annoying kid from her block finding her and yelling to the rest of the building about how that pissy woman with the tattoos had got herself killed.

She also knew, though, that she would never have deliberately deceived the police, even if she had thought it might put her in danger. She was too moral, always had been. Lying was not in her repertoire. But what she couldn't figure out was what she had told the detectives that could make someone want to kill her. All she had done was show them an article about Glint. They could have googled that themselves. Who would want to stab her to death over that?

Someone tried, though, didn't they? You've got a bloody great bandage to prove it! You almost didn't make it out alive.

Then Jenny realised that the receptionist had been talking. She had tuned the poor woman out, she was so wrapped up in her own thoughts.

'Come on, Jen,' Calvin said warmly, taking her arm and leading her to the small waiting area. At least the woman hadn't just told her to go to another station – that was something. She knew that members of the public weren't supposed to turn up at Scotland Yard, a quick internet search had told her as much, but she hadn't known what else to do, since she had misplaced DI Graves' card. She figured that at least they would point her in the right direction.

She slumped down and again scanned the doors, as though the detective would simply materialise any second and solve all her problems. Her leg was jumping, but she let it continue. It was nervous energy and she thought it was better out than in. She hated waiting. This time it was excruciating, enough so to distract her from her aching body. She was anxious to see the detective again. He had crossed her mind more than a few times since he had first visited the tattoo shop. There had been a spark there, she knew it, and he was cute – the kind of guy who seemed geeky but was okay with it. She couldn't let herself think about that, though. She had to stay focused.

The entrance doors opened and she turned to look at the man who walked through. He was late thirties or maybe early forties, dark-haired, and wearing a black hat and long black coat. As he entered, his coat fluttered open and Jenny saw the dog collar gleaming against his black shirt. So dark was his outfit that the white rectangle looked as though it was glowing. That was the first thing that surprised her: that a priest had just waltzed into Scotland Yard. Jenny suspected that this was not a normal occurrence, and was instantly fascinated with the man.

The next thing that took her by surprise was what he said.

'Good morning, miss. My name is Reverend Newman, and I must speak to Detective Inspector Daniel Graves right away.'

CHAPTER FIFTEEN

There was an awkward silence in the interview room as Daniel and Charlie sat down opposite Reverend Andrew Newman.

Daniel was dumbstruck by the situation, and a little light-headed. Whenever someone was brought in for questioning or was interviewed he felt a certain pressure to have things go his way, but this seemed different. Just when he thought things were complicated enough, in walked a priest.

When the receptionist had called to tell him that a priest was demanding to see him, and that so was Jenny Cartwright, Daniel had been sorely tempted to leave the priest to Charlie. He'd had his fill of demon talk already, and it wasn't even midday. The receptionist had said that Jenny claimed to have been attacked because of a case he was working on, and Daniel felt guilty about that. He unenthusiastically decided to give Newman priority, however, knowing he needed to speak to the man but also wanting to get it out of the way.

Reverend Newman had done nothing so far to assuage Daniel's doubts. He was yet to say anything beyond a brief hello, and he came across as cold, his posture rigid and his expression sharp. He was far from the homely, welcoming father figure Daniel had imagined. Dressed in black, Newman had a remarkably dominant presence despite – or possibly because of – his frosty demeanour. He seemed to be able to command attention without doing much. Daniel thought that must give him an advantage when delivering a sermon.

'So, Reverend, what can we help with? I presume this is related to the Whitmore Close case?' Daniel began, wanting to get things going.

Charlie had already brought up the obvious – that the priest was highly likely a fraudster, trying to capitalise on the murder for some reason. The fact that Newman claimed to know Catherine Delamar was what had garnered him a meeting, rather than being turned away. It was possible that he had simply seen her name in the press, but it was enough to make them want to talk to him. Now face to face with the man, Daniel was eager to find out what he wanted.

'Actually, I believe it is I who can help you. And yes, as I'm sure you know, I came because I spoke to Catherine Delamar.' Newman's voice was well educated and plummy but his words were clipped and matter-of-fact, as though he too did not care to be there.

'You do realise that Delamar is a suspect in this case?' Charlie asked.

Newman nodded and clasped his hands together, his face remaining firm, almost a blank slate. 'Of course. Like I said, I am here to help. I'm sure that you're very busy men and you don't have endless hours to follow up leads that will not prove fruitful, so I would like to eliminate one of those leads for you.'

'And which lead might that be?' Daniel said. A tingle of apprehension danced down his neck. The way Newman spoke was too calm, too direct; it was unsettling. Daniel had prepared himself for passionate talk about Christ and the Devil but the man across from him showed no bombast, instead cutting to the chase.

'Catherine,' Newman responded, a slight raise of his left eyebrow his only hint of feeling. 'She did not kill that man. The demon Adramelech did.'

Daniel rolled his eyes, unable to stop himself. He glanced at Charlie, who looked equally unimpressed by the answer. 'Forgive me for being rude or sounding dismissive, Reverend, but we have evidence that suggests that something far from supernatural was the cause of Darrell Morris's death. I'm not a man of faith so I do not believe in demons and devils. Evil, cruel, malicious people, yes, but not demons. I believe in what a crime scene shows me, and there is nothing to point to demonic activity being responsible for the victim's death.'

'Be that as it may, Detective, I also have evidence.'

'You do?' Charlie asked, sounding surprised. He narrowed his eyes at the man.

Newman nodded again. 'Yes, I do. Catherine Delamar and Marcus Spindler are not responsible for the death of that man, and I can prove it.'

'Okay, we'll bite. Why are you so sure they're not responsible?' Daniel said, his words full of doubt.

'Because it has happened before, and neither of them was there.' The reverend fell still, his words heavy in the room. Daniel and Charlie sat back in their chairs, stunned.

Sergeant Amelia Harding was beginning to feel like a stereotypical tech guy who was known for having greasy skin, unkempt hair and sallow, sun-deprived skin. The thought made her think of the goldfish she'd had as a kid. Buzz and Woody had started off glossy and orange, all shimmers of iridescence. They had died pale, white and flaky. She also felt uncomfortably pale and flaky; she had not slept well since she'd been working on the case, and it showed.

On the desk next to her were two notepads, covered in scrawls, their edges frayed from constant flicking between pages. One detailed everything she knew about the tattoo case, the other everything about the demonology victim. Large black question marks punctured almost every page.

The brick wall that Amelia had run into on the tattoo case seemed too large to scale. The words on her notepad danced around her vision, taunting her. No real suspects, leads that didn't go anywhere, and a motive that, while valid, could not be proved. The only real suspect was Cassandra Salinas, but beyond Daniel and Charlie thinking the woman could still be hiding something, there was no hard evidence that she was involved. Amelia was simply not convinced. The fact that Jenny Cartwright was downstairs waiting to be seen gave her hope of more insight. Unfortunately, she had to wait until Daniel had finished talking to the priest who had turned up out of nowhere.

She pushed the first notepad aside and went back to the one featuring the Morris family. This case confused her even more.

Darrell Morris had been poisoned. That was pretty much a certainty. Or at least as certain as the coroners could be. All signs pointed to it. That was a start. How the poison had been administered, though, and why – those were true roadblocks. She had gone through the house on Whitmore Close from top to bottom, questioning every crime scene guy in detail over the smallest things, but no hydrofluoric acid had been found anywhere, not even in the garden shed. She thought it may have been deliberately removed beforehand, but that still didn't explain how Darrell Morris had ingested the acid. All beverage bottles had been tested and had come back negative. She couldn't help feeling that the murder had been premeditated, but she needed more information.

Daniel had asked her to find out more about Catherine Delamar and Marcus Spindler. Amelia decided to start there. They were demonologists, they were in the press, there was more attention on them than probably ever before. The internet was a tool Amelia had faith in. She started with the typical searches, looking for social media accounts and the like, but came up empty-handed. She wasn't surprised. What would they be tweeting about? The newest demon on the block? Five simple ways to tell a demon from a ghost?

Next she searched online data records for UK citizens, first in London, then expanding outwards, before accessing the UK-wide database. She sifted through public records and lists of naturalised citizens, moved on to National Insurance listings, even put in a request to the UK National DNA Database from which she hoped to get a print match. A myriad of data warehouses gave snippets of information on millions of individuals. The problem was, she couldn't narrow any of it down to the two people she was hunting. Records showed numerous people called Marcus Spindler and a few called Catherine Delamar. Amelia jotted down notes on each person, matching files and data to form an outline of each individual listed.

'Except none of them bloody match!' she hissed when she had finished scanning through each profile. A few heads popped up like meerkats over neighbouring computer screens but she ignored them, instead double-checking what she had, trying to decipher her own handwriting.

Wrong age, or dead, or living far too far away. Amelia found nobody who matched what they currently knew about Spindler or Delamar – which, admittedly, was very little. She was well aware that it wasn't enough for the two not to appear on databases. Not everyone had a National Insurance number or a passport or driving licence, and most people did not have a criminal record. Still, it was highly unusual that they didn't feature on any database – bordering on almost impossible. She felt the red flag rising.

'Databases be damned,' she muttered as she started on plan B. Her fingers were a blur as she typed into Google: *Cases of demonic activity in the UK, 20th century.*

She groaned when the search threw back over four million results. She had no idea where to start, so she began by looking through the numerous 'Top 10' lists that plagued sites like Buzzfeed and Listverse.

The Enfield haunting cropped up in nearly all lists, being one of the most recent and widely reported cases. It didn't help that there was a new horror film out based on the story. Most articles were from outside the UK, but there were huge numbers of hauntings that had been retold either in films or television shows or that had books based on them. None of them seemed relevant, though. That was, until she stumbled on a Tumblr blog post two hours into her research, written by a demonology obsessive and amateur supernatural hunter, or so the profile said.

In the blog piece the writer, username DevilD, said they had decided to delve into some less well-known cases, claiming he was sick of the same old stories doing the rounds. Amelia was scrolling through the essay-length post, scanning its headings, when she froze, her finger hovering over her mouse. A photo that accompanied one of the cases had jumped out to her. At first she couldn't figure out why, and she leant closer to the screen.

Then she spotted the reason.

The photo showed a group of people standing in front of an old farmhouse near Denbigh in Wales, according to the caption. A woman had supposedly been terrorised by something in the farmhouse she and her family had moved into. This had resulted in the death of one of their children in a freak accident. The colours in the photo were faded and the outfits dated, the story having been recorded in the mid-1980s. The solemn group comprised a family of four, an elderly, somewhat overweight, farmer standing off to one side, a nervous-looking policeman and a woman bundled in a huge fur coat, her hair curled and a scarf masking the bottom part of her face, which was turned away from the camera.

Though the woman's features were hard to make out, and though the poor quality of the photo didn't help, Amelia was certain she had seen the woman before. She'd bet a month's salary it was Catherine Delamar standing next to that family. A family not unlike the Morrises. A family that had lost a child in an apparent case of demonic activity.

'How's that for evidence?' Amelia grinned, tapping the woman's face on the screen. Elated, she immediately began to look for more details on the case, silently thanking the internet and everyone who contributed to its ever-growing library.

Jenny Cartwright's words came out like a flurry of angry wasps disturbed from a hive. Daniel felt as if he needed to swat them away.

'Okay, hang on, can you backpedal a bit? Are you saying you know who killed Rogan Simmons and Jason Tagoe? And that it's the same person that attacked you?' Daniel tried to pick out the key words from the scrambled information Jenny had thrown his way.

'Yes! And it's because of Glint. Sort of. Well, I mean it's connected.'

Daniel had never seen Jenny so animated. Each time they had spoken she had been calm and collected and mildly flirtatious. The Jenny sitting across from him today was anything but. Her rich red hair was messy, strands falling out from a loose ponytail. Her cheeks were ruddy and flushed. Her accent seemed stronger, more northern.

'Okay, take a breath and explain.' Daniel had a pen and notepad ready, but a Dictaphone whirled quietly on the table between him in case he missed anything.

'So, Glint was supposed to have a lot of money, right? Like, hundreds of thousands,' Jenny started. 'A while back – a few months ago, at least – this guy I met when I came to London, Marvin Summers, he let slip that he had come into a load of money. He was just chatting, not really bragging or anything. He was a tattoo artist too and used to come into the shop – that's how I met him. But the thing is, a week later he was in a car accident and died. His motorbike was hit on the motorway near the Olympic Park. Out of curiosity I asked a few people, but no one knows what happened to his money. See, I think *he* was Glint and after faking his death in the fire, he waited a decent amount of time before planning what he was going to do next. You know, so no one would clock that he was really Glint.'

'Wait – I thought you said you didn't know who Glint was. Why didn't you tell me this before?'

Jenny's eyes widened and she looked exasperated. 'Because it only started making sense after I was knifed. I had no reason to think any more about it until then.'

'Fair point, carry on.' Daniel held his pen ready to scratch down more notes.

'Right, so I remembered that when Marvin was talking about the money, we had this guy working at the studio who was really sketchy. He used to weird me out, to be honest. I swear to God he had a dodgy past. I'm sure someone said he'd been in prison for assault or something. He might have been called Steve, something like that. I can't remember. After Marvin died, this guy started asking loads of questions – like a proper Spanish Inquisition. He was asking everyone all about Marvin and his money and plans. Then out of nowhere he left the studio. I think he was on a short-term contract or something, so no one really cared. I know a few other people didn't like him, so they were glad to be rid of him.'

'So you think this guy, this Steve, has come back to get the money?'

'Exactly! You said the killer is going after people with Glint tattoos, right?'

'Well, so far. Wait, do you have one?'

Jenny shook her head, looking dismayed. 'I wish. But look, you have two people that maybe knew Glint, both connected to the shop, both dead. I reckon he thought one of them might know about Glint – or Marvin, if I'm right about that – and he killed them when they realised what he was up to. I'm surprised he hasn't gone after Cassandra or any of the others that are connected to Needlepoint. She knew him, hated him too. I bet it's only a matter of time.'

'And he came after you because you knew Marvin but also because you've been talking to us? Shit.' Daniel could see the connections starting to fall into place.

'You didn't actually see him when he attacked you, right? You couldn't identify him?'

'Sorry, no. All I saw was a dark figure and, to be honest, I was pretty drunk. I wasn't looking for details. It was just a person, dressed in black, not massively tall. But I swear it's him, I just know it. Stefan, that's it – he was called Stefan.'

Daniel scanned his notes, making sure he had everything he needed. He could feel a tingle inside. Jenny Cartwright had handed him the best lead they had. Mixed with the adrenaline was hope: it flooded through Daniel like the welcome warmth that comes when you see a long-lost friend.

CHAPTER SIXTEEN

Charlie Palmer was driving like the proverbial bat out of hell. Daniel clung to the passenger door, his stomach threatening to jump out of his mouth and onto the dashboard.

'Jesus, Charlie, how many times do I have to ask you? Slow down!' Daniel pleaded as they swung round a bend, racing towards Mile End, the scenery blurring on each side. A lorry slammed on its horn as they shot past Stepney Green Tube station, pedestrians swivelling instinctively to watch them.

It had not taken long to find out who the Stefan Jenny Cartwright had spoken of was. Daniel had called Needlepoint Ink and spoken to the manager, Maxwell Cena, who they were yet to meet. He knew who they meant instantly, and gave them an address for Stefan Coen within minutes.

Charlie ran a background check on Coen and found a nice little list of petty – and not so petty – crimes against the man's record. Coen had been charged with assault twice, breaking and entering, indecent exposure, and handling and dealing of controlled substances. He had been in and out of jail a handful of times, apparently with no effect. Cena had hired Coen as a favour to someone he knew who worked on various community outreach programmes across the city, and had regretted it almost instantly.

According to Cena, Coen was renting a room on Strahan Road, just off Mile End Park. Daniel and Charlie jumped in the car immediately. As they hit the multi-lane junction at Grove Road Charlie finally slowed down a little, and Daniel breathed out. 'Thank God. You know driving in the city shouldn't be an extreme sport, right? Don't you get enough of that in your spare time?'

Charlie flashed him a quick grin before looking back to the road. 'I thought you were keen to catch this guy, get this case signed and sealed.' Charlie swerved past a pristine red Range Rover, a vehicle that had clearly never been tested off road. He tutted as they passed it. 'Waste of a car.'

'Catch him might be a little presumptuous, but yes. If any of what Jenny said is correct, then we need to get hold of him. Doesn't mean I need you to drive like you're being chased by the zombie apocalypse, though.'

'Okay, okay, quit your whining, Graves. I hear you. See? Nice and sedate.' As Charlie spoke, they bumped over a pothole in the road. Daniel sighed but made no comment, instead checking his seatbelt in the vague hope that Charlie would notice the passive-aggressive gesture.

'These cases are really getting to me, you know? My head is still spinning from that priest. If he gives us evidence that Catherine Delamar is innocent, then how do we link her to this one? We can't tell the superintendent that a killer demon is on the loose. I need to lock down what I can, and I have faith in what Jenny said.'

Charlie opened his mouth to speak. Daniel saw and stopped him in his tracks, knowing what was coming. 'And before you say it, it's not because I fancy her.'

'So you do admit you fancy her, then.'

Daniel glared at his colleague, who was grinning again, eyes deliberately on the road.

'We're here,' Charlie said as they pulled onto Strahan Road. The street was quiet. An uncomfortable feeling needled under Daniel's skin, chilling him.

'This looks eerily like Whitmore Close. If we come across another demonologist I'm done, I swear.'

Charlie parked and they got out of the vehicle. Daniel checked out the street. There was a constant buzz of nearby traffic, but on this road everything was still. He pulled out his notepad and checked the house number. Then he spotted the van.

'See that? I'm guessing we found the house.'

They walked slowly down the pavement, their eyes on the van, which stood out among the family cars that lined the street. The van was black, battered and had amateurish blacked-out windows: the wheels of someone up to no good.

'Subtle.' Charlie frowned. 'Like a X on a map. I hope we find treasure.'

The house that the van was parked outside was unassuming. It looked almost identical to those on either side, although it was considerably more rundown. The small patch of front lawn was dried out, angular twigs poked from the ground where lush hedges and flourishing roses should be, and paint peeled from the window frames. Curtains blocked out every window.

Charlie's gaze flitted around the street as they approached the house. Daniel knocked on the door and they waited. Hearing nothing, Charlie looked over at the downstairs window. A curtain fluttered.

'Well, whaddya know, someone's home after all,' he muttered, turning back to Daniel, who knocked again.

'This is Detective Inspector Graves. Open up, please, Mr Coen.'

They heard someone bumping around on the other side of the door, but it remained closed.

'We know that you're in there. We need to speak with Stefan Coen – please open the door.' Daniel tried again.

'Think we have a runner?' Charlie whispered, his hand hovering over his expandable baton clipped onto his belt. Daniel shrugged. He banged on the front door one more time. 'You know what? Go round the back, anyway. I'll take the front. Just be careful.'

Charlie nodded, then strode across the dead grass. A broken fence allowed entry to the rear garden and he stepped past it. Daniel heard a crash from inside – perhaps a window breaking or something being dropped. He decided the time to be hesitant was over. Putting his full weight behind him, he kicked the front door. The cheap lock broke with no resistance. Splinters rained down as Daniel raised his baton, stepping into the shadowed interior. He paused for a second, long enough to take in his immediate environment. A dingy sitting room to the left, littered with junk-food containers and beer cans, with old, worn furniture that looked ready to give up the ghost. A mist of stale cigarette smoke floated in the air. To the right was a dining room, clearly not used for hosting dinner parties: the cheap table was almost hidden under papers, magazines and other detritus.

Movement caught Daniel's eye. He whipped to the left, saw Charlie pass the back window off the living room, which looked out onto the overgrown garden beyond. Charlie caught his eye, nodded and continued out of sight, his shoulders hunched. The house was still quiet. Cautiously, Daniel stepped further into the house, his heart pounding. The floorboards underneath Daniel's brogues creaked, and he winced. Stairs led up to the first floor. No light came down from above, and Daniel was reluctant to go near the stairs, knowing he could be charged or jumped.

Where are you, you fucker? His muscles tight, he moved past the old sofa to get a better look at the kitchen.

A shot rang out, then a bullet whistled over his head. Instinctively, he dropped to the floor. Another two shots boomed, the walls lighting up with flashes. Daniel scrambled across the floor. He heard someone curse, the voice close to him. Crouching, his back to the end of the sofa, he stole a quick glance towards the kitchen, where he saw a man wearing a dark hooded top. Before he could decide his next move the man ran out through the back door.

Daniel jumped to his feet and followed the man towards the open door. He flinched as two more shots screamed out. Someone yelled, and Daniel's breath caught in his throat. He charged out of the kitchen into the garden – and stopped dead.

Charlie Palmer lay on the grass on his back, unmoving. Harsh red flowers bloomed on the white of his shirt.

Stefan Coen had gone.

'Amelia, if you don't have good news, can it wait?' Daniel said as the young sergeant swung open the glass door to join him in the dark meeting room. She had seen him duck into the room a few minutes earlier and switch the lights off, clearly needing to gather his thoughts in silence. She had hesitated, hugging a wad of papers and folders to her chest, then urgency had taken priority over sensitivity.

'It's kind of good and bad, but it can't wait – sorry,' she said, entering the room and pushing the door closed behind her. She flicked on the lights. Daniel groaned. Amelia placed the papers on the table next to him and pulled up a seat.

'How is he?' she asked, eager to focus on their work. She already knew the answer but Daniel needed to say it. She needed his full attention for what she was about to show him.

'The hospital called half an hour ago. He'll be fine. Nothing vital was hit.' Daniel's voice was low. He sounded exhausted and miserable.

'Well, that's great news. Why aren't you happier?'

'Because my partner got shot, he'll be out of action for at least a few days. And that bastard Coen ... where did he get a gun?' He leant back in his chair, facing the ceiling, and closed his eyes. 'I've effectively lost a partner and a lead, all in one morning.' His words were followed by a barely audible growl of frustration.

'Well, I'm here,' Amelia countered, opening the folders and spreading out the sheets of paper. 'So why don't I show you what I've got? Some of it is very good news!' She chuckled, hoping to dispel some of the tension. She knew what she had discovered would go down well, even if she did have some less great news to accompany it. Daniel didn't smile but his expression calmed as he opened his eyes again and scanned the mass of printouts.

'I'll lead with the bad news, shall I? While you were looking for Coen, we got some stuff through from that reverend. He emailed over loads of files. Old articles, photos, even a video of what seems to be another exorcism, although it's pretty poor quality. According to what he sent, there have been quite a few incidents over the last fifty years or so where someone has died in an apparent case of demonic activity – all linked to Adramelech, the demon Delamar claims is responsible for the death of Darrell Morris. It's not quite the smoking gun Reverend Newman claimed, but since neither Delamar or Marcus Spindler were connected to any of the cases Newman mentioned, it's more support for them being innocent. It also all looks quite genuine – not the stories themselves, but the reports.'

Amelia plucked out a few sheets of paper and pushed them over to Daniel, who looked over the collection of headlines and grainy images. He tossed more than a few aside and Amelia felt a ripple of worry that he was simply dismissing it without taking the time to read the articles properly.

'Okay. None of this is proof that they didn't kill Morris; it's all hearsay and stories. I suppose you're right, though: it does add to the argument that if this has happened numerous times before and our suspects have never been connected to those other incidents, then maybe we missed something. Maybe they aren't responsible.'

'And a demon simply can't be.'

'Because demons are utter bullshit!' Daniel answered quickly – Amelia thought a little too quickly – his voice harsh. She was aware of what Daniel thought about the existence of anything supernatural. He had been pretty vocal on the matter since the case began. She had tried to maintain an open mind, but had to admit it was practically impossible to believe that a demon had attacked and killed Darrell Morris. Something about the way Daniel prickled at the very mention of supernatural beings had stuck with her, though. It seemed like a real over-reaction. He was clearly rattled, but she didn't think it was just because he was pissed off. She chose to move on, knowing Daniel was not in the mood to be questioned.

'Indeed, I agree it is far more likely that a person killed Morris,' Amelia continued, 'so I've asked for all of this to be authenticated, particularly the video. Marsden and his team are on it. I hope to God it isn't real, because I watched it and it's really creepy. And of course it would totally undermine our investigation.'

'Good. Patrick should be looking into something for me too.

So what's the good news?' Daniel asked bluntly, anger bubbling under his words. He seemed to be running out of patience. Amelia was pretty sure his bad mood wasn't aimed at her, so she chose not to take offence, but she didn't like seeing him like this, snapping at her.

'Daniel, calm down, would you?'

'Sorry,' he said with a grimace.

Amelia retrieved the photo she had found earlier and slid it over to the detective inspector. It was time for what she hoped was their own smoking gun. She tapped the image. 'Recognise her?'

Daniel picked up the print and held it, squinting a little. His eyes widened as he looked over the sheet at her. 'Is that—'

Amelia nodded, feeling a tingle of adrenaline filtering into her system.

'Yep. Catherine Delamar. Around twenty years ago. And look at the case it relates to.'

Daniel scanned the article. 'Death of the youngest child ... holy shit. That demon, Adramelech, he's known for sacrificing children. Charlie and I were literally just talking about this. Does it say anywhere how she was connected to this?'

Amelia shook her head. 'But what are the odds of our lead suspect turning up connected to another death as a result of demonic activity? Not only that, but one where the victim links so directly to the demon she herself named?'

'I'd say slim to none.' Daniel locked eyes with her, smiling finally, the photo held tight in his hand.

The grogginess Charlie Palmer had been feeling was finally starting to clear when the nurse on duty came round to check up on him.

'How are you feeling?' the young woman asked as she poured him a glass of water. 'Have a drink, then I'll check your bandages.'

Charlie complied. 'I don't think it's bleeding any more,' he said, then lifted up the thin fabric gown he wore. He winced. The bullet had hit high, fracturing a rib before ricocheting. It had left a nasty gash beneath his left pectoral muscle that would no doubt scar, but he had been extremely lucky, escaping with wounds that would heal easily. The pain he could not escape so easily.

'Try not to move too much. The painkillers you're on may make it seem like you're healing faster than you are, so don't push it.' The nurse's voice was friendly but stern. She checked his bandages. 'You're right, looks pretty good. I'll come back in a few hours, okay?'

'Could you do me a favour and switch the television on before you go?' Charlie asked. She nodded and pressed the power button on the small wall-mounted unit opposite Charlie's bed, then handed him the remote.

'Enjoy, see you soon,' she said and with that she was gone, her pristine white pumps squeaking lightly as she went.

Charlie held up the remote, careful not to irritate his stitches, and began to scroll through the channels, thankful he had the room to himself. He stopped on a news channel when he caught sight of the red ticker-tape graphic at the bottom of the screen. The word 'demon' slowly made its way across the frame as a female journalist delivered a piece to camera. He turned up the volume.

'Following reports of strange activity in the house, the father said that his youngest child went missing in the early hours. Given what happened in the highly publicised case of the Morris family from north London earlier this week, the family are naturally fearful that they have been targeted by Catherine

Delamar and Marcus Spindler, the so-called demonologists believed to be suspects in the death of Darrell Morris. Local police forces have already started the search for Mary Ross, with neighbours and friends joining in. Neither Delamar nor Spindler have been taken into custody, casting doubt over just what happened at the Morris residence and what steps the London Metropolitan Police are taking in this very upsetting case. What is clear, though, is that if this case is related, it is vital that Mary Ross is found before it's too late.'

Charlie dropped the remote in his lap as the news cut to shots of the clearly terrified Ross family at their home.

'Fuck!' he yelled. He grabbed for the button next to his bed meant for summoning a nurse and pressed it repeatedly.

CHAPTER SEVENTEEN

A wide-brimmed hat pulled down low on her head, saucer-like sunglasses covering her face, Catherine Delamar entered the American-themed diner as quickly as she could. Marcus had told her he would be in a booth at the back. She headed quietly through the place, eyeing up the blue circular booths. Each featured a high back, making customers hard to see unless you were in front of the table. It was clear why he had picked the restaurant. She wished it was somewhere less private, but their rented accommodation was being plagued by journalists and they had worried about being seen together.

'Catherine!'

She turned and did a double take. Marcus was wearing a beige cap and had grown facial hair out of nowhere; it was obviously stuck on.

'Hardly conspicuous, dear,' Catherine muttered as she took a seat in the booth, rolling her eyes behind her sunglasses.

'Well, you didn't know it was me, did you?'

Catherine tilted her head, forced to admit he was right, even though she thought he looked ridiculous.

'This is getting too much for me, Marcus. We need to figure out what we're going to do. Did you see the news?'

Marcus picked up a wrinkled newspaper from the seat beside him and dropped it in front of her. 'I sure did. The whole city thinks we're kidnappers, for fuck's sake. On top of being murderers! I don't know what we do now. Can we leave? Just get the hell out of here? I mean, we got the money off the Morrises.'

Catherine startled at the sudden presence of a chipper waitress, looming over them with a beaming smile.

'Hi, guys, how are you both doing today? Ready to order?' the girl asked, her American accent too much for Catherine's liking. She had never been keen on the over-the-top happiness many Americans seemed to possess. She much preferred a waspish Brit.

'Just a coffee for me,' she answered curtly. Marcus ordered a milkshake and fries.

'And what happened with good old Reverend Newman? Has he called you?' Marcus continued when they were alone again. Catherine was thankful for the tinny music playing over the restaurant speakers, covering their conversation, allowing their voices to blend with the chatter of other patrons.

'Yes, he did.'

Marcus grimaced at her.

'Sorry, I meant to tell you. It was only a few hours ago. He's not sure he had much luck – said the detectives were dismissive of him. He sent the files over to them but hasn't heard back. It should hopefully get them off our backs for a while, then when they can't charge us with anything the press will die down and we'll get back to normal. That's what I'm hoping.'

Even as Catherine spoke, it was difficult to believe her own words. Worry churned inside her. She had barely eaten since they had been questioned, and had been regretting coming to

London ever since. She knew it had been a risk but the chance of a much higher payout had seemed worth it.

More provincial towns or villages had fewer police; it was easy to slip away in the night. Those were places where they could get money without too much trouble. It was never enough to sustain them, though, that was the eternal problem. Now she had pushed their luck. It was her fault that everything was crumbling around them. Just the act of disguising herself to go outside was more than enough to give her a panic attack.

'So, no leaving then?' Marcus said.

'I'm not sure it would be a good idea. We need our names to be cleared first. How do you think it would look if we're caught fleeing?'

Marcus nodded, his shoulders sagging. The waitress returned with their drinks but did not linger, perhaps sensing the air of depression hovering above the pair. Marcus took a swig of milkshake and a fry.

'Perhaps...' Catherine started before pausing, shaking her head. She blew on her coffee and took a sip, the bitter taste instantly making her feel queasy.

'Perhaps what? Do you have an idea?' Marcus asked around another fry. Grains of salt lingered around his mouth. Catherine pursed her lips, not sure whether she should say what had sprung into her mind. The thought was vague and the idea risky.

'What if ... what if we went to the police ourselves? Proved our own innocence?'

Marcus coughed, and milkshake dribbled down his chin. He wiped his mouth with a napkin, dabbing carefully at his fake facial hair. 'Seriously? How would that achieve anything?'

'They have no evidence so far, correct? That we had anything to do with Darrell Morris dying, I mean. They have nothing they can pin on either of us, or they would have charged us. They can't even charge us with extortion because Janine Morris paid us willingly.'

'I suppose so.'

'And we have nothing to do with this new missing girl,' Catherine continued, glancing at the front cover of the newspaper. 'We have never met this family, something they can quickly confirm. Add that to not having any evidence, and what can they do? If we show those detective inspectors that we're not hiding, that we have nothing to do with this other case, then they'll have to clear us. Sure, it will piss them off, but the press will be forced to move on and we can go back to what we do best. We'll leave the second they dismiss us as suspects in their investigation.'

'To somewhere smaller,' Marcus pointed out.

'Yes, exactly. Maybe even Europe. Marcus, I'm ... I'm so sorry I made us come here. I should have seen this all coming. I just got greedy – arrogant, maybe. I hope you can forgive me. Are we agreed, then?'

'I suppose so, but I'm not forgiving you until we're free and clear. And I'm not sure I like this plan, for the record.'

'Well, neither do I, but we can't just sit waiting for this to pass, and I don't want us to live our lives watching over our shoulders because we ran away from something we could resolve. So, eat up and let's go.'

'What, now?'

'No time like the present,' Catherine answered, a small smile forming on her lips. She didn't really feel any better and she had no idea if her plan would work. For all she knew, they could be about to walk right into the arms of the very people who wanted them. Something told her this was their best chance, though. If it worked as she dared hope, then they could move on, learn from their mistakes and avoid causing a media frenzy ever again. Perhaps they'd change up their approach...

'Honestly, we should be happy this didn't happen sooner. It was bound to at some point. People don't like what they can't explain. Demons are a hard pill to swallow. It's not surprising so much doubt has been cast on us.'

'What a comforting thought.' Marcus groaned and dropped some money on the table. He took a last gulp of his drink, then got up to follow Catherine, who was tugging her hat down over her eyes as she walked.

A Be On the Look Out order had been put out on Stefan Coen, and Daniel and Amelia were out looking for Catherine Delamar and Marcus Spindler. The unwelcome and overly familiar feeling of being up shit creek without a paddle washed over Daniel as they drove towards Wapping. The weather was dull, the pale grey sky seeping any energy out of the afternoon, seeping the energy out of Daniel.

Three times Amelia had tried to spark a conversation, either about one of the cases or just general chat, but he just couldn't muster up the words to engage properly. Daniel knew how easy it was to become overwhelmed by depression. After what had happened with his sister, he had been forced to go to weekly therapy sessions. He hadn't wanted to at first, but after a year or so he had started to feel better.

He had never got over the fact that he had killed someone, even though it had been ruled an accident, self-defence – and in defence of his sister. His therapist had admitted that while he could move past the incident and learn to live with the memories, they would still be there, and he would have to manage them. It did not help that his sister's opinion of things changed with the wind too. Sometimes she blamed him for everything; at other times she called him a hero. As a result he was constantly questioning himself, never sure what he was or what people thought of him.

Adam Spencer's death had affected Daniel so much that it had ended up dictating his career choice. Before then he had never longed to join the world of law enforcement. In fact, he had always been more interested in architecture and design. That changed in the blink of an eye.

Adam had come from an abusive family. Years of verbal and physical blows from his parents had infected his mind as surely as a virus. He had become a spiteful, vicious young man – and Amanda Graves was to be the last target of his venomous anger and twisted logic.

Daniel had thought that Adam was just nasty, a violent soul. Adam had stalked Amanda, threatened her, and finally tried to rape her. Although his death had been an accident, at first Daniel had thought that maybe the world was better off without the kid. That feeling dissolved almost instantly when he found out more about Adam's background. After Adam's death, the Spencer family had undergone scrutiny from all sides. The cruelty that they had subjected Adam to rapidly became apparent. Adam had been angry and bitter. His history didn't excuse Adam's actions, not really, but it had made them easier to understand. Adam could have grown up to become a much better man in different circumstances – if he had different parents.

Perhaps if he became a policeman, Daniel could prevent others from falling prey to the same cycle of self-loathing and aggression that Adam had succumbed to.

The guilt of taking a life still swam around inside Daniel, raising its head every so often. Sometimes he told himself he wasn't good enough to be a detective inspector, that he was a murderer, that he had tricked everyone, that it was only a matter of time before people realised and sent him packing.

When those feelings came up he would sit down and talk himself round, go through all that he had achieved. Or he would speak to Rachel, who would give him a mini therapy session.

So much had happened in just a few short days. Three bodies, Charlie being shot, an apparent demonic visitation in the middle of the night. Daniel was floundering. The water seemed that much deeper without Rachel or Charlie at his side. Now he glanced at Amelia, who was driving, looking extremely comfortable behind the wheel.

'You okay?' she asked, flicking her gaze to him for a second.

He wound the window down, enjoying the air flowing over his face despite the traffic fumes. He knew he had to talk to her, to help sort his mind out, to let her know what was going on. He took a deep breath.

'There's something I should tell you, something that has been driving me nuts all day.'

'Go for it,' Amelia responded, switching lanes but clearly ready to listen.

Daniel told her all about his past, about Adam and Amanda. He told her about the day he'd taken a life. How he had pushed Adam off the second floor of the half-built block of flats where he had taken Amanda. The sight of the teenager's broken, bloodied body in the rain-fresh mud, a piece of metal rebar sticking through his chest. How Amanda had sobbed into his shoulder as he tried to persuade her to leave the building site, and how guilt and anger ate at him like bacteria. He told her of his doubts and insecurities.

They were passing Wapping Station by the time he finished, with Amelia checking their GPS for Catherine

Delamar's address. Daniel felt exhausted, relieved, pathetic and more, not sure how his colleague would react.

Amelia pulled up outside the apartment complex on Wapping Wall, frowning at the small crowd of picketers and local journalists still camped outside. She turned to Daniel.

'You know, I get it. I get why you're worried, why the pressure of your job makes you nervous. You've moved to a brand-new city, into a high-stakes position with a new partner. Anyone would be stressed by that.'

Daniel nodded, feeling his throat go dry.

'You and Charlie have been assigned some pretty nasty cases since you got here. That one with the guy who had murdered his wife and girlfriend last month – that was horrific. I could see the impact it had on you; everyone could. Things like that don't often happen where you came from, but in London… And now here you are with two more cases that keep getting more and more complicated, with leads vanishing every time anyone tries to grab one. It's taking its toll on you. Not to mention the whole demon angle. And you're trying to resolve feelings from when you were a teenager – it's a hell of lot to deal with.'

'You're pretty astute, huh?' Daniel mumbled. He agreed with everything she said, and it simultaneously made him feel better and worse. He could tell where her words were aiming, that she was on his side, but he could feel his negativity fighting to be in charge, as usual.

'I am indeed. Can't help myself for shit, but I'm pretty good with other people. So I get it. But you know what? I struggle every day, trying to prove myself to people like you, trying to impress and show that I'm good at this, that I have what it takes to progress. And I've worked with a lot of different detective inspectors, and guess what? They all struggle too. The combination of dealing with cases like this, feeling responsible for putting killers away, helping victims, and just being human, with all the doubts and issues and baggage. I don't know if this will make you feel better, but you're not the only one who feels like shit sometimes. We're in this together. You, Charlie, me, Hobbs – the whole team. I can't see the future, I don't know how this is all going to go, but you're a good detective, Graves. You are. And you have me to help.' Amelia finished with one of the most genuine smiles Daniel had ever seen. A tear trickled down one cheek. He wiped it away and laughed.

'God, you really are good. Thank you. I think I needed that, needed to hear it out loud.' Daniel took another few slow breaths, calming himself, then stole a look in the wing mirror to make sure he wasn't too red-faced. He felt that he should be embarrassed for crying in front of Amelia, a colleague who ranked below him. He was supposed to be in control. But he had started to feel like she was his friend, and that somehow outweighed any embarrassment.

'You're welcome.' Amelia smiled again, giving him her signature gentle shoulder nudge. He was smiling back when her face changed in an instant, her eyes widening with surprise.

'Shit.' She nodded towards the apartment complex. Daniel swivelled in his seat to see what had surprised her. A taxi had pulled up in front of the building and the crowd had swarmed around it. Pushing through the over-zealous picketers, ignoring the man thrusting a camera into their faces, Catherine Delamar and Marcus Spindler strode down the pavement, aiming for Daniel and Amelia.

'Detective Inspector Graves,' Catherine said into the open passenger-side window before Daniel could say a word. 'Marcus and I would very much like to talk to you. We were just collecting some things before making our way over to your department. How handy that you are here waiting. Serendipitous, you might say. Can we get in?'

Daniel turned back to Amelia, at a loss for words. Her expression echoed his.

'Yes, yes, of course,' he stuttered. Amelia pushed the button to unlock the rear doors. As Amelia started the car, Daniel studied his lead suspects in the rear-view mirror. They were beaming with satisfaction.

CHAPTER EIGHTEEN

Patrick Marsden was waiting for Amelia and Daniel when they returned to headquarters, two alarmingly cooperative suspects in tow. Amelia felt her heart sing with hope: would he have something that could help them?

Amelia had long since stopped worrying about having to deal with unusual turns in her job. She had seen things she would never be able to unsee, and was often bemused by how odd or downright shocking people could be. Still, she had felt extremely unsettled with Catherine Delamar and Marcus Spindler sitting behind her in the car, making small talk about the weather, firing random questions at them about life in the Met. Only a few hours earlier Amelia had been digging through the woman's past, looking for a way to incriminate her, and all of a sudden there she was, chatting away like the situation was totally normal – as though she were not under suspicion of murder but they were off on a road trip. Amelia was concerned: what could it mean? She doubted that they wanted to turn themselves in. The fact that they were being so brazen worried her.

Amelia was glad to see Daniel and another officer take the

duo away. As soon as they were gone she grabbed Patrick, dragging him down to the IT department, telling him how weird the last half hour had been.

'You better have something amazing to show me!' she said, feeling a little frantic, aware she needed to calm down. Patrick gave an awkward groan, at which Amelia rolled her eyes. 'That is not the correct response,' she muttered, 'but go on. I'm all ears.'

Fingers clacked over keyboards frantically, a constant plastic chattering of activity in the background as Patrick led Amelia across his floor. She didn't really like going down to talk to the tech guys. It made her feel inadequate when they had to dumb things down for her. She knew she wasn't alone in that, but it bugged her more than it probably did others, so she tended to avoid being around such people.

Most of the windows had blinds pulled down. The light from the monitors cast an alien glow over everything, and Amelia tried to ignore the thought that she was an intruder entering a hive of supercomputers.

Patrick settled at his desk and Amelia wheeled a chair over to sit next to him. Then she saw what was on his monitors: the video that Reverend Newman had sent in, details of cases he had provided, with the aim of proving that Catherine Delamar and Marcus Spindler were innocent.

'I got Casey to look into the news pieces that the reverend sent over. He spent half a day calling up publications, searching on forums and online news pieces – even phoned a few names related to the articles. It was a mixed bag. All the articles were real, in that they were actually written and published as news pieces, but with more than a few there seems to be a lot of scepticism over whether the events actually transpired as reported.'

'Well, that's good. I mean, it sheds doubt over the stories, adds a point to the "demons don't actually exist" column.'

'True, but then one or two of the people he spoke to were adamant about what they saw, and one has had a career as a journalist since then. She may be harder to ignore, given her reputation.'

'And the video?' Amelia asked. Patrick pressed play, and the video filled one screen of the dual set-up. Amelia shivered in anticipation, knowing what was to come and not too pleased to be watching it again.

The clip was just over five minutes long. It looked to have been filmed in a kitchen in a fairly modest house. The quality of the video was poor, with nearly all colour bleached out and scratches and degradation giving it a rough texture. The kitchen looked to be from the 1970s. A woman in her early twenties had been bound to a chair. She looked dirty, dishevelled. The camera zoomed in on her angry, crazed eyes. Amelia shivered. An elderly man began to talk to the woman in the chair, and she tracked his movement around her. Her head was not moving but her eyes blazed with animosity. There was no audio on the video, so they couldn't be sure what was being said, but Amelia suspected it was the same stuff she had heard countless times in nearly every demon- or exorcist-related film: the woman was accused of being possessed by something, or causing terror and panic. *The power of Christ compels you!* Another woman was present in the shot then: she had harsh features, her hair scraped into a tight bun. She spoke briefly before sprinkling water over the bound woman. Instantly the scene descended into chaos. A wind whipped into the room, and the seated woman's long hair flew around her face. As the camera panned around the room, cupboard doors opened of their own accord, a chair was pulled out through an open doorway by an invisible force, a projectile flew towards the camera operator, causing the camera to sway. When the camera turned back to the woman, Amelia could see how crazed she seemed, her lips moving ever so slightly, hair writhing around her. The lights above her flashed and a shower of sparks rained down over her head. At this point the camera was wrenched violently across the room. It slammed into something and the video cut out.

'Please tell me it's fake, Patrick. It's so bloody creepy. I can't bear to think about that being real.'

'We passed this thing through every test we have, looking for anything odd at all. I'm not going to lie, we struggled.'

'Shit, what does that mean?' Amelia burst out.

'It means that we don't really know. Logic and reason tell us it has to be fake. The things that are shown in the video are preposterous, not possible in real life. That said, we couldn't find anything to prove that it was staged either. It seems likely that it was done with ... I don't know ... practical effects. People behind the scenes pulling the strings, probably literally, but still...' His voice petered out.

'Fuck, Patrick, I need evidence against them, not more things to cast doubt over the case. We don't have anything that can pin Delamar and Spindler to the murder, beyond the fact that they were there at the time.'

She was exasperated. How on earth did everything they have seem to point to the supernatural being more real than fake?

'Do we know who the people in the video are, at least? Can we track them down and talk to them?'

'Unfortunately not. We don't know who apparently conducted this exorcism, and the woman in the video, Margaret Johnson, died in the late 1970s of liver failure.'

'So that's it?' Amelia asked, defeated, unable to hide her

disappointment. She reached out and broke off a piece of the Dairy Milk bar open in its wrapper on Patrick's desk. He frowned but didn't say anything, and she gave him a 'thank you' shoulder hunch as she chewed.

'Well, no, hence why I was waiting for you. I know you wanted an answer about the video, so that was partially it, but Detective Inspector Graves asked me to look into two calls that he and Palmer received in the early hours of this morning.'

'What calls?' Amelia asked suspiciously, taking another piece of chocolate without thinking. Patrick pushed the whole bar over to her and she took it without hesitation. She needed the sugar. She had not heard anything about any weird calls, and her mind flashed back to Daniel snapping earlier.

'They both got a call at around three in the morning, from unknown numbers. I don't know what the calls concerned, but they were adamant that I find out where they came from – I think because they may relate to this case, somehow. Anyway, Porter and I did some digging, went through the records and such. The calls came from burner phones.'

'Does that mean we can't trace them?'

'A mere burner phone can't stop me, Amelia. We got the numbers – that wasn't hard, but it also wasn't helpful. What may prove handy is that the calls came from two different phones, both bought at the same time from the same store, and they are very likely the same model too. The shop is in Brent Cross shopping centre.'

He gave her the name of the shop.

'And it will have CCTV!' Amelia said a bit too loudly. A few heads turned to her. 'Patrick, I could kiss you! Okay, I've got to go, thank you.' She flew out of her seat, newly energised, but kept hold of the Dairy Milk as she headed to find Daniel.

He barrelled into the warehouse and pulled the heavy metal door closed. Stefan Coen took a deep breath and fell back against the wall, his lungs burning and his calf muscles on fire. He hadn't stopped running for over an hour in his attempt to get the hell away from the police. The panic that had flooded through him when they had turned up on his doorstep had been like a fire under him, and instinct had taken over.

A lot of people were after Stefan Coen. He didn't know how it happened, but everything seemed to be snowballing. He'd always been in trouble, that was nothing new, but charm and luck had, time and again, pulled him through. He knew how to play people, was highly adept at getting what he wanted and worming his way out of tricky situations. At least, he used to be. The past few months had signalled a worrying turn in his fortunes.

If anyone asked Stefan when the turning point was, he'd have struggled to pinpoint an exact moment, but one name had certainly become a painful thorn in his side. Glint. He found it laughable that no one had cottoned on to who Glint was. That fucking smug prick Marvin Summers was so obvious – at least, Stefan thought so. The guy was always going on about how he idolised Glint's work and his style, how he envied the riches Glint had won from all that mystery bullshit.

But when had Stefan's lightbulb moment been? Marvin had been more than simply pissed off when an arts and culture journal had shredded the enigmatic Glint, criticising the 'wizard behind the green curtain' effect. The journal had lambasted Glint as a cheap, tacky facade to make up for less than stellar tattoo work. Not six weeks after Stefan witnessed Marvin having an apocalyptic blowout at the audacity of the writer, Glint was mysteriously 'killed off' at a convention. Stefan wouldn't have been surprised if Marvin had started the fire himself.

At first he didn't care. He had never rated either Marvin or Glint. But then Marvin started going on about the money that he had apparently inherited, all the plans he had. Stefan owed big money to more than one person – and he saw an opportunity. He'd been plotting the best approach to bribe Marvin, threatening to reveal him and Glint as a sham and score a payoff in the process.

It was supposed to have gone smoothly. He'd planned to confront Marvin at his house, maybe giving him a light roughing-up. Stefan had dealt with the sort before. Marvin was a gentrified idiot and Stefan knew he would be a pushover. He'd give Stefan a wad of cash and tell him to beat it. Maybe Stefan would even be able to get a few more thousand if he threatened Marvin again. The royalties alone that Marvin was getting would ensure he wouldn't want the truth coming out. But that was not how things had panned out. They had fought, things had been broken, Marvin had literally kicked Stefan backwards across his sitting room. Stefan had pulled out a gun, not even thinking about what he was doing, with no intention of shooting Marvin, but the gun had gone off. The bullet had gone wide but Marvin had charged, almost knocking Stefan out, dragging him out of his house. By the time Stefan's vision had cleared, Marvin was on his bike, no doubt heading for the nearest police station. Stefan had given chase. He couldn't go back to prison; Marvin had to be stopped.

The rest had been a daze. He didn't even think he had clipped Marvin's bike, but the ensuing crash was proof enough. As life had taught him to do, Stefan had fled, ditching the battered truck near a scrapyard. He had been on the run ever since. He had no money to pay off the heavies, was terrified of being found out by the police. And then shit, suddenly people he knew were being murdered.

When the detectives had turned up in Mile End, that

familiar panic had set in, taking over Stefan so much, he'd felt like he was possessed. He knew the charges for manslaughter; there was no charming his way out of that. When the second detective inspector had appeared from nowhere, blocking his escape route, he'd done the only thing he could think of. He pulled the trigger and ran.

He caught his breath as he made his way across the warehouse, past the makeshift chairs and shredded old sofa. The place was a dump but it did the job well – a safe hideout in a place no one would ever bother looking. There were loads of empty units in Deptford and he'd taken one that no one seemed to own. Barely anyone knew about it; he'd had a few hook-ups there with half-blitzed junkie girls, but they didn't count.

After playing around with a socket point in the warehouse Stefan had managed to get electricity in a few places, effectively stealing it from a neighbouring unit. He'd bought a cheap-ass mini-fridge off Gumtree and – bada-bing, bada-boom – chilled drinks. He retrieved a can of Carling and slumped on the sofa, shuffling over to avoid a spring busting through the fabric. After a few swigs and another few deep breaths he started to relax and plot his next move. Hiding out for a while was an option. He'd only attempted to kit out one room of the warehouse but it had a small working bathroom left behind from whatever it had been before, and two rooms up a metal staircase that had presumably been offices or something similar. A couple of empty files and old receipts were all that remained. It was hardly cosy, but it would do for a while.

Stefan closed his eyes for a moment, savouring the cold beer, then he heard footsteps.

'You're a hard person to find, Stefan Coen,' came a voice

from behind him. He spun around. Beer sprayed out across the back of the sofa when he registered the glinting machete in the intruder's grip.

CHAPTER NINETEEN

Constable Alan Mitchum felt like the dogsbody of the department. Whenever someone had a job they weren't interested in doing, they called good old reliable Alan – and for some reason he always said yes. This was partly because confrontation made him nervous. His mother had been prone to tantrums that could last for days, and he had grown into an adult who had an almost pathological need to please. Then there was the fact that he had no real aspirations in life; he had a tendency to coast.

Alan had never really known what he wanted to do. He had floated through secondary school with average marks across the board but no real aptitude for anything, and this had led to similar in his work life. His problem was, he got bored easily, couldn't focus on anything for long, yet he had little idea of what would keep his attention. An online employability test his mother had forced him to take had suggested that he needed some structure when it came to a job: a career with specific, achievable goals. He had joined the police force with only average interest. He was as surprised as anyone to find he enjoyed it, that it was a profession that engaged him. Six years on, however, he had made barely a whisper of progression, and he suspected this was why people gave him the important, but straightforward, jobs they didn't have time for. A number of colleagues and superiors had mentioned his lack of ambition. Sometimes this didn't bother him. Today, however, he had been rushing from pillar to post doing nothing of great importance – in his opinion. He had been in his car for most of the day, only stopping for a late lunch consisting of a beef burrito and a sugar-free Pepsi. He was swiping left and right on Tinder as he ate, relishing the break, when the call came in. He had to go and check on some woman, apparently to make sure she and her family were okay, then sit outside her house until his shift was over, when another officer would take up the duty. That seemed easy enough.

After scoffing his food he made his way to the address in Haringey, drifting through the afternoon traffic for what felt like an eternity. He hated driving in the city – was not a fan of driving at all, in fact – but he made it to Green Lanes unscathed.

Alan was used to doing house visits. In fact, he had done two already that morning. As he approached the front door of this house, though, he felt that something was off. Not sure what it was, he pressed the doorbell and waited. Nothing happened. No one answered, and he could hear no movement inside. He knocked on the door, which opened slightly.

'Goddammit,' he muttered. He had a sixth sense for things being out of place, not quite right. The door being open backed up his gut instinct that something was wrong. The woman was supposed to be home, that was what he had been told. There was supposed to be a kid too. He pulled his radio off his shoulder and buzzed in.

'Natasha? This is Mitchum, I'm at the place and there's no one here. Front door's unlocked too. You sure they're supposed to be in?' He was hoping Natasha would say there was a mistake. He didn't want to have to go into the house, at least not by himself. Front doors left open in London was never a good sign.

'One second, let me check.'

Alan took a step back onto the pavement as he listened to the tapping of a keyboard on the other end of the call. The house seemed totally still. It unnerved him.

'Hey, Alan – yep, she's supposed to be home. She was called a couple of hours ago, according to the log, told that someone would be round. If the door has been left open, there's a good chance something is wrong,' Natasha said, her voice lowering. 'She's involved in a potential serial murder case. I take it you haven't gone in there? Do you need me to call for assistance?'

Alan thought about that for a moment. Half of him wanted to wait, but it dawned on him that could be an opportunity to prove that he was more than a dogsbody. Wasn't it about time he seized such a moment?

'No, it's okay, I'm pretty sure the place is empty. Stay on the line, though, okay?' Holding his radio in his left hand, he stepped back up to the house and pushed the front door with his right. 'Hello? Anyone home? This is Police Constable Mitchum, I believe you were expecting me.'

'Anything?' Natasha asked.

'Nope. Hello?' he called again, leaning in through the door. He waited a few more seconds before stepping over the threshold and into the house.

'There's no one home, Natasha, and I think we need to call this in. The house has been turned over. Someone must have come looking for Cassandra Salinas, and recently.'

The words hit Daniel like spears to the chest. He struggled to form a response, his mind racing to make sense of it.

'I don't ... I don't understand. How can this be? How is it possible? Are we seriously just going to let this happen?' He sagged against the wall of Superintendent Peter Hobbs' office, the cold of the concrete seeping through his shirt. The man looked pained, not relishing delivering the bad news.

'I just spoke to them. They were just here, for Christ's sake, in the building! We had them!' Daniel raged, his voice louder than he knew was professional, but out of his control. He simply couldn't believe what he was being told.

'Except we didn't, Graves, that's the whole problem. I know how hard you've been working to connect them to the death at the Morris household, but there's simply no presentable evidence. It's all speculative. We can't charge people with murder based on opinion.'

'Oh, come on, you can't possibly believe they're innocent. Are you going to tell me a demon did it after all? The veil between this world and hell opened up and out popped one of Satan's minions to unleash death on an innocent family?' Daniel threw back.

'Please don't take that tone, Detective. You know as well as anyone that it doesn't matter what you or I think. It's the evidence that needs to speak volumes and I'm sorry, but you just don't have enough on Delamar or Spindler. And now that missing girl Mary Ross has turned up, safe and sound after having thrown a tantrum and run away, there was no way I could convince the CPS to be swayed.'

'Swayed on what, exactly? It's not like I'm asking to arrest them, but we need more time. I know they did it; I just need the smoking gun.'

'Swayed on that, exactly that. Time. With the press harassment that Delamar and Spindler are being subjected to, the libel printed in the national press, and the fact that we're being pushed to make statements about the case – how could we be seen to be trying to hold people as suspects who have no more than a circumstantial connection to the death? You know the public often distrusts the police, and all these stories about supernatural goings-on are making things worse. The press know we don't have enough evidence or we would have gone ahead with a criminal prosecution.'

Daniel threw his hands up. 'Really? Circumstantial? You know I'm not big on swearing, but fuck that! They were at that house conducting an exorcism – a bloody exorcism! And at that exact same moment the father of the family dies under very suspicious circumstances? If they didn't do it, who the hell did? Then there's the fact that Sergeant Harding has found evidence connecting Delamar to previous cases of so-called demonic activity where people have died. How can that possibly be dismissed?'

Daniel sat down in the free leather armchair opposite Peter's desk, ran his fingers through his hair and took a deep breath.

'Okay, look. I know we don't have anything that can truly, without a doubt, prove that they did it, but what about the leads we're currently looking into? Surely they count for something.'

'They do, if you manage to turn up some real evidence, but until then we have nothing to justify prosecution, and without that our hands are tied when it comes to restricting either Delamar or Spindler. Even if we had arrested either of them at the scene, we'd be out of time by now and we wouldn't be able to charge them, which would reflect even worse on the department.'

'Because that woman is playing us. Don't you find it a little odd that she's suddenly being so co-operative? That she and Spindler came to us directly to clear their names? I was in that room, speaking to them, I heard all that crap about the press hounding them, ruining their names. I bet you any money she'll be making a statement to the same bloody outlets within an hour about how they were victimised, that it's not their fault that their beliefs aren't shared by the Met. It's the type of crazy shit the press go wild for. They did something stupid, too public, too outlandish for their own good, and now they're snaking out of it, using the strange aspects of the case to distract attention and cover up the truth.'

'Maybe you're right, but you haven't been able to find anything that can nail them for it. If they did it, then why can't we figure out how? Why can't we prove it? Has it crossed your mind that maybe they are actually innocent? Take the wife, for example. She currently has full-time security after her episode at the hospital. Maybe she snapped. Or maybe he committed suicide. Or maybe it was an accident.'

Daniel had been trying to keep calm, but with each word Peter Hobbs spoke he could feel his blood boiling more and more. The wife? An accident? He had heard enough. Maybe the Attorney General and Hobbs had their hands tied, but it wasn't over yet.

'I'm not going to let them get away with this. We've got a few leads still, and I'm not going to drop this. What's the alternative? We release a statement saying a demon must have done it because we're all out of clues? You'll see – they did it, and I'll prove it.'

'I hope for all our sakes you can, Graves, but you'd better come up with something fast. This case needs to be closed before it evolves into the beast the press are trying to make it. You may be new here, but you must know we run on success records. Either you find me something to use *now*, or this case needs to be dropped quickly and smoothly and we'll pray that it gets forgotten soon.'

Daniel yanked the office door shut as he left, the slam echoing down the corridor. He winced, but didn't stop. He needed air, needed to clear his head so he could think. His mind was screaming with images, wild thoughts, a chaotic mass of doubts and fears. The shadowy figure outside his house, the calls he and Charlie had received, all the stories Reverend Newman had sent them. It was crazy, but why couldn't he refute their legitimacy? Then there was the theory about Delamar targeting the children, using the legend of the demon Adramelech as a cover. If that was true, why had it been the father who had died? Why was there no evidence? Was Delamar just a crackpot after all? What if someone else had used the Morrises' desperation against them?

He knew he would have to tell Charlie what was happening. He practically ran to the lifts, phone in hand, feeling sick and anxious and angry. And most of all helpless.

CHAPTER TWENTY

For a horribly long moment Sergeant Amelia Harding was at a loss, not sure what to do. Everything was falling apart. One boss was in hospital, one was so angry she thought he would implode at any moment. Two suspects had been released; another two were missing. She felt like both cases were like sand, trickling through her open fingers so fast that just a few grains would remain to say that anything had ever been there.

Daniel had been fuming when he passed on the news to her. Amelia had never seen anything like it. She had seen him down, depressed, but never furious. She wasn't sure what to make of it. But she wasn't surprised, given the turn of events.

Amelia was not one to give up, however. She prided herself on her determination. She had told Daniel about the phone store lead, and he had demanded she look into it immediately. When he had found out that Cassandra Salinas was missing and no one had been able to locate Stefan Coen either, he had screamed down the phone about yet another bloody body waiting to turn up. Part of her thought that might be a good thing – eliminate a suspect, maybe result in a new lead – though she quickly admonished herself. Something needed to materialise in their favour, but it shouldn't take the form of another bludgeoned corpse.

All Amelia's training thus far had taught her to be practical, to think logically, to tackle what she could and get help for what she couldn't. She had gone over the evidence for both cases a hundred times. Although she knew she had been helpful on numerous occasions, she wanted more. She wanted to be the person to find that breakthrough, the piece of the puzzle that turned things their way, cracked the case. She was hopeful that was exactly what Daniel had handed to her by giving her responsibility for the lead. She wanted to be a detective inspector herself, and maybe this would push her in the right direction.

Amelia had analysed her options. The Tattoo Killer case was still up in the air. She could spend time looking for Stefan Coen and Cassandra Salinas, but others were already doing that – and probably more efficiently than she could. She could also look for more clues on the case, but so far she had drawn a blank.

On to the demon case. There was no evidence against the suspects Delamar or Spindler. The articles and video from the reverend had got them nowhere beyond connecting Delamar to older demonic stories that may or may not have been true. The mother was, for all intents and purposes, a no-go, faltering between catatonic and crazed. It had been decided that the children should not be formally questioned beyond the brief interview they had taken part in, and that they were not reliable witnesses, given the emotional, intense situation they were in. Searching the house had revealed nothing either. Sure, the coroner had proven that Darrell Morris had been poisoned, but by who? For what reason?

That left the phone store lead. She was determined to make

it come to something, though she was worried that it would be a waste of time, leaving her with nothing.

Patrick Marsden had told Amelia the name of the shop the phones came from – even told her the likely models that were used for the calls made to the detective inspectors. That gave Amelia an objective.

The day was grey, sunlight struggling to penetrate the blanket of clouds and city smog. As Amelia crossed the car park to the entrance of the Brent Cross shopping centre, the place felt hollow and cold. Some teenagers were chatting under the canopy covering the revolving doors and a few evening shoppers milled about, but it was quieter than normal. She suspected the gloomy evening was partially to blame.

Amelia had called ahead and arranged an informal meeting with the head of security for the centre, but she had half an hour to spare so she made her way to MobileU, glancing into shop windows as she passed them.

The phone store was small but well spaced out. Bright lights showcased various models of smartphones, tablets and accessories. It made her want to buy a new phone, but she shook off the thought. Instead she looked up, taking note of the three CCTV units mounted above the entrance, cash desk and centre of the store.

'Hi, can I help at all? Looking for a better deal or a new handset?'

Amelia looked at the small, plump young woman who had addressed her. She had long hair on one side of her head, and the other side was shaved. She looked desperate to make a sale, not just to engage in friendly chatter. Amelia thought that Lydia – as her name badge indicated – possessed the worn-out appearance of someone who relied almost solely on commission, and felt bad that she was about to disappoint. Lydia's face dropped as she took in Amelia's uniform, clearly not having noticed it before she approached.

'I'm afraid, neither of those things. My name is Sergeant Amelia Harding, and I'm with the Metropolitan Police Force. I'm actually investigating a case.'

Lydia frowned. 'Here? I'm here all the time, and I can assure you, nothing police-worthy ever happens here. The handsets are all dummy models so we don't even get shoplifters really.' She sounded curious, clearly perking up at the hope of possible excitement, a story to tell.

'Do you work here full-time?'

Lydia nodded.

'Maybe you can help then. I'm meeting with the head of security for the shopping centre shortly, but I'm looking for details on a customer. Do you keep records of sales of different types of phone?'

Again Lydia nodded, raising her eyebrows as if to indicate this was a stupid question. 'Anything that goes through the till is recorded.'

'Are you able to check a purchase for me then?' Amelia asked, sidestepping to let a teen with blaring headphones pass her on his way to the iPhone section.

Lydia turned and called to her colleague. 'Pete, can you man the store for ten?'

The guy who was leaning against the counter going through some papers gave a noncommittal nod. Lydia led Amelia to an office at the back of the store, taking a seat in front of an old computer. 'So what am I looking for? And when?'

Amelia peered over her shoulder at the screen. 'Two burner phones, probably Nokia, sold at the same time within the last week, maybe week and a half.'

Lydia tapped the keys, finding the result almost instantly. 'Looks like ... four days ago. Wow, on a day I actually had off,' she muttered. 'They were sold at quarter past three, the cheapest pay-as-you-go phones we have. The customer paid cash.'

'Are there any other customers that it could be? Like on another day?'

Lydia shook her head. It was the only time in the last month when two same-model basic phones had been sold together. It was exactly what Amelia needed. She felt a surge of hope. She had the time and date of the sale, which meant she would be able to find CCTV footage of the buyers in a heartbeat. She thanked Lydia profusely and shot out of the store before the girl could say anything else, aiming for the agreed meeting point with the security man. She was early, but so was he. He headed straight for her.

'Sergeant Harding? Nice to meet you. I'm Neil Spencer, head of security here at Brent Cross.'

As she shook his hand Amelia thought the man was in his forties. His short cropped hair was greying around the temples, but he had a baby face that made him instantly seem welcoming. She was glad he seemed willing to help out. She had come across people in similar roles who could be quite uncooperative, butting heads with the police almost instinctively.

'Hi, yes. Call me Amelia. Thank you so much for helping me. I don't want to waste too much of your time, but as I said on the phone I'm after CCTV footage.'

'Not a problem. Do you know when and where in terms of recordings?'

Amelia filled Neil in on what she had found out at MobileU as he led her towards the security office. Inside, a bank of monitors greeted them, with a younger man at the helm. Amelia smiled a hello, which he returned before looking back to the screens.

'This here is Miles, one of the two technicians. If the footage is there, he'll find it,' Neil said.

'What are you looking for?' Miles asked without turning around, his gaze flitting between the screens that monitored the shoppers and stores within the centre. Amelia glanced between them too, noticed that each screen was flicking through at least three cameras. It didn't take long for one of the MobileU cameras to appear. She could see half of Lydia, cut down the middle by the frame as she helped a customer. The image vanished after a few seconds, and changed to a view of an escalator.

'What I need to see is footage from inside the phone shop four days ago, from around three to three thirty.'

'Okay, hang on a sec,' Miles answered. He typed something into a bank of keys much larger than a standard keyboard, then drew their attention to two screens on the far right. Both were filled with shots of the store from different angles. With a twist of a dial, Miles began to scroll through the footage, the time ticking through at speed in the corner of each screen. He slowed down on Amelia's command. The time was 15:08.

They waited, all eyes on the screen. Amelia could feel her heartbeat starting to accelerate and her palms become clammy with anticipation. She jumped as the figure appeared on screen – the only customer to have entered in a ten-minute window.

'Shit, he's wearing a cap,' Amelia said as she took in the details. It looked like a man, the height and body shape suggested that much, but was it Marcus Spindler? She couldn't tell. The figure moved out of shot, walking over to a sales assistant, and Miles switched views.

The camera gave a perfect view of the back of the man's head. His coat collar was pulled up around his neck, obscuring his hair and face.

'Miles, switch to the cash desk, move forward a little,' Neil requested. 'Maybe we can pick him up as he pays.'

When the view of the register came up and the man came into shot, he kept his head down, angled away from the camera. It was impossible to tell who it was. She could already hear Daniel's voice in her head, his anger and frustration at her failure, their last lead slipping through her fingers. There was nothing she could do with this footage. It proved nothing.

'This chap obviously knows where the cameras are – must have staked the place out beforehand. Smart move,' Miles said, sounding impressed, but adding salt to Amelia's wound. 'Fear not, though, all is not yet lost.'

It took Amelia a second to realise what the technician meant: different views of the shopping centre replaced the phone store, showing wider shots of shoppers on the same day. Then she saw the figure, small but definitely the same person, hunched and with their cap pulled low, walking out of the store and back into the throng of shoppers. Miles was tracking the man. For what felt like an eternity they watched as the cameras flicked again and again, the man disappearing in and out of shot, passing behind pillars and plants and people, never in full view.

'Got you!' Miles exclaimed with pleasure. He had paused the video. Amelia leant in closer, so close she could see the cells that made up the image. The figure was a blur, with no features discernible. How was that helpful? She looked at Neil, who had a small smile on his face. He held up a finger, telling her to wait a moment. She was impatient, not understanding what she was missing. On one of the screens the image changed, then again and again, showing fifteen shots in quick succession. Then it stopped and there he was, stealing a quick glance over his shoulder, his head raised just enough.

Amelia's jaw dropped.

'I take it you know who he is then, Sergeant?'

'Yes, yes I do ... holy shit...' Amelia stuttered.

CHAPTER TWENTY-ONE

The afternoon had been a complete waste of time. For the last two hours Daniel had been fuming, could feel his skin practically burning with anger, but a deadly cloud of apathy had begun to descend.

As Daniel grew older and wiser, he knew that he would never take such a drastic measure as ending his own life. That didn't mean he was always good at climbing out of a quagmire of gloom, however.

Night was falling as he pulled off Kennington Road, heading for his apartment. His stomach rumbled at the sight of the Chinese takeaway on the corner, but he wasn't in the mood to eat, despite his hunger. A dark mood always had the same effect on him. It made him want to hide. As he pulled onto his street, his mind drifted to the four-pack of Heineken in his fridge.

As he halted outside his building Daniel sighed, resting his head in his hands. He growled and slammed his palms on the steering wheel until the action felt futile and his hands twinged in pain. A woman walking her dog on the other side of the road glanced towards him, but sped on when he locked eyes with her.

He stared at the folded newspaper that lay on the passenger seat, headline in view.

A Supernatural Failure by Scotland Yard

He had been right about the press. They had jumped on a brief statement made by the General Attorney's Office admitting that the Met had no evidence with which to charge either Catherine Delamar or Marcus Spindler. It had hit the news in seconds, with all evening papers carrying the story. He knew it would be all over the papers the next day too. Some of the pieces had simply explained the facts. Some had torn into the police force, either to accuse them of letting guilty people get away with murder or to show their disgust at detectives supposedly entertaining the idea of supernatural goings-on.

Peter Hobbs had tried calling Daniel twice, but Daniel had ignored his calls. He'd had one from Charlie too, and three from Amelia, and texts. He knew it was unprofessional but he needed some downtime, time to wallow.

Grabbing the paper and his bag, Daniel got out of the car and trudged up the steps to his front door. He couldn't help glancing back at the spot across the street where something – someone – had stood less than twenty-four hours ago. He shivered, and not just from the chill in the air. He still couldn't explain what it had been.

He knew Amelia had been looking into the lead with the phones. That was probably why she was calling. On the one hand he felt guilty for ignoring her. Perhaps she had found something, perhaps not, but either way he knew it was rude. He was well aware of how hard she was working, trying to crack the case, trying to impress him and Charlie. On the other hand, did he care any more? He felt thoroughly defeated. He told himself that once he'd sat down and had a beer he would check his messages. He felt a small release of tension as he closed his front door and shut the world outside.

A banging woke Daniel up. It took him a while to figure out where he was. The space around him was dark, dripping in shadows. He shook the sleep from his eyes to see that he had passed out on his sofa, three empty beer cans on the coffee table in front of him.

The banging came again, but this time he knew what was causing the sound. He got up, his joints stiff after sleeping in an awkward position, and flexed his neck and shoulders as he headed for the door.

A red-faced, frantic-looking Sergeant Amelia Harding was waiting for him. 'Thank God – I've been calling you for ages! Didn't you get my messages?' she asked. She pushed past him and flicked on the lights to the sitting room and kitchen. He winced.

'Sorry, I saw the missed calls, I just – what time is it?' he asked, following Amelia into the small kitchenette.

'It's quarter past eight. What happened to you? How come you fell off the radar?'

'Shit, is that all?' Daniel muttered, focusing on the cheap plastic clock ticking away on the wall. 'I must have fallen asleep ... only for an hour or two, though.' He saw that Amelia was frowning at him. 'Sorry, I just ... I needed some time. I must have been exhausted. Came back feeling sorry for myself and ... well ... I guess I just passed out.'

Amelia glanced at the cans, but didn't say anything.

'Anyway, sorry, I should have said something. What's so urgent?' he asked. His brain felt incapable of connecting any dots.

'Apologies for my bluntness, Graves, but for Christ's sake, I found the evidence we need!'

The words shot instant sobriety into Daniel. 'Wait, what? Seriously? Like *actual* evidence?'

'Yes! That's why I'm here!' Amelia exclaimed.

With that sentence, Amelia had smashed through the gloom that had settled over him. It was a miraculous feeling, unsettling. At once he felt revived yet ashamed, refreshed with new hope but embarrassed at letting himself spiral so quickly and easily.

'Tell me, tell me everything,' he demanded. 'I'm just going to change my shirt, but I want to know everything.'

Amelia began to talk as he ran into his bedroom. Daniel listened intently as he grabbed a clean shirt and started to change.

'After I spoke to you I went to Brent Cross like you asked, following up on the phone lead. I met the head of security there so I could see the footage for the store where Patrick said the phones were bought. God knows how Patrick even knew those details, but I guess that's why he's a tech wizard and I'm not.'

Daniel sped back out of his bedroom and into the bathroom, needing Amelia to get to the point. 'Tell me! What did you find?' he urged as he loaded his toothbrush, cleaning his teeth and running a hand through his hair at the same time, trying to flatten down the tufts.

Amelia stood in the bathroom hallway, a wide smile slapped across her face. 'The link we needed. Irrefutable evidence. It took a while. I thought there was a chance it would come to nothing, but the technician at the shopping centre found it. We got the guy on camera, undeniable, clear as day.'

'Amelia, come on.' Daniel spat out toothpaste. 'Who was it?'

'Reverend fucking Newman, that's who.'

Daniel coughed in surprise, minty foam running down his chin.

CHAPTER TWENTY-TWO

Droplets of sweat trickled down Stefan Coen's forehead as he came to. His head pounded and his vision was spotted with fuzzy black circles. He realised he was still in the warehouse – his supposed safe house. He could taste blood in his mouth, felt with his tongue a wet, ragged gap at the back of his mouth where at least one tooth had been knocked out.

He was sitting down, and tried to get up. He couldn't move. He realised there was duct tape binding his hands to the arms of the wooden chair; his ankles were also fixed in place. Wriggling, Stefan tested the tape, hoping for some give, but he was bound tight. His head was not restricted so he turned it to both sides, surveying his environment. In an instant his memory flashed back. The intruder, coming up from behind, the crowbar glinting in the air as it came at him. That was why his head hurt, why his skin felt tight around his left eye.

The person responsible for giving him the brutal concussion sat alarmingly casually on a stool in the battered kitchen area; it was really no more than a scratched countertop with two cupboards and a tarnished old sink. He knew who it was – and he was furious.

'You knocked me the fuck out!' Stefan snapped, his throat full of gravel and coppery spittle. 'What the hell? Why'd you attack me?'

'Welcome back. And quit your whining. I had no choice.'

'No choice? You could have just knocked.'

'Oh yeah, sure, and you'd have welcomed me with open arms and a cup of tea.' The comment came with a raised eyebrow and a sneer. 'Anyway, I need you compliant.'

'Compliant?' Stefan asked nervously. He knew that being strapped to a chair wasn't a good start, but 'compliant'? That dialled everything up a notch. 'For what?' he continued, though he wasn't sure he wanted to know. He scanned the room for a means of escape as his uninvited guest hopped off the stool and retrieved the crowbar from the counter. The metal sang as it scraped off the counter edge, sending shivers down his spine. He had no idea what to do, could see no way out.

Be patient, be co-operative. Put that charm to good use and it'll be okay. His inner chat failed to convince him but he took a slow breath, trying to remain calm.

'I believe you know where something is, and I need you to tell me. Rogan didn't know, nor did Jason, but I think you do.'

The statement came with a smile, but there was nothing friendly about it. In fact, Stefan got a sense of madness, of rising desperation. It made him gag. He quietly swallowed the bile that had risen into the back of his throat. With each second that passed, the tension in the air was building.

'Okay, sure, I'll help. Full co-operation. I'm sure whatever it is isn't worth fighting over,' he said, trying to sound chirpy and light. Maybe if he was jovial and chatty he could stop anything worse from happening.

'Glad to hear it. I'm going to get right to the point. Where is Marvin's money?'

So that was what this was about. Marvin Summers.

'Glint, you mean? I don't have his money. I tried to get it but failed.'

The slow, deliberate footfalls on the stained concrete echoed as Stefan watched the crowbar get closer.

'Stefan, I don't have time for lies. You promised you would co-operate.' The crowbar jumped from hand to hand, just waiting to be used again.

'Honestly, I don't have it. Any of it. I tried, I thought I could blackmail that dumb twat, at least get a few thousand out of him. You think if I was rolling in cash I would be hiding out in a shit tip like this?' Stefan rolled his head around, indicating the warehouse.

'So you're telling me you don't have the money and you don't know where it is?'

Stefan didn't want to answer. If he said no, then that was it. He was of no use. Would that mean lights out, like Rogan and Jason? He felt sweat drip down his back, and the tape around his wrists suddenly felt tighter.

'Er, well...' he started, pausing as he thought frantically for something to say that might give him an advantage.

'Not sure? Then let me jog your memory!'

Before Stefan could react, the crowbar was swinging down in front of him. Pain shot through him as he heard, as much as felt, something crack in his right thigh. He bellowed in agony, choking as the sharp tip of the weapon pulled back out of his flesh. His jeans were stained red in an instant and he could feel blood running down his leg. He gasped for breath, struggling to get past the pain. The room swayed around him and he thought he might pass out with the pain, but he stayed lucid.

'Please, please stop,' he stammered, tears streaming down his cheeks. 'I swear I don't ... don't know anything.'

'I'm sorry, Stefan, I just don't believe you.' The weapon rose into the air again, ready for another go. Stefan yelled out, spittle spattering down his chin. 'Wait!'

The crowbar paused, an animal needing to feed but curious to see what its prey was about to do next.

'There's ... one person ... who might know...' he started, not wanting to name names but desperate for this to stop.

'Who? Who, Stefan? I just need the name and we can be done here.' The voice almost sounded caring. Maybe if he just said it, he would be okay. Bloody and hurting, but okay. Sure, it would put someone else in the firing line, but if it saved his own arse he reckoned he could live with that. Even as he mulled over his options, the crowbar was getting heavy. As it rose above his head, he couldn't help blurting it out.

'Jenny! Jenny Cartwright! If anyone knows, she does.'

The crowbar halted. Stefan allowed himself a deep breath, trying to ignore the excruciating agony in his leg.

'Seriously? Jenny Cartwright? That doesn't make any sense. Are you lying to me, Stefan?'

'No, I promise. She was close to Marvin. No one knew it, but she was. I honestly don't know where the cash is, but if anyone does ... it has to be her.'

'Okay, okay. I can work with that. I guess, if I think about it, it makes a weird kind of sense.'

'Of course it does, yeah,' Stefan said. 'That bitch, she was always sticking her nose in. She's the one you want.' He felt like this was it, his opportunity. He had done the right thing. He had nothing against Jenny, but who cared? It was over; he could breathe easier. 'Can I ... can you let me go now?' he asked. 'You know, we used to be friendly. You know me. I won't tell anyone about this. Shit, I need to stay low myself anyway.'

'Well, I suppose you did help me out.' The crowbar lowered, as though it had changed its mind. No kill today, after all.

Thank God! Stefan thought.

'But then again, I don't trust you one bit, Stefan Coen, and I'm not about to let you get yourself out of a hole by giving the police my name.'

'Wait what?' he stammered as he realised what the person had just said. 'But you said I helped!'

'You sure did, but this has to be done. I'm sorry.'

Just like that the crowbar was awake again, energised by the blood still on its tip. It was above Stefan in a flash, moving faster than he thought possible.

'Cassandra, wait!' he screamed, but his words were stopped short as the metal chewed into the side of his head, digging deep, finding skull and brain matter. His eyes wide, blood gushing down his face, Stefan was dead in seconds.

The team that had been pulled together to help Daniel were operating in hyperdrive. Everything had changed so quickly since he'd connected Reverend Newman to the demonology case. Daniel had never trusted him, but had been forced to dismiss the feeling after Patrick Marsden's research had shown him to be honest. Now Daniel wondered if any of the stories the man had fed them were true, and even if he was a reverend. Newman had to be a persona used to divert attention, to muddle the truth.

Daniel had tasked Patrick's team with digging deeper. Who he really was, and why he was helping Catherine Delamar – that was so far undiscovered. He hoped they would uncover this information in the process.

Knowing that Newman had bought the phones used to call Daniel and Charlie, he thought that the figure outside Daniel's apartment had probably been Newman too. That seemed to make sense. Even if it wasn't him, it could have been Spindler or

Delamar. The three were clearly in cahoots. He instantly felt better at realising this, at knowing that they had deliberately been trying to make him doubt himself. He had to admit that there had been moments when he had worried about his mental well-being. Now the case was back in the comfortable, familiar realm of the real world – and that he could work with.

There were so many unanswered questions, though. Why had they done it? How had they convinced the Morris family to hire them in the first place? Had they tricked them too? How did they kill Darrell Morris without leaving any evidence? And who the hell were they, if not who they said?

Then there was an even more urgent question that Daniel desperately needed answering: where were they now? After Catherine Delamar and Marcus Spindler had been released, they had vanished. The flat she had been renting in Wapping was vacant, they had no record of where either Marcus or the so-called reverend had been staying, and the search for any of the trio had so far been fruitless.

Superintendent Hobbs had been happy – ecstatic, in fact – at the discovery of the footage from the phone store, because suddenly there was a link strong enough for them to reignite the case, and he had offered up all the resources Daniel needed. The General Attorney had warned that they still needed better evidence, but Daniel knew that would come. He was hoping for a domino effect: that finding one clue would lead to another, then another, until the whole picture finally made sense.

He and Amelia were working with a profiler, Martia Franklin, who was a prim and proper woman with a businesslike air. Together they were trying to get a sense of what these people might do next, and how they could anticipate where they could go, in order to be able to greet them with open arms and a squad car.

'We have to assume they have fled the city, given the fact

that they have been under intense scrutiny both from us and the press. If we're correct in assuming that their normal goal is to swindle people out of money by pretending to be demonologists, then they must travel a lot,' the profiler suggested.

'That's backed up by the photo I found of a woman who we assume is Catherine when she was younger. Shame I couldn't find a name to go with the photo. I bet her real name is not Catherine Delamar,' Amelia added.

'So if they've left the city, where are they going? They have – what? A five-hour head start, maybe?' Daniel asked, checking the time. 'They had to get all their belongings first, maybe together, maybe separate. They could only have been on the road for a few hours tops, surely. And it will take them ages to get out of central London.'

'I suspect they will stay together,' Martia responded. 'Certainly Catherine and Marcus would. From what we know, they are rarely apart. Their bond must be a strong one. Newman seems a little outside of them; perhaps he will have gone his own way. Having said that, we still don't know how they're actually connected. There's a chance he may have left with them too. If they have gone into hiding they won't be using any public transport, as it doesn't allow for freedom or spontaneity as much as their own wheels would. Also, there are security cameras in every underground and mainline station, even on the buses. They would be trying hard to stay under the radar. Do we know if any of them owns a car?'

Daniel and Amelia shook their heads. The footage of Newman at the shopping centre had shown him hop onto a bus, and they hadn't seen either of the others with a vehicle.

'Then there's a good chance they're renting one. Even if one of them had already rented a car, we have to assume they're smart enough to have switched.'

Daniel knew what needed to be done next. 'Amelia, can you contact every car rental place within a reasonable radius of the flat that Catherine was staying in? She's the ringleader in all this, so the men would go to her, I reckon.'

Martia nodded. Amelia jumped into action, heading back out to the open offices with renewed energy. Daniel said a silent 'thank you' to the world in general for having her there to support him.

Martia was standing in front of a huge map of London, marking up exit routes, when Patrick Marsden burst into the glass-walled office, waving a handful of papers. 'Detective, you were right, I'm sorry we didn't spot it the first time,' he said breathlessly. 'That man you met, the one in the footage, is definitely not Reverend Newman. We don't know who he is yet, but the Reverend Newman we have been able to trace died three years ago from lung cancer. As you can imagine, there aren't that many white British males working as reverends today who deal with demonology and who share that name. It was our assumption that he was who he claimed that stopped us from doing a more thorough background check. The basics stacked up without scrutiny the first time round, so we didn't go any further. The real Reverend Newman was hard to track down, but we found a few images of him. He was sixty-seven and bald. Not quite as youthful as your supposed reverend.'

'Shit – okay, good work, Patrick. So what can we do with that? Run what we do know through our databases and hope that he comes up?'

'Actually, we have some pretty impressive tools at our disposal. Two of my guys are trawling the internet for facial matches for him and the other two, and also any related content that seems to match their descriptions or similar situations. It's slow going, but if there's anything out there, if they have been careless before, we might get lucky.'

Patrick dropped the papers onto the table next to Daniel and headed back out. Daniel was trying to keep his hope in check, but his heart was singing. They were close to a revelation, he could feel it. *If only the other case would crack too,* he thought before turning his attention back to Martia, praying she would be able to help before it was too late.

CHAPTER TWENTY-THREE

Traffic had been brutal for a solid two hours, but they had finally reached Maidstone and were pulling off into a petrol station to rehydrate and grab some snacks. Google Maps told them it was less than a two-hour drive from Wapping to Dover, but it had failed to take into account massive closures for maintenance on the M2 and a HGV driver falling asleep and colliding with a roadside barrier on the M20. According to the radio, four lanes had been closed until the lorry could be moved.

Their aim was the ferry to Calais. They had estimated they could be in a shitty hotel in Dover by two in the morning, but only if they didn't stop anywhere for longer than a quick breather.

'I'll go in. What do you want? I'm going to get a few bottles of Coke, some Quavers or something.'

'Oh, Marcus, I don't care – get whatever. Maybe something healthy? You eat far too much junk. And please be quick.'

'I'll be quicker if you stop calling me Marcus. We're out of there now, you can drop the act,' he snapped back, rolling his eyes.

'Fine. Dominic, please try and get something healthy too.'

Sitting with her hands in her lap while Dominic jogged across the forecourt into the brightly lit store, Jane Benson had a brief moment of quiet, the first in what felt like forever, to simply be herself again. Dominic was right: they were out of there, their backs to London and the threat of imprisonment that her actions had led to. She needed to shake off the persona of Catherine Delamar and allow herself to be truly herself for a moment.

She knew she had made a mistake, she knew they had become too cocky, that she should never have suggested taking on a city like London. It was time to go back to what they knew best: the small, quiet nowherevilles – this time in Europe, where detective inspectors would not hound them and the national press would not be around every corner. They had come too close to losing everything and she would not allow that to happen again.

Pulling the sun visor down, she checked her appearance in the small mirror. She'd have to change her hair, and maybe she'd change her make-up too. But not yet. She knew she would soon need to become someone new, but for a moment she allowed herself to be Jane Benson – the plucky, inventive woman who had made the most of what she had been given. As Dominic returned to the car, laden down with two plastic bags, she felt a burst of pride. Her son was a difficult one, always had been, but she had somehow managed to keep him safe, alive and well, and out of trouble. If she had lost him back there, if he'd been charged with anything – well, it didn't bear thinking about. She hadn't: that was what mattered.

The car shook as Dominic settled back in, slamming the door.

'What's up?' he asked her as he put the bags down in the footwell and buckled his seatbelt. 'Your mind still on everything? It's okay, Mum, we're out. Just relax. We did what we needed to and still got out. I think that's a pretty good outcome.'

Jane nodded. 'I know, I know. It'll just ... I need some more distance between us and all of that. Then I'll be fine.'

Jane smiled as Dominic passed her a cup of fruit salad with a side of Maltesers, glad for the healthy snack but also thankful for the sugary treat.

'By the way,' he said, 'I reckon we should change the car again before we get to Dover, if we pass anywhere. And we need to do something about that.' He pointed a thumb at the sleeping figure in the back. 'He can't keep wearing the dog collar and crucifix.'

Jane turned to look back at her other son, who was snoring gently, his eyes flickering in his sleep. She knew that Steven hated being involved in what they did, and he would no doubt be as mad as a rabid dog at her when he woke, but he would come around. He always did. He would never do anything to reveal the truth about his brother – or what they did to support him.

'True, but let's let him sleep a bit longer. You know he struggles with all of this more than we do. Now, let's get going again, shall we?' Jane started the car. In moments they were on the road again, getting further and further away from London.

Jane had failed to spot the cashier in the petrol station frantically making a call as their car had pulled away; she had been too busy thinking that, in too many ways, the real Bensons were far worse than the characters they had created.

Bad things always came in threes. It was a universal rule, unwritten but familiar nonetheless. The first two blows that

Jane Benson had suffered were bad enough, but the third? Well, that changed her life forever.

First had been the death of her husband in 1976 – an event that started the cracks in the foundation of the Bensons' world. Patrick Benson was Jane's first husband. Although he wasn't the biological father of either of her sons, he was instantly part of the family. Steven was ten, Dominic seven, and they had taken to him so much that when he was killed in a car accident coming home from work one night they had been devastated. Suddenly a single mother once more, Jane had not known what to do, or how to comfort her grieving children, even as she struggled to get through her own shock and distress. Though her romance with Patrick had been somewhat of a whirlwind, fast and intense, she had also seen in him the ability to provide, to keep her and the boys secure. It was as though the floor had crumbled from beneath her the moment the policeman had delivered the bad news.

Over the following months, Dominic and Steven began acting out, refusing to obey her, becoming argumentative and more temperamental. Steven was suspended from school twice for bad behaviour – once for punching a boy and again for stealing a classmate's homework and shredding it before throwing it in a drain and spitting in the crying girl's face. Both incidents had taken place in full view of other children and teachers, and it worried Jane greatly that Steven cared so little about being caught. He was deliberately difficult at every opportunity, and a constant pain for the teachers who had to deal with him.

It was Dominic, however, who kept Jane up at night, who filled her with dread and doubt. Always a quiet child, Dominic had started to withdraw even further after Patrick's death. He had also become obsessed by death. Jane had assumed he was simply trying to make sense of what had happened to Patrick, to understand how someone close to him could just one day not be there any more. She figured it was a natural reaction. After all, Steven had asked her a fair few questions about it too. It didn't take long before Dominic's interest took a darker turn, however, and these actions were the second of the three blows she would have to deal with.

It started with the jars full of insects, caught in a nearby field and the woods that ran past the back of their home. Jane had encouraged Dominic's hobby, thinking he was using the jam jars to catch snails and beetles to study them. She was relieved that he was willing to take part in an activity that got him out of the house, taking in fresh air and learning as he went, instead of cooping himself up in the house with the curtains drawn. When she realised that he had been killing the beetles, the spiders, the other creepy-crawlies he'd caught, pulling off their wings and legs and mixing the body parts to fill numerous jars to the brim, then she began to worry that this was not a phase. Nervous about his behaviour, Jane acted in the only way she knew how: a stern telling-off and a swift ban of bug dissection. She hoped this would put an end to this new, unsettling habit.

Two weeks later, Jane came home to find Dominic in their garden, blood all over his T-shirt. She rushed over to him, terrified that he had been horribly injured somehow. The sight of the cat's head and tail, viciously severed and lying on the ground alongside an old football and a tattered comic, made her scream so loudly that the whole neighbourhood must have heard. Shaking as she dragged her son into the house, struggling to understand how he could have committed such an atrocious act, she decided to tell the police that a dog had attacked the cat and that her son had been so upset he had scooped up the remains.

What Dominic had done remained a secret. The family

who owned the cat had accepted the story with sadness but understanding, even buying Dominic a bag of sweets and a comic to alleviate his upset at the death of the animal. Dominic had behaved as though he had done nothing wrong, and he never mentioned it again. Even Steven had no idea what really happened to the cat.

Unfortunately for the animal population of Helmsley, the cat was just the start. More pets went missing: carcasses of guinea pigs appeared, shredded, on the school sports field, two rabbit heads were left outside the town hall. Jane knew who was responsible, knew something was horribly wrong with her son, and Dominic did not deny it. When she looked into his eyes, all she saw was a calculating coldness: a mind that did not – perhaps could not – accept that what it was doing was wrong.

It wasn't long before Jane was afraid to let Dominic out of her sight. Steven also felt like he had to play babysitter after he found out about his brother's sick obsession with death. He loved to pull creatures apart to study their innards, to have control over whether something lived or died.

At the end of a tense, uncomfortable summer for the Bensons, the third blow came: the one there was no hiding from, the one that would change everything for their family forever.

Steven had taken his younger brother out for the afternoon, keeping him occupied while Jane cleaned their home and went into town to shop. As usual she had returned home with trepidation, feeling guilty for wishing she didn't have the boys, wishing that she didn't have to constantly worry about them. The house had been silent. She thought her children were still out playing somewhere, and she relished the quiet. She cracked open a can of the cheap beer she had bought and snacked on some crunchy pickles, her favourite.

Steven's screams and shouts interrupted her before she was even halfway through her drink.

'Mum, Mum! You've got to come quick! It's bad, real bad,' Steven babbled as he launched himself into the kitchen. Jane had just enough time to register the splash of red across her son's T-shirt before he grabbed her hand and yanked her outside. The afternoon sun was still hot but a sharp chill ran through her as Steven tried to tell her what had happened.

Steven led her across a small field. Tall grass and weeds whipped at their legs, bugs darting up in the air with every footstep. Something caught her shin and scratched it, drawing blood, but her son was not about to let her stop.

'Where are you taking me, Steven?' Jane asked, hearing the panic in her voice. The second Steven had mentioned Dominic her skin had iced and her mind had filled with dreadful images: of animals gutted and strung from trees, her son covered in blood like Carrie at her prom. As it turned out, the last part was not far off.

As they broke into the woods, Jane spotted Dominic: flashes of colour among the browns and greens of nature. Red – she saw a lot of red: too much red. When they reached the small clearing, Steven let go of Jane's hand and stayed back. His brother stood stock-still, dappled light falling over him, illuminating the blood that covered his arms, that had spattered across his face and hair, that had smeared the front of his dinosaur-emblazoned T-shirt. He looked up at her, slowly, calmly, with a slight show of surprise that she was there. Then he looked back down at the beaten, mangled body of Jimmy Green. The earth underneath him was soaked in blood, a pool of darkness.

In her head Jane was still screaming two days later when the body of local child Jimmy Green was found by a couple out for a walk with their dog. The story hit the papers immediately. It was all anyone could talk about: on the radio, in the street, people gossiping, rumours spreading. The kid had been a weirdo, an outsider, into rock music and the devil. His father was a drunk, his mother a junkie. It must be their fault – they should never have moved to Helmsley. Apparently Jimmy had books on Satanism in his room. He was worshipping the occult. Got involved with a cult. Attacked by the very devil himself.

The theories got more and more extreme, but the police had no evidence and could not decide what had happened. Demon fever was in the air – paranormal investigators Ed and Lorraine Warren had not since visited Enfield in north London, hot off the back of their most renowned cases in Amityville, Pennsylvania, and New York. While many dismissed the Warrens as clever tricksters, spinning press attention into a valuable source of income, plenty of people could not forget the claims of the famous duo so easily. A town with so many Anglicans was like kindling to a bonfire when the Green household was searched by police: images of rat skulls were pinned on Jimmy's bedroom wall, pentagrams were scratched into his desk top, well-worn books on Satan worship and demon summoning were all the people of Helmsley needed as evidence to either pin the kid's death on the occult or to put it down to a troubled, disturbed kid who had killed himself.

The weeks following the incident in the woods were traumatic for Jane, to say the least. The stress of knowing what she did, the pressure of lying every time someone brought up Jimmy's name, the shakes that took over her body every time she picked up the newspaper. She could barely even look at Dominic; she had to rely on Steven more than ever.

One morning, as she stood in the kitchen watching Dominic pour himself an orange juice and read a new comic, one she had bought him in a desperate bid to keep him busy, she realised something. He seemed happier, more animated than usual. When he saw her watching him, his face lit up with a smile so bright that for a second she forgot what he had done. Forgot that she'd had to help him wash blood off his arms in the middle of the woods, strip him bare and get him to change, that she'd been forced to light a bonfire to burn his and Steven's bloodied clothes. She felt like maybe she had her son back.

'Sweetie, can you ... can you answer something for me?' she asked, nervous about the answer but eager to test the theory that was swirling around her mind. Dominic nodded.

'Why did you do it? You never told me. Why did you hurt Jimmy? Did he try to hurt you? Was it self-defence?' As she waited to see what he would say, Steven stepped into the kitchen. She threw him a look. He understood immediately and stopped, leaning against the door frame, not drawing attention to himself.

'No. He didn't hurt me. He was mean and weird, but he didn't do anything.'

It was not the answer Jane was hoping for.

'So why, Dom? I need to know.'

'Because I had to. Same as with the animals. I had to do it.'

Again this was not what Jane had wanted to hear. It didn't make sense, made her boy seem crazy. Was he hearing things? Were there voices in his head? She asked him.

'No, Mummy, it's not like that. I just ... I had to. It just seemed like ... the right thing to do. I felt strange before, but I feel better now.'

Jane didn't fully understand the answer, and clearly nor did Steven, given his expression, but something fell into place for Jane.

Dominic would do it again. Of this Jane felt certain. His actions had escalated so quickly to killing the boy, yet he showed no real emotion about it. The way he had spoken just then – he could have been talking about the need to drink a glass of water to quench a thirst, or to go to the bathroom, or to cry at something sad, as though he was just getting something out of his system. Was killing to him something he had to do to feel better? If so, if she knew how it worked, knew what to look for, then maybe they had a chance. It was the start of a thought that, despite its outlandish nature, seemed to make a strange sort of sense, followed by the bud of a plan of action, the return of a semblance of control.

The next year was almost peaceful. Dominic did nothing else so violent as what he had done to Jimmy, with the exception of a few wild-animal kills. He even chose to leave neighbourhood pets alone. He seemed happier, less withdrawn, and he was performing a little better at school. The knock-on effect on Steven was positive too: he was less angry, less combative, with his marks rising as well.

Jane was glad, but she was never truly relaxed. She had instructed Dominic to tell her the next time his dark feelings came back, and every morning she woke up thinking that this could be the day. As expected, he finally did, but she had a plan, one she had been concocting over time. It was crazy, reckless, seemed ridiculous, yet something inside her told her it might work.

She had been reading everything she could about Ed and Lorraine Warren's cases. She had read about demons and evil spirits, their connection to religion. She had even researched exorcisms and rituals, reading every story she could find on so-called real cases from around the world. With Dominic's dark feelings returning, it was time to put her plan to the test. She needed to keep her boy, her precious Dominic. When he was good, he was her everything, him and Steven. She couldn't face losing him – or Steven – if the truth about Dominic ever came out. If anyone discovered what she had covered up, their family unit would be destroyed. Jane could not let that happen.

And so it began, the Bensons' new life. Jane ended her rental contract on their house, quit her job, packed the boys into her battered old Ford and headed to the residence of the Perkins family just outside Leyburn. She'd read that they thought they were being targeted by an evil spirit – a deadly one. The influence of the Warrens was still everywhere: people were convinced that they needed a demonologist, either for real or perhaps to get on television. The Perkins family seemed genuinely terrified that someone would end up dead.

It was Jane's job to make sure someone did.

CHAPTER TWENTY-FOUR

It was almost midnight when the call came in, direct to Daniel's mobile. He had been downing mugs of coffee to stop himself from drifting off. The call had him hyper-alert instantly.

'Oh, thank God you answered! Please, I need your help!'

The voice was hushed but laced with fear. When Daniel realised who it was, his skin chilled.

'Jenny? Is that you? What's the matter? Are you okay?'

'No, I'm in real trouble. You need to help me! She's going to kill me!'

His heart started to race. 'What? Who is? Who is trying to kill you?'

'It's Cassandra! It's been her all along. She murdered Rogan and Jason, and I think she killed Stefan Coen too!'

The words punched through Daniel. Cassandra Salinas was behind the murders? Why? What was her motive? The money? She hadn't admitted any knowledge of the thousands that Marvin Summers had racked up, had claimed to know very little about his alter ego Glint either, beyond what was publicly available. She had pointed them back in the direction of

Needlepoint Ink. They had eventually found out about Stefan Coen – a man boasting a history riddled with police run-ins and a proven interest in Glint. And of course he had shot Charlie, then done a runner. Surely Coen was the obvious choice – surely Jenny was wrong.

Then a theory played out like a silent movie in fast-forward across Daniel's brain, twining together all the strands of his conscious and subconscious knowledge into something that made sense.

Cassandra must have heard Marvin talking about the money, put two and two together, and figured out that Marvin was the mystery tattooist Glint after seeing Stefan's sudden interest in the man. She may have seen an opportunity to bribe Marvin herself but Stefan beat her to it – and in doing so, got Marvin killed. Stefan had then gone underground, maybe with the money, so she tried to track him down. After failing to find Stefan she had flirted with Rogan Simmons to get info out of him, knowing that he knew Marvin and that he had a Glint tattoo. Had she got too close and let too much slip? When Rogan cottoned on to what she was doing, she killed him. Maybe they had met in Finsbury Park that night on a promise of some outdoor, under-the-stars action and she had seized the chance to silence him. Daniel and Charlie had gone to speak to Jason Tagoe, Rogan's employer, who threw Cassandra's name into the ring as a suspect in Rogan's murder. After they had spoken to Cassandra she killed Jason too, taking him by surprise at the garage to make sure he didn't say anything else and as revenge for being fingered as a suspect. That brought her back to Stefan, but who else knew him that she could harass for information? Maybe she'd hit a brick wall, but then Jenny Cartwright had sent the police in Cassandra's direction again. Once more trying to stop the flow of information, she attacked Jenny but failed to shut her up. Jenny then raised the whole

Stefan connection, not knowing it was Cassandra who had tried to kill her but remembering Stefan's fascination with Marvin. Stefan had panicked when the detective inspectors showed up on his doorstep, shot Charlie and instantly became a most-wanted with the Met. Maybe Cassandra went through a list of places where Stefan might go and got lucky. There she threatened him and presumably he had then sent her after Jenny again. She had deliberately left her house a mess, to look like something had happened to her; she knew that would distract the police from where she really was for a while. She killed Stefan to cover her tracks and then she baited Jenny into meeting her somehow, which brought Daniel back to the desperate woman on the other end of the phone.

Holy shit! his mind screamed. Cassandra was about to claim a fourth victim and he was all that stood in her way.

'Where are you, Jenny?'

'I'm in a warehouse near Hackney Wick Overground. I don't know the exact address, it's near Wick Lane. She told me she was looking into a new tattoo studio, but when I got there she went fucking crazy!'

Daniel scrawled the address on a sheet of paper before rushing through the open-plan office looking for Sergeant Amelia Harding.

'We're coming for you right now. Are you hurt?' he asked, his voice gravelly and dry. Amelia was at her desk, scrolling through archives of news stories, looking for details on the demon case. He signalled for her to come with him. She pulled a confused face but didn't ask any questions, scooping up her jacket and tailing him to the lifts.

'I hurt my leg – she went for me and I fell. I can't really walk. Daniel, she has me trapped! It's pitch black in here, the warehouse is massive, and I don't know where she is. Please hurry!'

'Okay, Jenny, we're on our way. We'll be as fast as we can, but it could take up to an hour with traffic.'

'Shit, are you kidding? I can't wait that long!' Jenny sobbed, her voice shaky.

'Just do your best to stay away from her. Can you do that?'

Amelia's eyes went wide as she realised what was happening. The lift doors pinged open and she raced in ahead of Daniel, pulling out car keys and her radio, requesting all nearby and available units to head to Wick Lane, as well as any authorised firearms officers.

'I'll try,' Jenny whispered, tears audible in her voice. Her fear pierced Daniel, spurring him forward yet scaring him to death.

'I'm coming, Jenny, just hold on!' He hung up and ran after Amelia into the cold night air. Amelia was already starting the car. He jumped in after her, dialling Patrick Marsden before he even had his belt on.

'Patrick, I need you to run GPS on this number immediately.'

As Amelia pulled out onto Horseferry Road, aiming to cross the Thames, Daniel waited for Patrick to get a hit, tapping his foot as he tried to keep calm. He forced himself to slow his breathing. His adrenaline spiked when Amelia flicked on the siren, the red and blue lights splashing across the tarmac racing by underneath them.

'Found it,' came Patrick's voice after an agonising wait. Daniel typed the address into the car dash, thanked Patrick and hung up. As they raced past the shadowy offices lining Waterloo, it was everything Daniel could do not to vomit. He gripped the passenger door of the car until his knuckles went white, the sound of the emergency siren screaming through his brain.

The air was silent, thick and oppressive like a black velvet blanket. She didn't dare make a sound, barely even breathing, but her racing pulse boomed in her ears. Jenny had pulled herself under a small staircase and behind a pile of splintered wooden pallets, hoping the deep shadows would keep her hidden. Though it was unsettling, the darkness was her friend, and she prayed it would protect her.

She had been sitting there for what felt like forever, but must only have been half an hour. She hoped it was longer. After Cassandra had swung at her, the teeth of the crowbar just missing her face, Jenny had fallen off the concrete platform they had been standing on – the area Cassandra had claimed would be perfect for a mini design studio. Jenny had hit the ground hard, twisting her ankle. A rogue strip of metal had bit into the back of her thigh.

Cassandra had actually laughed as Jenny had run, her leg screaming with pain. Her cackles got louder when the lights went out. With the warehouse suddenly treacherous in the dark, Jenny had stumbled blindly down a corridor, Cassandra calling after her.

'Run, bitch! I'm right behind you!'

Jenny's blood went cold at the woman's voice. She sounded crazed, unhinged. She knew that she was the mouse in this game and Cassandra wouldn't stop until she had found her, silenced her like she had the others.

The warehouse was larger than Jenny had at first thought: a maze of abandoned rooms and halls, strewn with boxes and broken furniture. She had found only one exit: the door was bolted from the other side. Desperate to get away from her pursuer, Jenny had made do with the best hiding spot available. Certain she needed help, Jenny had risked the call, phoning

Daniel Graves instead of 999 in the hope he would be quicker. She was terrified that Cassandra would hear her but somehow she had remained undiscovered, and now she knew that Daniel was on his way, with backup. She just had to hold out for a while – an hour at the most. Easier said than done. The warehouse was big, but would it take Cassandra an hour to search it top to bottom?

Jenny's leg was throbbing, and she could feel blood dribbling down her calf. She clamped a hand over the wound, hoping that would help. She had no idea how bad it was, but it didn't feel like she had done too much damage. If she had to make another run for it, she might be able to. As a last resort.

Jenny wasn't sure what was more unsettling: that Cassandra was hunting her or that she had done something to put herself in this situation in the first place. She had been racking her brains for a reason Cassandra would attack her. While they had never been friends as such, they had got on okay whenever they met, so surely it couldn't be personal. Jenny couldn't think of anything she had done that warranted such a response. Then it clicked: Cassandra had kept saying she was going to come into money, that soon she would be free to do what she wanted, but Jenny knew she wasn't a wealthy woman and couldn't figure out where the money would come from. How was she planning on setting up a tattoo studio with no finances? Then Cassandra had mentioned her ambition: to be as famous as the legendary Glint, her studio the go-to place for celebrities and rich tattoo fans everywhere. In a flash it was obvious. Jenny was the only other person to have witnessed Stefan Coen's Spanish Inquisitions of Marvin Summers and his money, and she was the last person standing who may know where his money was. That was the real reason Cassandra had summoned her. When this dawned on Jenny, Cassandra had attacked her. The weapon came from out of nowhere and a twisted grin spread over Cassandra's face.

The scuffing of feet on concrete pulled Jenny from her thoughts and she froze. Instinctively she huddled into her hiding spot, her leg screaming as she tried to make herself even smaller. Another sound. She held her breath. Her lungs burning, she listened for any indication of where Cassandra could be. The warehouse fell silent, with not even the vague hum of traffic in the distance breaking through. She let out her breath slowly, unable to hold it any longer.

Peering through gaps in the stack of pallets, Jenny could just make out a few details. The doorway she had come through, another closed door off to the side, a mound of rubbish left by the previous business. It was then she spotted the rebar – a dull but heavy-looking piece of metal poking out of the rubbish. She needed a weapon to defend herself. Should she stay in hiding or go for it? She froze when a shadow moved just outside the room. Cassandra stepped through the doorway, a dangerous silhouette ready to wipe Jenny out. Jenny clamped a hand over her mouth.

'Here, Jen, Jen, Jen,' Cassandra said, her voice low but clear, with the hint of a giggle. *Is she insane?* Jenny thought.

The sound of the crowbar tapping against the door frame made Jenny jump. Her eyes widened as she fell back against the wall. The crowbar froze mid-tap and Cassandra leant forward into the room.

'You in here, Jenny? You know I can't let you leave, not now. Why don't you come out so we can get this over with?'

Cassandra almost sounded normal. Jenny found it horribly disarming. It made her skin crawl. She was trying to control her breathing and desperately wanted to take a lungful of air, so she was relieved when Cassandra took a step backwards out into the hall. Jenny let her body relax. Her leg twinged and she slipped, steadying herself with a hand on the cold, dirty concrete. The dark outline of Cassandra swung back around.

'That you, Jen?' she asked, her voice too cheery. Jenny had

frozen once more, but the pain in her leg was getting worse and she was shaking. *Please turn around again!* she willed silently. Cassandra reached into her pocket for something. For a moment Jenny was confused, then she realised what was about to happen. With a soft click the torch on Cassandra's phone bloomed into life, its harsh white glow washing over everything. It swung back and forth. Jenny ducked down as far as she could. Then the light stopped on the pallets.

'There you are!' Cassandra shrilled.

Terror flooded through Jenny as Cassandra stepped forward, the beam of light from the phone hiding her attacker. Her stomach flipped and her brain raced as her body fought to decide: fight or flight?

As the light got close, forcing her to squint, Jenny pushed at the pile of wooden pallets with all her strength. The top few fell forward and landed with a heavy crash.

'Bitch!' Cassandra spat, the light shaking and throwing leaping shadows as she jumped back to avoid being hit. Jenny knew what she had to do. Pain burning through her leg, she pushed herself off the wall and ran towards the mound of rubbish in the corner of the room. Cassandra whipped round to follow her. Her leg giving up already, Jenny stumbled and shot out her hands to break her fall. The rough concrete floor scraped the skin on her palms and she hissed. Shoving herself up, she launched herself at the rebar, twisting towards her attacker even as she grabbed it.

'Where's the fucking money?' Cassandra screamed, her voice booming around the room. She still held her phone out. The light showed Jenny where she was but still kept her outline hidden.

'I don't have it, Cass, I don't! Please, you have to believe me!' Jenny begged, shuffling back to gain some space between them. The rubbish crunched under her feet.

'Come off it, Jenny. Stefan told me everything.'

It was what Jenny had feared. Stefan had told Cassandra that she knew what Marvin had done with the money. She had no idea; she had only realised what was probably going on after talking to the detective inspectors about Glint and Stefan. Evidently Cassandra thought differently, though.

'It was you, wasn't it? Who attacked me at my flat,' Jenny started, her brain finally connecting all of the dots.

'Bingo. What a smartie-pants you are,' Cassandra shot back.

'But then ... wait, if Stefan told you I know where the money is and that's why you brought me here, then you didn't know before, so why did you attack me then?' Jenny was desperate to buy time, knowing Daniel was on his way. She also wanted to know. If Cassandra really hadn't suspected her of hiding the money until Stefan told her, why had she already tried to kill her once?

'Because you have a big mouth, Jen. Just couldn't keep your mouth shut, could you? I don't know what you told those detectives but they kept snooping, wouldn't leave me alone. I was worried you knew something, so I wanted to shut you up. You're lucky you got away once. You won't again. Now tell me where the money is!'

Still gripping the rebar, Jenny edged to her feet as slowly as she could. She had to be ready to run again, and was horribly aware that she was very close to being cornered. She could hear the seconds ticking away, but knew that Cassandra could go for her any minute.

'It's...' she started, panicking when she couldn't think of a convincing answer.

'Spit it out. I'm running out of patience.'

Jenny's ears pricked. Had she just heard sirens? She was worried she had imagined it, but what if she hadn't? Her heart was thudding, scared to hope.

'Come on, Cass, I thought we were friends. What if we split it?' Jenny said, willing to try anything. The pain in her thigh threatened to overwhelm her as she struggled to stay in a crouch; she knew her injury was getting worse. She could feel blood trickling down the back of her leg, collecting in the heel of her trainer.

'Cut the shit!' Cassandra yelled. 'Tell me where it is!'

And just like that, Jenny knew she was out of time. Act now or die by crowbar to the face.

'Fuck you!' she bellowed, swinging her arm as hard as she could. The rebar whipped through the air. The metal caught Cassandra's arm with a crack. She screamed, her phone spinning out of her grip, the torch flickering but staying on. Cassandra looked rabid in the light that flashed across her face. Jenny didn't wait for the follow-up attack. She got onto all fours and burst for the door, an athlete out of the starting blocks, but the wound in her leg meant she struggled to get upright. As she careened into the hallway, Cassandra recovered and was on her. Jenny felt the woman's weight slam into her back. They hit the opposite wall and went down in a flash of agony.

The sirens were back, howling outside somewhere, definitely not imaginary. Like an animal Cassandra growled, grabbing at Jenny's hair, pulling her head backwards. Her nails found Jenny's throat and raked across her skin. Blood welled immediately. Jenny threw one arm back as hard as she could and felt her elbow connect with ribs. Cassandra roared in pain, the sound deafening in the small hallway. The woman's weight on Jenny lessened, her grip falling away. Jenny crawled forward immediately, her body burning with pain. She scrambled up, found her footing and was running before she knew it, barrelling down the corridor towards the open doorway. She didn't know where she was going or how long she could run, but pure adrenaline was carrying her.

'Get back here!' Cassandra spat, her voice deep, possessed. Jenny could already hear the woman coming after her, her footsteps getting faster, echoing and reverberating behind her. Then a man stepped out of nowhere, suddenly filling up the space in front of Jenny, blocking her exit. He held out a gun. Jenny skidded to a halt, her momentum threatening to plough her straight into the man.

'Get down!' the man bellowed. As he aimed the gun, Jenny let herself drop. The sound of the shots tore past her as hot orange fire flared out. She pulled her arms over her head.

The sudden silence that followed was so all-encompassing that Jenny thought for a second maybe she had been hit. Was she dead? Was that what it felt like? Slowly she lowered her hands, daring to open her eyes. Just metres from her lay Cassandra, blood pooling out from her chest, the crowbar still at last. Jenny jumped when a pair of arms wrapped round her. She heard Daniel's voice in her ear and sensed people around her.

'It's okay, Jenny, you're okay. She's gone.'

Two uniformed officers stepped past the man holding the gun and crouched down by Cassandra. She lay totally still. Exhausted, numb despite the pain vibrating through her, Jenny felt herself relax. She closed her eyes, shutting out the warehouse that so easily could have seen her last breath.

CHAPTER TWENTY-FIVE

By the time Jenny had been taken to hospital, by the time Cassandra Salinas's body had been bagged and tagged, Daniel was ready to drop. He felt elated and utterly drained. His team and he had stopped a psychotic, homicidal woman in her tracks, and they had saved a life in the process. It was a time for champagne and cheering, to revel in a true sense of achievement, yet his exhaustion was so all-consuming that he just wanted to sleep. He didn't hear Sergeant Amelia Harding speaking until she snapped her fingers in front of his face.

'Graves!' she shouted, startling him. She was waving something in front of him, gesturing for him to take it. It was only when the object was in his hand that he realised it was his phone.

'What? I don't...' he mumbled. He would have been embarrassed to be so out of it if he hadn't been too tired to care.

'You left it in the car. You have nine missed calls. All from Patrick. You might want to phone him back,' Amelia urged. It was the last thing Daniel wanted to do. He was tempted to drop the mobile in his jacket pocket, but something clicked in his brain. He knew why Patrick had been trying to reach him.

'Shit, the other case!'

Amelia nodded, clearly way ahead of him. Daniel unlocked the phone and returned the missed call, noticing it was almost one in the morning. The sky above him was rippled with blues and blacks as silent clouds passed overhead, stars hidden by light pollution from the city. *How am I still standing?* he thought as the call rang through.

'Finally, Graves, did you catch Salinas? Is the other woman okay?'

Daniel told him that Jenny was injured but would recover, that Cassandra was no longer a threat, but before he could start to tell him what had happened, Patrick was hurrying him on.

'Listen, fill me in later, okay? I have big news. You might want to get your GPS ready, because your night's not over yet.'

'What do you mean?'

'We got them – we bloody got them! The profiler sent photos of Spindler, Delamar and that fake reverend to a forensic sketch artist, and you'll never guess what. They're only bloody related. This woman spotted it in a heartbeat!'

'Seriously? How the hell did we miss that?' Daniel asked, dumbfounded. The information surprised him and then quickly and suddenly became obvious: a connection that made total sense.

'They changed shitloads about themselves. Obviously they made up their names and history, but they made physical changes too. Hair colour, skin tone, contact lenses. The artist reckons Delamar may even have had minor cosmetic surgery. She stripped everything back to facial details and structure and knew instantly that they had to be related, so we threw everything and everyone we had at our disposal at this thing. It took some of the best online trackers we know, but matching their ages, their appearances, cross-referencing with the picture of Delamar from that old newspaper story – we had them in half an hour. Jane, Dominic and Steven Benson. Mother and two sons.

'And it gets better. I had another team crawling the internet looking into any similar cases to the Morris family to help us find more links to the Bensons. What a surprise – just a few hours from Helmsley, a town they moved away from out of the blue, a case of supposed demonic activity was reported in Leyburn. A woman with two children was recorded as having helped the family, but not before the eldest son, reportedly a troubled youth with a drug problem, went missing, never to be seen again.'

'Shit,' Daniel stammered, not capable of anything more profound as he processed Patrick's findings. 'So the kid just disappeared?'

'Yep, just vanished. A small story ran in the local papers about it – an opinion piece mainly about Ed and Lorraine Warren, thanks to the Enfield haunting, but mentioning the missing teenager and this woman with her kids who had claimed to be a demonologist. We couldn't find anything else with any detail that could relate to the trio again until that story with the photo of Jane Benson that Harding found. There was no name reported, and no mention of children with her, but again, the family in the story lost a child. And, Daniel, we found five more stories between then and now, all in rural towns around the country, where a woman and a young colleague had attempted to help a family suffering from supposed supernatural activity. In every single story someone either went missing or ended up dead.'

Daniel felt like he had been winded, as if someone had just punched him in the stomach. He rocked back. Amelia put a hand on his shoulder to steady him. They had been totally wrong about everything. These people weren't con artists. They weren't trying to swindle gullible families out of their savings.

Sure, the money obviously paid their way but the truth was much worse. This trio, this mother and her sons, had been travelling the country for more than thirty years, tricking people, deceiving them, with one agenda in mind. Murder.

'Patrick, you said GPS – please tell me you know where they are.'

'Yes, we do. Total luck, but someone called the hotline. He'd seen them on the news, didn't know they had been cleared of being suspects, and rang in their location in case they were doing a runner.'

'Which is exactly what they are doing. How far away are they?' Daniel asked, his body fizzing, his blood pumping a mile a minute. Patrick gave him the location they had been seen in, and how long ago.

'Okay, got it, we're on our way. Have you called in local support?'

Patrick said he had – that four officers from the Maidstone Police Department were heading to the location and would wait for instructions. Daniel hung up as he ran to his car, Amelia close behind.

'What's going on? I couldn't hear Patrick's side of the conversation,' Amelia said, her voice frantic as she buckled her seatbelt. Daniel's foot was already on the pedal as he reversed, gravel from the warehouse car park kicking up against the vehicle's undercarriage. Her eyes were like saucers as Daniel filled her in.

'But ... how?' she started, unable to find the words.

'How have they been getting away with it? How did they kill Darrell Morris? And why?' Daniel answered, filling in the blanks. 'That's what we're going to find out.'

The car whipped out onto the A12. Daniel put his foot down, suddenly glad it was the middle of the night. The road was clear ahead of him.

'Wake up!'

If the shout was not enough to snap Steven out of his sleep, the bag thrown onto his chest certainly did the job.

His brain cleared slowly as he pieced together the details of his surroundings. The worn brown leather armchair, the cheap, mismatched lamps, the not entirely comfortable mattress underneath him with the springs poking into his spine. The shitty budget hotel off the A20 on the outskirts of Maidstone clearly had no aspirations to be any more than cheap and basic. It was, however, a better choice of rest stop than the Premier Inn down the road, as it didn't have CCTV, night porters or a steady flow of customers.

'What? What's going on? I was asleep,' he complained, rubbing his eyes and watching Dominic shoving stuff in his rucksack.

'They found us, so get the fuck up! Mum!' Dominic yelled. Steven turned to see his mother, groggy, shuffling to sit up in bed next to him.

'Darling, we're not due to set off for another few hours,' she said quietly, her gaze on the black plastic alarm clock. It read 2:54.

'I know, but we have to go. Now! The police are outside!' Dominic's voice was panicked and he was shaking. 'They have their lights off but they're parked pointing right at us. Just waiting for the right time.'

Steven clambered off the bed and made his way to the window, moving aside the curtain a crack to see out. The night was still dark and the mostly empty car park was still. The road outside the hotel was barely lit, the streetlamps few and far between on what was effectively a country road. He thought he could make out a car or two a way down, but couldn't be certain what they were. Hedges and trees lined the road in both directions, obscuring the cars in shadow. It was odd to have vehicles parked at the side of such a road, though, especially since there was a car park at the hotel.

'Are you sure–' he started. Dominic's shout cut him off.

'Yes, I'm bloody sure! Now get your shit together – we have to leave right now!'

Steven and Jane began to gather up their belongings. Dominic called to them. 'We can get out of this window. Come on!'

Steven wanted to complain then. How were they going to get away if they were being watched? Surely someone would see them clambering out of a window at the back of the hotel? Was their mother even up to this? She seemed exhausted. How would they get to their car?

Steven had led his life living by someone else's rules. He had done everything his mother had told him, done everything he could to keep his brother safe and protected. Out of prison.

The familiar feeling of wanting to give in hit him as he watched his mother shove on her coat, her hair a mess, looking the very picture of a hard-done-by parent. They had both sacrificed so much. Had it been worth it? Really? Sometimes Steven did think so. They were as close a family as possible, had supported each other through thick and thin. Dominic was able to function in the real world as a vaguely normal human being, thanks to their lifestyle, which allowed him the occasional release of his inner demons. That was down to Steven and their mother facilitating it. Without them he would be rotting away in a maximum-security prison.

But then, there was everything else. People had died because of them, because of what they had done. Too many people. Sure, many of them were no-hopers, violent, guilty of numerous crimes themselves, but not all. And Dominic wasn't

Dexter; he couldn't get away with murder just because he thought the victims deserved it. To Steven, it was not a valid justification. Should they have informed the police about Dominic when all this started? Before he had the chance to ruin so many lives? To ruin their own? Perhaps the best thing for everyone would be for Steven to hand Dominic over to the authorities, put an end to everything. Even if he was arrested too, which he surely would be, at least then it would stop. Maybe he could atone, or at least be satisfied that he had finally spoken out and stopped something that should never have started. He could stop anyone else from being killed to satiate Dominic's sick need.

He glanced at the cheap wooden door that stood between their hotel room and the real world. How easy it would be. He could be out of there in a heartbeat, knocking on the door of one of the police cars, could tell them everything. What a relief it would be.

'Steven, come on, please hurry up,' came his mother's voice. As he turned to look at her, love, fear and concern were all too readable in her eyes. He knew he couldn't do it, could never give them up, could never break the toxic, guilt-ridden but utterly invaluable bond the three of them had. He shoved his feet into his battered Nikes, slung his bag over one shoulder, and hurried to the cramped bathroom to join the two people who meant more to him than anything else in the world.

The drive to Maidstone had been agony. Daniel had pushed the car to its limit. They made good time, but he was desperate for this to be over, to have the Benson family in his possession.

For most of the ride Amelia had remained quiet. Daniel was glad she had let him think, allowing him to focus on what was about to go down. His heart was in his mouth the second the satnav woman announced that they had reached their destination.

The roads leading into Maidstone had quickly changed from motorway to smaller roads, fields and trees replacing the concrete, then the night had taken over. The shabby hotel stood out easily, the only building on the road.

Daniel still couldn't believe that Patrick Marsden had tracked the Bensons simply from a description of their car given by the petrol station employee, but somehow he had. Their vehicle had been rented from Europcar and had on-board GPS, apparently. Whatever. The tech team had come through again.

'There are the cars from Maidstone police station up ahead on the left – see them?' Amelia leant forward in her seat to peer out of the windscreen. As Daniel pulled up next to the police cars, cutting his headlights, one of the men was already getting out, his outline just visible in the dull moonlight.

'Detective Inspector Graves? I'm Officer Hill. You're just in time: we've got movement. I think they know we're here. We need to act fast.' Hill had one hand on his gun. Daniel was glad to have two armed response officers to assist. The Bensons would surely be panicking, and that made them extremely dangerous.

Hill explained as quickly as he could their set-up: two cars this side of the hotel, another further down where the road connected to the motorway, blocking the road, and another circling the roads near Maidstone West in case the targets got past them.

'We've kept our distance, but the curtains twitched a few minutes ago.'

Daniel squinted at the lone hotel: a small, one-storey building with perhaps six rooms, all dark except for the reception office. It was old and dilapidated, a weird 1960s knock-off of a classic American motel. Clearly, it was losing business to the nicer, cleaner, newer hotels Maidstone had to offer. The building looked seconds away from shutting up shop entirely, lacking any of the olde English charm that kept other similar establishments competitive.

'Does the owner know we're here?' Daniel asked, pointing to the lit-up window a few down from the room the Bensons were in.

'Yep. We phoned him, told him to stay put, not do anything. He can lock himself in his office if needs be, but he said they didn't seem threatening when they checked in.'

'They rely on charm – have done all this time. They can't be trusted. We have to assume they're armed and lethal. We need to do this right.'

Quickly, efficiently, they agreed an on-foot flanking approach, aiming to cut off escape in all directions.

'Ready?' Daniel said, baton in hand, hoping it would be enough. Everyone nodded. 'Then let's end this.'

Officer Hill and his partner diverted off to the left, aiming for the left rear side of the hotel. Daniel and Amelia went straight, heading for the front, their eyes like hawks on the one room with light behind its curtains.

'Shit, they're coming! Run!' Dominic yelled, ushering his mother and brother along the back of the hotel. They had to get to the car, then they had a chance.

As they ran past two old rubbish bins, their contents threatening to spew out over the broken tarmac, Dominic risked a look back over his shoulder. Two officers were running towards them from the other end of the building. He could just see the guns in their hands. His heart fluttered painfully as he realised how serious they were about stopping him. The police only carried guns in extreme circumstances.

There was a crash. The sound of the door to the room they had just left being kicked in, he assumed. Distracted, he lost his footing, stumbling on a crushed Coke can that had fallen out of the bin. He fell hard, gravel cutting into his hands, dry earth billowing up into his eyes and mouth.

'Dom!' his brother shouted. Dominic could hear Steven running back to him. As he desperately tried to blink grit out of his eyes Steven grabbed him and yanked him up, pulling him after their mother.

'Stop right there!' one of the officers warned, his voice horribly close, but Dominic knew they couldn't stop.

Jane disappeared around the end of the hotel, aiming for the car park, Steven hot on her heels.

'I said stop, you son of a bitch!' the officer yelled again. As Dominic took the corner, he knew he had to act. He pulled his handgun out from his belt. It was a cheap .22 that he had bought a year back, a secret he had kept ever since. That didn't matter now, though. He had to protect them. They had done so much for him and he could never repay them for that, but if he could keep them safe, keep them free, he would.

As he spun round, Dominic was raising the gun. He had six shots, and he needed to make them count. The first exploded in the darkness as the closest officer came charging towards him, so close that Dominic could see the fear flash in the man's eyes. The bullet punched through his neck, splashing inky sprays of blood across the peeling white paint covering the back of the hotel.

As the splintered door swung inward, Daniel knew the room was empty, that the Bensons had gone out the back.

'Go!' he roared at Amelia, racing out into the car park. Amelia was just ahead of him. A figure shot out from the edge of the building, speeding towards the car parked near the exit to the road.

'Stop where you are!' Amelia bellowed. The runner paid no heed, vanishing behind the car. Daniel nodded to Amelia, hoping she knew what he wanted. He hunched over and ran to the right, aiming to flank their target.

'We have you surrounded. Give up now before anyone gets hurt!' Amelia continued. Daniel slid to a halt behind a huge old pot left out in front of the hotel to fade and crack over the years, a dead shrub still sticking out of the soil, and peered around it towards the car. He was about to move when a shot rang out. Someone screamed.

Steven knew he was trapped, pinned against the wall at the end of the building. To his right was the car – so close yet so far. His mother was desperately gesturing for him to follow her, but he had heard the policewoman shouting. The second she saw him he was done for – especially after Dominic had fired the first shot. Before that maybe they would have been okay – arrested but alive. Not now. Now the police would shoot to kill if they had to.

His heart sank as he glanced left. His brother was hunkered down behind a corner of the building, the gun in his hand. *Where the hell did he get that?* Just past Dominic he could see the police officer, motionless and lying on his back. He didn't know if the officer was dead or not, but he feared the worst.

What the fuck do I do?

He had two options. Help his brother take out the other policeman, who had ducked out of sight after his colleague was shot, or risk getting to the car, where maybe he and his mother could make a break for it. The key was already in the ignition. They had thought ahead.

There was just one problem, apart from the possibility of getting shot or caught. Who was more important to him? His mother or his brother?

There was no time to hesitate. If he waited too long, he'd have neither option. He made a choice. He got up and ran, praying he had made the right decision.

The next thirty seconds happened in slow motion for Daniel. He sped out from behind the potted plant and ran to the car, his grip on his baton firm. When he reached the back of the vehicle, the woman inside pleaded with him. 'Please don't hurt me.'

Crouching in the shadows, moonlight frosting her hair and face, Jane Benson was sobbing. She knew it was over. Daniel stood up to motion Amelia, then a flash of movement drew his attention.

'No!' the man shouted, charging towards Daniel. He had just enough time to register which brother it was before another gunshot boomed through the night. The man dropped to the ground. Next to Daniel, Jane Benson began to scream hysterically.

Then suddenly there was the other brother, right behind the first, raising his gun, aiming at Daniel. Instinctively Daniel dropped, readying himself for the inevitable impact. A shot rang out around the car park, echoing off the hotel's walls.

The bullets punched into Dominic Benson's back. His own gun flashed in the dark. As he fell, his bullets tore through the air. The car window beside Daniel exploded, and glass showered out around him. Daniel saw Officer Hill step out from behind the corner of the hotel, his gun raised. Dominic Benson was down, not moving, and the night was suddenly still, but for the soft whisper of wind.

Next to Daniel lay Jane Benson. Her eyes were open and staring up at the night as though she were star-gazing. A tear glistened on her cheek. Daniel knew she was gone, saw the blood seeping from the wound in her stomach. Her own son had accidentally taken his mother's life.

Daniel fell back onto the hard ground, dropping his baton onto the concrete. He was short of breath and still stunned. A hand fell on his shoulder and he jumped. Amelia stood over him.

'It's over. We got them.'

Daniel could hear the low howls of Dominic Benson, who was still alive. The combination of agony and loss was all too clear in his cries, which punctured the night air.

CHAPTER TWENTY-SIX

'I'm so sorry I missed it, Danny, but it sounds like you proved yourself more than capable. You both did.' Charlie Palmer smiled at them from his hospital bed. 'You didn't even need me.'

'We always need you.' Amelia laughed from her position on the window ledge.

'Yeah, Charlie, don't make us go through that without you again. No more getting bloody shot halfway through a case.' Daniel frowned, though his smirk undermined the serious tone in his voice.

'I'll try.' Charlie glanced down at his bandage. 'But you didn't tell me, how did they actually do it? How did they convince the Morris family there was a demon in their house?'

'Years of practice, partially, but Dominic Benson told us everything once his gunshot wound had been treated. He had no reason to hide anything any longer. They played on the family's desperation multiple times, and then while they were out one day they broke in. They had put a Dictaphone in the vent system of the house, had candles that lit by remote control, mechanical crosses that fell over with the push of a button. It was all pretty elaborate. It's no wonder it worked for so long.

They teased out the family's fears and doubts and made them feel real, showed them just enough for them to believe that what they had experienced was really the work of a demon. It's no wonder the Morris family fell for it. We didn't figure it out at the time because no one believed the demon story, and the Bensons had cleared most of their stuff away before we got there, so there wasn't much for us to find. Apparently Jane Benson chose each family, based on local news reports and online chatter, and they would move from town to town. Dominic doesn't even know how many people he's killed over the years – can you believe that? He actually lost track. And it was him I saw outside my flat. Turns out no one visited Janine Morris, though. That was genuinely a hallucination, by the sound of it.' Recounting the story to Charlie made Daniel shiver.

'But we stopped it,' Amelia interjected. 'He'll be behind bars for life, and the others – well...' She tailed off. Amelia wasn't sorry they were dead. Still, Daniel knew that the case would stay with her for some time. Seeing people killed right in front of you affected you. Officer Hill wasn't feeling much better, by all accounts, having lost one of his own men. It had been rough on everyone involved, and none of them would forget it in a hurry.

'And how did they kill him? Darrell Morris?' Charlie asked.

'Poison, as we thought. Dominic saw how much Darrell had drunk the first time they visited the Morris family. He filled the whisky bottle with hydrofluoric acid, just like the coroner said, then switched the bottle with another before we arrived. It was simple. They took the evidence with them. We were so wrapped up in the whole demon thing that he got away without being searched. We'd have found the dodgy crosses and Dictaphone then too if only we'd searched him at the time.

Without any evidence at the scene that proved they poisoned him...'

'God, they were so close to getting away with it – thanks to an oversight on our part. It makes me sick,' Amelia said, her voice low but full of venom.

'It's shit for the Morris kids too. I take it their mother is still in the crazy ward?'

Daniel frowned at Charlie but nodded. The doctor looking after Janine Morris had deemed her unfit to look after the children, at least for a while. Her mind had snapped: she had bought into a lie that she didn't seem able to escape from.

'So much collateral damage. But we did it. The Bensons, Cassandra Salinas. Guys, we stopped a serial killer and a psychopath in the same week. Well, you and I did anyway, Amelia,' Daniel said, bursting into laughter as Charlie swore at him.

It had been one of the most intense weeks of his life. But even though so many people had been hurt, and even though he knew that if they'd acted faster, maybe a few lives would not have been lost, Daniel couldn't help feeling a surge of pride as he looked at Amelia and Charlie. They had done good. As the bright summer sun washed over them through the window, he felt a sense of warmth and comfort he had not experienced in a long time.

───────

'Don't you think I deserved to sleep in?' Daniel laughed as he pinned the phone to his cheek, pulling his jeans up in an awkward hop.

'Nope,' Charlie said. 'I'm out of hospital and we're going for breakfast to celebrate. Full English. I'll meet you at the usual place, okay?'

'And then I have to go to work while you skive off, I get it.'

'Hey, get shot and then see how jealous you are. And here I was thinking that gun crime in this country was all but gone.' Charlie laughed.

The sound of the doorbell interrupted them. Daniel told Charlie he would see him in an hour before chucking the phone on his bed. The bell sounded again as he was reaching for a shirt.

'Hang on, I'm coming!' he called as he fiddled with the buttons, not wanting to open the front door half naked.

He swung the door open, frowning when he couldn't see anyone outside. He stepped onto the porch and looked down the steps to the street. No one was there either.

'Weird,' he mumbled and turned back to his apartment. He stopped when he saw the small box sitting by the door. Kneeling, he inspected the package. It was wrapped in shiny blue paper with white stars dotted over it. A curly silver sprig of tinsel glittered in the sunlight, and a small card poked out from under it. Daniel pulled the card off the box and opened the envelope to read the message.

A little piece of me, to say thank you. J x

He smiled. Daniel had not seen Jenny since the incident at the warehouse. It had been just three days ago, but it felt like another lifetime. He picked up the box and headed into his flat, excited to see what was inside.

Placing the gift on the kitchen counter, he carefully tore away the wrapping, exposing the brown cardboard lid, which he flicked open. He felt nervous. He had texted Jenny to see how she was. She had said that maybe she would be up for a pint once she felt a bit better. Perhaps this was a sign that she would be ready soon.

Inside the box was a layer of blue shredded paper. Daniel began to lift it out. He froze when he realised his fingers were sticky.

'Oh God, please no...' he stuttered, his heart pounding. He pulled out more of the paper. Pieces stuck to his fingers.

His throat caught as he saw what lay inside. It was a piece of skin, its neat edges lined with red, that had been cut tidily from a body. On it was a bluebird – a tattoo Daniel recognised immediately. Jenny. He remembered seeing it the first time they met. Someone had ... had cut it from her chest.

There was something underneath it. Not daring to touch the piece of skin, he risked tilting the box, then saw the unmistakable fleshy shape of a human heart. Blood had soaked into the blue tissue around it. He turned to the sink and threw up. He hadn't seen the unsigned note that was tucked inside the box, scrawled in scratchy black ink.

You took something of mine, Graves, so I took something of yours. An eye for an eye, so to speak. And guess what? She's just the start.

Game on.

THE END

A NOTE FROM THE PUBLISHER

Thank you for reading this book. If you enjoyed it please do consider leaving a review on Amazon to help others find it too.

We hate typos. All of our books have been rigorously edited and proofread, but sometimes mistakes do slip through. If you have spotted a typo, please do let us know and we can get it amended within hours.

info@bloodhoundbooks.com

Printed in Great Britain
by Amazon

84750408R00150